FORGOTTEN

F-BOMB: SEALS LOVE CURVES, BOOK 2

MARY E THOMPSON

BluEyed Press

F-BOMB: SEALS LOVE CURVES

Welcome to the world of F-BOMB where a group of former SEALs have come together to protect the curvy women they love and the country they call home from the dangers of the world. They have the training and the knowledge, and they have the ability to kick some ass when needed. And it'll be needed.

F-BOMB: SEALs LOVE CURVES
Freedom
Fiancée (subscriber exclusive)
Forgotten
First
Failure
Friends
Family
Forbidden
Future
Finally

SUBSCRIBE NOW AT MARYETHOMPSON.COM

To everyone who's wondered if you would be missed...you would be

1
―――――

KELSEA ARNOLD LOCKED HER OFFICE DOOR AS A CHILL RACED up her spine. She looked around, but no one was in the hallway. Dark classrooms lined both sides, with doors long closed and locked. Her colleagues had families to see, lives to live. Things she hadn't had ever, if she was being honest with herself.

She glanced down the long hallway again and shook off the feeling of being watched. She was imagining things. She had to be. No one was there. No one was ever there when that feeling crept up on her.

Darkness blanketed the grounds of Erie University, like it usually did by the time she left work. She had papers to grade and lesson plans to finalize, and then there were the research papers she had to write. To say she had a lot on her plate was an understatement. It was one of the many reasons she worked late every night. That and it was easier to get work done at school where, once in a while, someone was around instead of her silent and empty home.

She was almost to her car when that feeling of being watched slithered up her spine again. She stopped and listened, straining to hear footsteps or some other noise that would tell her where the closest person was. A shuffling drew her attention to the sidewalk she'd stepped off of moments before.

She spun and stared long enough into the shadows that her eyes played tricks on her. She thought she saw a man near the bank of trees, but no one was there.

Right?

"Hello? Is anyone there?"

Silence met her question, but silence didn't mean she was alone.

She stared for another second, then convinced herself she was crazy. With a deep breath, she turned back to her car, not running, but not taking her time either.

As soon as she was in her car, she locked the door and forced herself to take a deep breath, then cranked up the car and drove off.

She watched her rearview mirror constantly on her drive home. Her heart raced as she changed lanes and took the long way home. At every intersection, she swore someone was following her, but she lost them at the next turn. By the time she pulled into her driveway, her palms were so wet they slipped on the steering wheel. She pulled her car into the garage and closed the door behind her, watching the mirrors to make sure no one got in the garage with her.

Kelsea turned her car off and sucked in a deep breath. She was safe. She was in her home. No one was there. She was okay.

She got out on shaky legs and made her way to the door. She unlocked it and went inside, locking the door behind her. She leaned back against it and breathed deep. Slowly, her heart stopped pounding and her breathing returned to something normal. It was sad to admit running from an imaginary stalker was the most exercise she'd had in months. She was painfully out of shape, something her ex reminded her of the last time they spoke.

Screw him, she told herself. She didn't need the man who thought she was fat. She was changing the world, and she didn't need any man for that. She was happy on her own.

Liar.

Kelsea rolled her eyes at herself and pushed away from the door. It was an ongoing internal battle. As a psychology professor, she knew her pride was bruised more than her heart. She'd studied enough to understand how people thought and why certain things bothered you when others didn't. Like the fact that she was pissed off that he said she was fat, but not bothered in the least that they were done. Pride, one. Heart, zero.

She stashed her double-x coat and oversized purse in the closet, imagining Maxwell's sneer. Everything about her was too big. She groaned. He wasn't worth another thought. And after the night she had, she didn't need one more thing to mess with her head.

Kelsea's home was her sanctuary. She meticulously chose every item that went into the house when she bought it. It was a true fixer-upper, and she painstakingly remodeled every room until it was everything she ever imagined her home would be. Her kitchen was definitely one of her favorite rooms. It was the first one she completed, and she loved the beauty and simplicity of the pristine white cabinets and matching smooth countertops. The only color came from the copper cookware that hung above the large center island.

It was also where she kept the wine, so of course she loved the kitchen. More than that, it made her feel good. You could be fat in the kitchen and no one thought twice about it. No one trusted a skinny chef. Not that Kelsea was a chef, but she told herself it made sense as she moved around her kitchen, heating up leftovers from the night before and pouring herself a large glass of wine.

She carried her computer bag, wine, and dinner to the blue-gray living room and sank onto her insanely comfortable couch. She finally took a deep breath. She was safe. She was possibly crazy, but she was safe in her home.

She ate in silence, letting the sound of the movie on TV fill her home and convince her she wasn't quite so lonely. If she had friends, she would call someone to come over once in a while. She had her work and her students and a neighbor a few doors down that she talked to, but mostly, she was alone.

After she finished her dinner, Kelsea pulled out the tests she had to grade. It wasn't long before she was dozing on the couch. A loud commercial startled her. She looked at the clock and realized how early it still was. She didn't care, though. She was exhausted. An early day combined with irrational fears did that to a person.

She went to her room and flipped on lights. Her dirty clothes went into the hamper in her closet, then she padded to the bathroom. She glanced longingly at her soaking tub and debated taking a bath. It would definitely soothe her nerves, but she was so tired she worried she'd fall asleep and drown.

She sighed and promised herself a long, hot bath over the weekend, when she wasn't so exhausted.

She finished up in the bathroom and debated sleeping naked, but decided she wanted clothes on to give her a sense of security. Just like snuggling under the covers wouldn't help if someone broke in, she knew it was irrational, but fears weren't rational so she gave in to them and pulled on a pair of yoga pants and a t-shirt. She threw an Erie University sweatshirt on with a pair of thick socks and told herself she was going to roast. But she felt better, so she kept all the clothes on.

She went back to the front door and double checked that she'd locked that and every other door and shook her head at herself. She was being paranoid.

In her bedroom, she pulled her hair up into a ponytail and wished, not for the first time, that there was a man sliding into bed with her. Being lonely sucked.

With a sigh, she turned off the light, and swore she saw a flash outside her bedroom window.

Jaymes Ford leaned back in his chair and laughed at something his mom said. He rubbed his stomach, enjoying the full feeling. It was another thing he'd learned to appreciate. His brother, Archer, told him he'd only been gone a little under two weeks when Archer's psycho former commanding officer, Brady Williams, kidnapped him, but for Jaymes, it had been a lifetime. They only gave him food when he couldn't sit upright any longer, and water was restricted so he didn't dump it on the computer.

The fuckers were smart.

"You shouldn't say things like that, Mom," Jaymes chastised.

His mom spun on him and rolled her eyes. "Neither should he. He's a grown-ass man, and he should know better than to proposition an old lady like me. And at church of all places."

Jaymes laughed again, because she was right. But that

didn't make it any less funny that one of his mother's fellow parishioners grabbed her ass and told her he wanted to take her on a hot date.

"You're right, Mom. Are you going to tell on him?"

She waved her hand at him and scoffed. "You know no one would care. Those old bitties would be jealous that they weren't the ones getting felt up."

Jaymes choked on his water. "Felt up? Mom, that's sexual harassment. I mean, him grabbing your ass is also, but feeling you up definitely is."

She gave him a funny look. "There's no difference, Jaymes. Feeling me up is grabbing my ass."

Jaymes held her gaze for a second then slowly said, "Mom, feeling you up is grabbing your breasts, not your ass."

She turned scarlet and busied herself with the dishes in the sink. "Oh, no. I didn't mean that!"

The doorbell rang and saved them both from further embarrassment.

"Will you get that, honey? A neighbor is supposed to be bringing something over tonight. That might be her."

Jaymes was more than happy to escape his mother for a minute, and her felt-up ass. He chuckled on his way to the door, wondering who was showing up at his mom's house at almost nine at night.

Jaymes opened the door and stopped dead. He expected an old lady, someone close to his mom's age.

Instead, it was another friend of hers. Jaymes met her a couple times but only briefly. He couldn't remember her name. It was something pretty, simple but not very common. It suited her, but Jaymes still couldn't think of what it was.

But it wasn't her name or how beautiful she was that had

Jaymes stopping dead. It was the look of pure terror on her heart-shaped face when she saw him standing there.

"Are you okay?"

She took a step back and started to turn away.

"My mom's inside. Hang on a second."

She froze and slowly turned back to look at him. Her eyes ran down his frame, taking in every inch of him.

He wondered what she saw. His white socks stood out against his dark jeans. His t-shirt was a little tight after the muscle he added the last few months, but it was comfortable. He edged his glasses up his nose, a new addition after spending so many days in dark basements and straining his eyes to look at computer screens.

He wasn't the same man he was before he was kidnapped, but the woman before him obviously didn't remember him anyway.

"Jaymes, right?" she asked tentatively.

He nodded. So much for her not remembering him. "Do you want to come in?"

She shook her head. "No, I should—"

"Come on. My mom was just getting dessert out. I think she made a chocolate cheesecake because she knows I'm a sucker for chocolate. You're welcome to join us."

She glanced down the street, then chewed on her lip, and finally nodded.

Jaymes stepped back and held the door so she had plenty of room to get around him. He didn't know what she was running from, but it was obvious to him that she was doing exactly that. Running. From someone or something.

Before they walked into the kitchen, he stopped her. "Are you okay?"

She nodded stiffly, as though regretting her decision to come inside. "I won't stay long."

"I think you should. Did my mom tell you I was kidnapped a few months ago?"

Her swift intake of breath told him she either didn't know or didn't remember, but either way, it was too close to her fears.

Enormous green eyes looked up at him and filled with tears. She was scared, trembling as she stood in front of him.

"Nothing will happen to you here. I promise."

She sucked in another breath, fortifying this time, and nodded sharply, just once. Strength stiffened her spine and dried up her tears. When she met his gaze again, she was a different woman. Determined, strong, pissed off.

He liked that one better.

She followed him down the short hallway to the dining room. The kitchen sat just beyond, but his mom was already bringing cheesecake back into the dining room.

"Kelsea, honey! How are you? I didn't know you were stopping by tonight. Did I?"

Kelsea nodded. "No, Cecelia. I'm sorry. I just wanted to... say hi. I scared myself and wanted some company."

Her cheeks pinked like she was embarrassed by what she admitted. Why, he couldn't understand. If anyone knew fear, it was definitely him. He wouldn't judge her, and neither would his mom.

"You're always welcome here, Kelsea. You know that. I've got two spare bedrooms these days, and my boys are both in town so I don't have any reason to fill them up."

Kelsea smiled and looked relaxed for the first time since Jaymes opened the door. He wondered what was going on with her, what or who she was running from.

She gave him a sideways glance, so he smiled, hoping she thought he looked trustworthy.

"Sit and have some dessert with us, Kelsea," his mom said, waving Kelsea toward a seat.

"Oh, I should go. You love your time with your boys."

Jaymes moved toward the table and took a seat. He cut a large piece of cheesecake and set it in front of the empty chair next to his. Then he cut another one and set it in front of the chair his mother used for dinner. Finally, he cut a piece for himself.

When he looked up, both women were watching him. He speared a bite of cheesecake and shrugged. "What?" Then shoved it in his mouth.

Kelsea met his gaze and finally settled into the seat he left for her, between him and his mother.

Both women forked a bite and ate it. Jaymes watched Kelsea out of the corner of his eye. She had one of those curvy hourglass figures that drove him crazy. She was wearing a pair of yoga pants that threatened his sanity and an oversized sweatshirt with Erie University on the front. Her dark hair was tied back from her face in a knot kind of thing on top of her head with tiny pieces falling down around her face and along her neck. Her emerald eyes darted around the room as she ate, taking in everything and focusing on nothing.

He hated that she was so scared, that she wasn't sure if she was safe. He understood that feeling and wanted to keep her from it.

"What were you teaching your students about today, Kelsea?" his mom asked when the cheesecake was half gone.

Kelsea set her fork down and folded her hands together. "We're still early in the semester, so I'm convincing half of them that I'm not crazy and telling the other half that they are. It's always an interesting time of year."

Jaymes smiled with her and slowly ate his cheesecake while his mom peppered Kelsea with questions.

"Are these freshman again?"

Kelsea nodded.

"They all think they know everything."

She laughed. "Some of them, yes. Since it's the second semester, many of them have mellowed out. They already know that they aren't the kings and queens like they were in high school. They're in a much bigger pond now."

His mom nodded. "Well, that's good. They don't need to go into it all cocky like they own the place. How many classes do you teach this semester?"

"Five classes. Two undergrad and three grad school."

"And how many students have projects with you?" his mom asked pointedly. She turned to Jaymes and said, "Kelsea is the most popular professor in the psychology department. She studies the brain side of psychology and interprets what people do because of their brain. It's where the field is going."

Kelsea blushed and met his gaze. "I'm a neuroscience psychologist. I study how the brain works in relation to psychology. I have the best toys. That's why I'm so popular."

He smiled at her, waiting for the realization of what she said to sink in. When it didn't, he simply said, "All the beautiful women I know have the best toys, too."

She choked on her cheesecake.

2

———

Kelsea could not believe she said that to so many people and never realized just how dirty it sounded.

Her cheeks heated instantly, and she sputtered for something to say to make it better, but there was nothing. She just had to run with it.

"Well, we smile and ask nicely, so people tend to give us lots of money."

Then it was his turn to choke on his cheesecake.

Cecelia looked at the two of them like they were crazy.

Kelsea finally felt better. When she turned off the light in her room and saw a flashlight outside her bedroom window, she freaked out. She snuck out of her room, tugged on her sneakers, and ran like hell to Cecelia's house. She didn't have her purse with her or anything, just her keys. Which was really stupid because if someone really was out there and they killed her, the police wouldn't be able to identify her body.

But she was operating on pure instinct when she left her room. Terror raced through her, and she knew she wasn't being paranoid or crazy. Cecelia was the closest neighbor to her that she'd gotten to know, so she sprinted the three houses down and panicked when a man opened the door.

But Jaymes was funny and sexy and kind. She'd forgotten that he was kidnapped months ago. If anyone understood how terrified she was, it was definitely a man who'd been there.

And instead of continuing to freak out, she was flirting with him.

His brown hair was neatly trimmed, but his beard was a little long. She'd always been attracted to men like him, men who were a little scruffy and a whole lot of sexy, but with a nerdy side that came out in small ways. The way his t-shirt stretched across his pecs had her mouth watering even as she shook with fear. He definitely had a nerdy side, as evidenced by his wire-rimmed glasses and bright white socks, not to mention the career working with computers, if she remembered correctly. But she was a psychologist who chose to teach others how to be psychologists, so she was no stranger to being a geek.

Jaymes took a drink of his water and smirked at her, tipping his glass in her direction.

"Are you two all right?" Cecelia asked, tossing her gaze between the two of them.

Kelsea and Jaymes exchanged a grin and nodded.

Cecelia rolled her eyes. "I swear, it's like having two children again. What is going on between the two of you?"

Jaymes recovered faster than Kelsea did. "Nothing, Mom. We're just talking about Kelsea's work. I'm guessing you teach at Erie University?"

She nodded. "I do. This is my second year."

"Wow. And you have a PhD, I'm guessing, if you're teaching grad students?"

She nodded, a little impressed that he would know that. "I do. In psychology. The neuroscience part of it wasn't all that common when I was going to school, but I was a premed major for my undergrad and planned to be a neurologist."

"Well, damn. That's impressive."

Kelsea grinned. A lot of people were shocked when she told them she wanted to be a neurologist, but not as many thought psychology was quite so fascinating. There was definitely something about brain surgery that was sexy, but she was learning how the brain controlled what a person did. She thought that was pretty damn sexy, too.

"I decided going to medical school, then getting into a residency program, and having to do a fellowship, and then studying under someone for years was too long for me to wait. It wasn't as important to me to be able to cut open a brain and fix it as it was to understand everything about how it works. So, I gave up neurology and went into psych. I love it."

Jaymes smiled at her. "It's better to love your job."

She sensed something in him, something that said he used to but it changed. She wanted to ask, to push, but before she got the chance, he turned to his mom.

"My mom was telling me about the dirty old man at church that felt her up the other day."

Kelsea gasped and met Cecelia's gaze. "Tell me he's joking."

She rolled her eyes. "My son likes to pick on me. The man grabbed my ass."

Jaymes scraped the last of his cheesecake off his plate and licked the spoon. Kelsea's nipples tightened watching the very tip of his tongue clean the fork. Damn, she really needed to get laid.

"Mom thought getting felt up meant she got her ass grabbed. It was a concerning few minutes. I figured I'd share with you."

Kelsea chuckled at the glint in Jaymes's chocolate eyes. He winked at her, as though they shared a secret. She looked back at Cecelia, who scoffed and got up, carrying the cheesecake back to the kitchen.

"Where are you taking that?" Jaymes asked.

"To the fridge. You're done."

"Mom! I wanted another piece."

Jaymes jumped up and followed her. He begged and pleaded with her until their voices dropped too low for Kelsea to hear what they were saying.

She sipped her water and her mind wandered back to whoever was following her. It had been six weeks, since just after Thanksgiving, since she started thinking someone was following her. She was sure she was crazy at first, but seeing that light outside her window, and all the times she heard someone behind her, felt someone watching her... She wasn't crazy.

But she was alone.

Her parents still lived in Ohio where she grew up. She wasn't close to them, and hadn't been her whole life. She didn't have any siblings, and her coworkers mostly all thought she was crazy anyway. Her only friends weren't human, but she loved the furry friends she made at the shelter every day.

And Cecelia. She met Cecelia the day she moved into her house. She came over with a casserole and homemade cheesecake and introduced herself. She offered her son, Jaymes, to help Kelsea move in, but Kelsea denied the help. She was used to doing everything on her own. She always had, and always would.

But Cecelia kept coming back. Once a week, she'd stop by with food in a plastic container with the excuse that she made too much and didn't want it to go to waste. She slowly wore Kelsea down until they became friends.

Jaymes and Cecelia came back into the room, Jaymes wearing a triumphant smile as he carried the cheesecake back to the table. He cut himself another large piece and plopped it on his plate, then offered her one.

"Oh, no. I can't. I'm trying to lose weight."

"Kelsea, you've been trying to lose weight since I met you. You're beautiful. You don't need to lose weight. Tell her Jaymes. Maybe she'll believe you."

He looked at her, his dark eyes going even darker as he scanned her body. She felt his gaze over her like a lover's caress, touching every inch of her curvy figure. She'd always hated that she wasn't smaller, that her hips were too wide and her boobs too big and her belly wasn't flat. But the look in his eyes made her feel stunning. Like if she changed one thing, lost one pound, it would be a mistake.

"You're perfect," Jaymes said, his voice husky. "You definitely don't need to lose any weight."

Kelsea trembled at the lust in his voice. She clenched her thighs together to stop the pulsing between them. Just the sound of the man's voice had her ready to go off. What was wrong with her?

"See, Kelsea," Cecelia interrupted her thoughts, "I told you. That Maxwell doesn't know what he's missing breaking up with you. He was lucky to find a woman like you, kind and smart and beautiful. And it's not like he was a real catch. With his scruffy face and all those muscles. Did he think he could do better than you? That he was really that perfect?"

Kelsea sighed. She thought he was that perfect. When

she met him at least. It baffled her that a man like him wanted to be with her. A man who rippled with muscles when he moved. He was confident and strong and smart. And he wanted her. He was perfect, until he wasn't.

"Who's Maxwell?" Jaymes asked quietly.

She avoided his gaze. It was bad enough that Cecelia told Jaymes she got dumped. She was thankful she never shared the real story with her friend. She hated lying about why they broke up, but Kelsea needed a shoulder to cry on when things ended between them. She never expected Cecelia to tell her hot son she got dumped.

"He was this guy Kelsea met over the summer and dated until a couple months ago," Cecelia supplied. "You wouldn't have liked him. I didn't like him. He was cocky and arrogant and never talked much."

"Sounds like a few other people I know," Jaymes said with a half-grin for his mother.

"Your brother is not like that," Cecelia argued.

Jaymes laughed. "Really? Because he's living with and engaged to *my* best friend, so I see him an awful lot. He's pretty damn cocky, and he's never talked much."

There was something deeper in his comments that Jaymes wasn't saying. The best friend comment set Kelsea on edge. She didn't know who Jaymes's best friend was, but she was pretty sure he wasn't happy his brother was with her.

"You know the cocky is because he's a SEAL and the not talking is because of your father. Trust me, he's nothing like Maxwell."

Jaymes shrugged, but it was clear he wasn't buying it.

"Well, I find it hard to believe you could raise a man who is anything like Maxwell. Jaymes is very kind, and I'm sure your other son is, too."

"You haven't met Archer?" Cecelia asked.

Kelsea shook her head.

"Oh, we all need to get together sometime. And he can bring his... well," she glanced at Jaymes, "Lily."

Jaymes gave her a tight-lipped grin that said a lot. Lily used to belong to Jaymes, but she was with Archer. And he was still upset about it.

Guess the flirtation between them was all in her imagination. And if that wasn't real, maybe her stalker wasn't either.

A grandfather clock chimed, telling them it was already ten o'clock. Cecelia looked at it and gasped. "I didn't know it was so late. I have to get to bed. Jaymes, make sure Kelsea gets home, okay?"

Jaymes nodded and got up. He carried the cheesecake to the kitchen while Cecelia grabbed plates and cups from the table. Jaymes helped her put everything away quickly, then she shooed them out the door and into the cold January night.

Jaymes looked around for a second, then back to her. "Where's your car?"

Kelsea shook her head. "I only live a couple houses down. I, uh, I walked here."

He looked down at her feet and nodded slowly, like he knew exactly what happened. "Why don't I give you a ride?"

Kelsea shook her head and ducked her chin into her sweatshirt. She walked down the steps and started to the sidewalk.

Before she got more than a few steps away, his hand landed on her shoulder and startled her. She jumped and spun on him.

He stepped back, staring at her.

One more person who thought she was crazy.

"Are you okay?" he asked slowly.

There was fear in her eyes. Just like when he opened the door an hour ago. That fear went away when he told her who he was, but this fear? This fear had hooked into her and wasn't letting go.

"I'm... I'm sorry. I was... you startled me."

"Kelsea, it's cold, and you're clearly upset about something. Let me drive you home, check out your house, make sure everything is okay."

She shook her head. "You don't have to do that."

He smiled. "I know, but you're a friend of my mom's. She asked me to make sure you got home. And I know how it feels to worry if you're safe in your own home. Let me check it out, Kelsea."

She stared at him for a long minute, then finally nodded.

He unlocked his truck and waited for her to get in before he joined her. He cranked the engine and blasted the heat so she'd stop shivering. After a minute, he backed out of the driveway, but her shivering got worse.

Terror, not cold.

"Which house is yours?"

She pointed to a light colored ranch three doors down. Jaymes pulled into her driveway and put his truck in park, then turned it off.

"Kelsea, let me come with you."

She held his gaze, then nodded again.

Jaymes hung back and let her go first. He looked around, checking for footprints or anything suspicious as she walked to her door.

He thought he saw something, but instead of scaring her, he followed her inside.

"I'm sure it's nothing," she said immediately. "I think I've been working too many long hours and I'm starting to lose it."

"What happened, Kelsea?" Jaymes asked softly.

She shook her head. "It's nothing."

He moved closer to her and reached for her hand. She stiffened for a minute, then sank into his chest, surprising him.

He wrapped his arms around her and held her. She trembled, clinging to him. It had been a long time since he felt able to take care of someone else. He ran his hand down her back and held her close, hoping he could take some of her fear away. She smelled like cherries and fresh air, and he couldn't resist a whiff of her.

"Are you okay?" he asked after a minute.

She nodded and stepped back, meeting his gaze with her own troubled one. "I'm sorry. I... I thought I saw someone outside my house earlier, and I've been thinking someone was following me, and I just worked myself up over nothing."

Jaymes shook his head. "When I was kidnapped, I thought someone was following me for a couple days. I brushed it off as nothing, but they took me anyway. From outside my home. Don't discount your feelings and your fears." He looked around. "Let's check everything out inside, then you can show me where you thought you saw someone outside. It hasn't snowed in a few hours, so we might find some footprints."

She shivered and looked up at him. "You don't think I'm crazy?"

He shook his head. "No. Not even a little."

She nodded and walked him around her home. The kitchen was simple and clean, all white. The clutter on the counter told him she enjoyed cooking. The living room had a very lived-in feel to it, with books on the coffee table, a TV above a short fireplace across from the couch, and a bookshelf nearly overflowing with a variety of books. They passed a hallway bathroom, where he checked behind the shower curtain, and a spare bedroom, where he checked under the bed, before she walked into her bedroom.

The walls were a steel blue color with light gray curtains breaking up the dark color. Candle holders filled with half-melted candles, pictures of different places around the world, and dogs and cats lined her walls. He smiled, enjoying the peek inside her.

What struck him was that nowhere in the house did he see a picture of a person. Family, friends, even herself. No pictures existed. Which told him something, too.

She was a loner. Kind of like him.

"Sorry," she said, moving to the corner of the room.

He watched her, wondering what she was apologizing for. She snatched a bra off the coatrack in the corner and shoved it in a drawer, then slammed it shut.

Too bad he got a damn good view of the purple lace. Now he was picturing her in it. And only in that.

He cleared his throat and turned away from her bed. He hadn't ever had the urge to throw a woman down on her bed and ravage her like he wanted to do to Kelsea. But he would be an asshole if he actually followed through. She was scared, and there was no way in hell he could take advantage of her.

With her room clear and the house empty, Kelsea led him outside. Jaymes stopped her on the driveway and pointed to what he'd noticed earlier.

"Are those footprints?" she gasped.

He nodded. "Yeah, and unless you were walking around your house earlier today, you weren't crazy. Someone was definitely here."

3
____

Kelsea thought she was going to lose it. The cheesecake she ate at Cecelia's house turned in her stomach and threatened to make a repeat performance. She choked back the urge to sob and turned to Jaymes.

"I thought I saw a light outside my bedroom window. This would have been where he would go."

"Kelsea, we don't have to go back there. We can call the police now and let them deal with it."

She shook her head. She had to know if there were footprints leading to her bedroom window. She had to find out if she was crazy.

Jaymes stepped in front of her and reached for his boot. He pulled a knife out of it, the shiny blade glinting in the moonlight.

Kelsea sucked in a breath. Until that moment, everything was in her head. It wasn't real. But this? This was very real. She was following a man she'd only met a handful of times around her house at night, in the dark, to see if a psycho was waiting for her, watching her.

Jaymes walked slowly and carefully, avoiding the footprints that were already in the calf-deep snow. When they got to the corner of the house, he paused and took a deep breath.

She held hers, waiting for him to make his move.

He peeked around the corner and brought his head back just as quickly. "I don't think anyone's here anymore," he whispered.

He peeked out again but didn't pull his head back right away. He stepped forward, sweeping the line of trees that separated her house from the ones behind it with his eyes, and moved around the corner.

The footsteps in the snow led all the way to her living room window. There was a small circle, like the person who was out there was watching her for a little while. Another circle was under her bedroom window.

A shiver ran down her spine, fear choking her. She glanced toward the trees, seeing dots of light from the houses behind her. She always loved that she couldn't see the homes on the other side of the trees, but standing behind her house, looking at footprints on the ground, she hated that her house wasn't closer to others.

"Let's go," Jaymes said, pulling her back the way they came.

She followed behind him blindly, stumbling in the snow and stomping onto the driveway.

Jaymes pulled her right to his truck and unlocked it. "Get in."

"What? No. Why?"

"You're coming home with me."

She shook her head. "I can't. I barely know you."

"I'm not leaving you here alone when someone was outside your bedroom window watching you."

She sucked in a breath, the reality crashing down

around her. She was close to tears and ready to pack it in. She couldn't do this. She couldn't stay in her house. But she couldn't go home with a guy she barely knew either. She'd never done that before, for a really, really good reason, or a bad one.

"This is my home. I need to call the police."

"I agree. Then you're coming with me."

He pulled out his phone and dialed 9-1-1 before she could say anything else. They waited inside for a police officer to show up. He prowled her house, checking out windows and looking around before he paced again.

The officer knocked on her door nearly an hour later. He asked her a bunch of questions, made some notes, and offered her a placating smile.

"I'm sorry, Ms. Arnold, but it's highly unlikely we'll ever catch whoever this was. And it's probably an isolated incident. I don't think you have anything to worry about."

"Are you fucking kidding me?" Jaymes asked in a soft, menacing voice.

"Excuse me?" the officer said, raising to his feet to square off against Jaymes.

"This woman has had someone following her for weeks. Someone watching her, standing outside her bedroom window. And the best you can do is say it's probably isolated. I repeat. Are. You. Fucking. Kidding. Me?"

The officer's face turned red. His eyes narrowed. His shoulders bunched. "How do I know it wasn't you? Maybe you're the peeper. And now you're playing big, bad protector so you can get her alone."

Jaymes scoffed. "Really? Is that what you think?"

The officer shrugged. "Who knows? Where were you earlier tonight?"

Jaymes crossed his arms over his chest and stared down

the officer. Jaymes had two or three inches on the guy and used them to his advantage. "I was at my mother's house, having dinner with her. Which is exactly where Kelsea found me when she ran from here in terror."

The officer glanced at Kelsea for confirmation. She nodded.

"Like I said, it's probably an isolated incident, but if you'd feel better, Ms. Arnold, I'll drive by a few times tonight."

Kelsea nodded, but Jaymes shook his head. "She's staying with me tonight."

"No, I'm not."

The officer looked between them. His hand went to his side. "Ms. Arnold, do you feel safe with this man?"

Jaymes laughed. "Oh, come on. Of course she's safe with me."

"I need Ms. Arnold to answer herself."

Both men turned to face her.

"Yes, I feel safe with him."

"We can protect you, Ms. Arnold. You can tell me right now if he's threatened you, and I can take him down to the station immediately."

Kelsea shook her head. "No, please don't. He's been wonderful. I know I can trust Jaymes."

"Then are you going home with him tonight?"

She sighed and nodded. "Yes."

JAYMES UNLOCKED his front door and went inside ahead of Kelsea. He turned lights on as he moved through his apartment, then stopped in the living room to talk to her.

She almost ran into his back.

"Sorry," she whispered.

He shook his head and hugged her with one arm. He was trying to be friendly and comforting without being a creepy asshole who wanted to sleep with her.

Although he was that, too.

"It's fine. My place isn't all that big, and it's kind of a mess because Archer's friends all hang out here most days."

"Archer's friends?" she asked. There was more than a little curiosity in her gaze.

Of course she'd want to know about Archer's friends. The badass SEALs who saved his life and would protect her better than he could ever dream of.

Jaymes took a step away from her and busied himself cleaning up the remote that was thrown on the edge of the couch, the dislodged cushions, and the blanket Lily used to sleep with. It didn't smell like her anymore since she hadn't spent the night with Jaymes since she and Archer got together.

"Yeah, seven SEALs found me and Lily, and they stuck around. They used my place as a home base for their search, and all of them come back here to hang out on a regular basis."

"You don't like them being here? I'd feel so much better if I was surrounded by men like that."

Jaymes shook his head. "It's not that. They're great."

He didn't elaborate, and she didn't seem to notice.

"Anyway," he grabbed her bag, "I'll show you the bedroom and you can get settled if you want. We'll figure out a plan tomorrow."

She nodded and followed him to his bedroom. He put her bag on the bed and went to his dresser to grab something to sleep in, then unplugged his phone charger to take that to the living room.

"Is this your bedroom?"

He nodded. "Yeah. There's a second one, but I have my computers in it instead of a bed."

"Where are you going?"

"I'm going to sleep on the couch. You're staying in here."

She shook her head. "I can't. No. Jaymes, you've been protecting me all night. You took me home, looked around my house, and offered me a place to stay. You don't even know me, and you're going out of your way to help me. I can't take your bed, too."

He rolled his t-shirt and shorts up around his charger and met her feisty gaze. "Kelsea, my mother would kill me if she found out you stayed here and I made you sleep on the couch. I was raised to treat women with respect, and I'm not going to have you out there."

She kept shaking her head. "It's not fair to you. That couch can't possibly be big enough for you."

He smiled. "I fit just fine."

She looked at him like she knew he was going to get a shitty night's sleep, but she stopped arguing. "Are you sure?"

He nodded. "Absolutely. Do you need anything?"

"Bathroom?"

He nodded to the hallway for her to follow him. He turned on the light to the bathroom across from his bedroom.

"Thanks."

"Sure. We passed the kitchen. Feel free to get anything you want. Um, I have to be at work at nine tomorrow morning. Do you have classes to teach tomorrow?"

"Shit," she groaned, dropping her head back to stare at the ceiling. "I didn't even think about work. My computer and everything I need is at my house." She met his gaze. "I have to go back tomorrow morning."

"What time is your first class?"

"Nine-thirty."

"We'll go when we get up. I don't want you going back there alone until I know what's going on."

She nodded, relief obvious in the set of her shoulders. "Thank you, Jaymes."

He nodded once, then moved toward the living room. "Good night, Kelsea."

"Good night, Jaymes."

He turned and walked away before he did something ridiculous, like try to kiss her.

JAYMES BARELY GOT any sleep all night. The couch was horribly uncomfortable to sleep on, but he was not going to put Kelsea there. Lily always took the couch when she stayed the night because they were best friends for more than a decade, and she always bossed him around. He barely knew Kelsea, and he was trying to keep her safe.

Jaymes laid on the couch and debated making a pot of coffee. He was exhausted, but he couldn't sleep. He had no idea what time it was, but he could do some digging into Kelsea's background if he got up. Maybe he could figure out who was after her.

Jaymes almost talked himself into getting up when someone pounded on his door. His heart jumped, fear paralyzing him for a few seconds. When the person outside pounded again, and yelled for him to "get his lazy ass up," Jaymes finally breathed.

Jack Farrell.

Jack was a former SEAL and friend of Archer's. He'd become a friend of Jaymes's in the months since he and the rest of their team saved him from his kidnappers the previous summer. All seven of them stuck around and created a task force known as F-BOMB to help with US / Canadian border concerns.

That and make Jaymes's life more difficult.

He tossed back the blanket, cursing when it wrapped around his feet and he still couldn't get up. Jack pounded on the door again, then tried the knob.

Jaymes knew it was only a matter of a few seconds before Jack would be inside the apartment on his own. He'd almost managed to get the blanket off his feet when he was tackled.

Warm, soft woman landed on his lap and wrapped her arms around his neck. "Don't let him take me, Jaymes," she whispered against his neck, tears already streaming down her cheeks.

"Shh," Jaymes said, trying to calm her.

"I'm sorry. I'm so scared."

The lock flipped, and Jack turned the knob, letting himself into the apartment. "Where the hell are you?" he muttered.

Kelsea gasped and tried to crawl deeper into Jaymes's lap. She shook in his arms, crying and fighting to stay with Jaymes.

His body liked all the movement and hardened. He cursed himself for getting turned on when she was so scared, but he knew they were safe.

Jack turned on the light in the dining room and moved toward them.

Kelsea squeaked and buried her face in Jaymes's neck. "Don't let him take me. Please, God, keep me safe."

Jaymes rubbed a hand down her back and tried to

soothe her, but she was beyond help. Instead, he called out to Jack.

"Turn off the light. She's freaking the hell out in here."

Kelsea gasped. "You know him?"

Jack didn't do as Jaymes asked, but instead, he walked into the room. He stood where the living room became the dining room, staring at Jaymes and Kelsea, tangled up on the couch. A slow smirk curled his lips.

Kelsea scrambled off Jaymes's lap and looked between the two men. "That cop was right. You tricked me. Oh, my God, I'm going to die. You're here to kill me."

Tears poured down her cheeks, and Jaymes realized she thought Jack was her stalker. She thought he was working with Jack to kidnap and kill her.

He jumped up from the couch the same moment Jack demanded to know what cop.

Jaymes flashed him a glare and moved toward Kelsea. She held up a hand to stop his movement, and he stopped in his tracks.

"Just tell me why. I need to know."

Jaymes sucked in a deep breath. He nodded toward Jack. "This idiot is Jack Farrell. He lives downstairs. He's a former SEAL, and a friend of Archer's. He and I go running together in the mornings, but since I didn't show up this morning, this dumbass decided to let himself into my apartment. He didn't know you were here. He's not here to kidnap you. You're safe with him. He's one of the guys who helped find me."

Kelsea's gaze flipped between the two men, trying to decide if Jaymes was telling her the truth or not. "You didn't set this up?"

Jaymes shook his head and held her gaze, ignoring Jack. "I told you I was kidnapped. When they took me, I thought I was going to die. I never want to feel that helpless again, so I've been running with Jack, I lift weights with Slade, and Dunn has been teaching me everything he knows about guns. They're all former SEALs and helping me to keep myself safe."

Jaymes could feel Jack's penetrating gaze on him, questioning everything he just revealed to Kelsea, but he couldn't focus on Jack in that moment. Jack didn't know about the other two, about the weights or the guns. Jaymes didn't tell any of them that he was working with someone else, but he had to feel safe. He had to know he could outrun someone, he was as strong or stronger than anyone, and he could shoot to kill if he needed to.

The only reason he took a knife around Kelsea's house the night before instead of the gun from his glovebox was because he believed the man was gone.

"You're safe?" she asked.

Jaymes nodded.

"And I'm safe?"

Jaymes nodded again.

"He won't hurt me?"

Jaymes shook his head.

"Okay," she finally whispered, her voice as shaky as her legs. She collapsed a second later, falling like a heap to the floor.

"Fuck," Jack said, moving to Kelsea.

Jaymes got to her first and scooped her into his arms. He carried her to the couch and held her while he patted her cheek and tried to get her to wake up.

"Why didn't you tell me about Dunn and Slade?" Jack asked, watching Kelsea with a trained eye.

Jaymes shrugged. "I didn't want you to know."

Kelsea finally stirred and blinked her eyes open.

Jaymes brushed the hair from her cheeks and smiled at her.

She struggled to sit up, and he helped. She perched on the edge of his lap and sucked in a ragged breath. She finally looked up at Jack and said, "I'm sorry I thought you were trying to kidnap me."

Jack grinned. "I get that all the time. I'm Jack Farrell, by the way. It's nice to meet you, although a little head's up that he has *company* would be nice, too."

Kelsea looked at where she was sitting, and what she was wearing, and scrambled off Jaymes's lap. He missed the heat of her pressed against him as soon as she stood up, but then she turned to him, bringing her nipples right to his eye level. Her tiny shorts did little to hide her curvy legs, and the tank top she wore clung to the rest of her body, leaving very little to his active imagination.

"We weren't... It wasn't... Jaymes is a nice guy. He let me stay here last night, but we're not together."

Jaymes stood and moved around them. Kelsea's stammering explanation told him all he needed to know. He was about to lose another woman to one of the SEALs that invaded his life, but he didn't need to stand around and watch it happen. He headed into the kitchen to figure out something for breakfast while Jack and Kelsea talked.

It wasn't long before Jack had her laughing. That was Jack. He always made everyone laugh and charmed the pants off more women than Jaymes had ever known in his life. Being jealous of Jack was useless because Jack would always win if a woman had a choice between the two of them.

Jaymes tossed a couple slices of bread into the toaster, then moved past the happy couple to take a quick shower. He washed, rinsed, and dressed in the space of five minutes.

They were still talking and laughing when he pulled his toast out of the toaster and slathered peanut butter on it.

He grabbed his computer for work and finally turned to Jack and Kelsea. "I'm going to head to work. I'll see you guys later."

"Wait. I thought you were going to take me back to my house so I could get stuff for class?"

Jaymes shrugged. "I figured you'd rather have Jack, so I'm going to head out. Let me know if you need a place to crash again. Stay safe, Kelsea."

He left before she could say anything else.

4

———————

KELSEA STARED AT THE CLOSED DOOR AND WONDERED WHAT the hell she was supposed to do. The one person she chose to trust deserted her the first chance he had.

She turned to Jack. "What just happened?"

Jack shrugged. "I really have no idea. But there are a few things I didn't know about Jaymes, so I might not be the best one to ask. You need a ride somewhere?"

Kelsea shoved down the hurt and nodded. She was on her own. She was always on her own. Jaymes walking away was a blip on a very busy radar. It happened to her all the time. People always left, and she just had to deal with it.

She took a quick shower, dressed for the day, and collected her things, then followed Jack to his SUV. He chatted and tried to make her laugh on the short drive to her house.

"Someone's following you?" he asked when she let them in her house.

She nodded, feeling foolish all over again. "There was someone outside my windows last night, watching me. Jaymes... no one else ever believed me."

"You reported it?"

"Well, I said something to my ex once, and he thought I was crazy. And there was another professor. I mentioned it to him, but he said all psych professors imagine whatever they're teaching at some point. Jaymes was the first person who didn't think I was crazy."

"And the police didn't believe you?"

She shook her head. "We called them last night, and the officer accused Jaymes of trying to manipulate the situation so he could get me alone. It wasn't Jaymes. I trust him."

Jack looked around her house, peering out windows and testing that everything was locked. "Do you know Jaymes well?"

Kelsea shook her head. "Not really. I've met him a couple of times. His mom lives a few houses down. She's a friend of mine."

Jack nodded but didn't reply.

Kelsea collected her things and went to put her overnight bag back in her room when Jack stopped her.

"Get stuff for a few days. I don't think you need to be here alone. Not until we find out what's going on."

Kelsea shook her head. "It's fine. I can stay here. I'm probably just being paranoid."

Jack leveled her with a glare that said she was anything but. "Pack a bag, Kelsea."

She ducked her head and admitted the rest of the truth. "I have nowhere to stay. Cecelia is my only friend, and I don't want to put her at risk."

"Then it's a good thing her son offered to let you stay with him again."

Kelsea laughed mirthlessly. "Um, no, he didn't."

Jack shrugged. "That's what I heard. Get your stuff.

You're going to be late for school. I never thought I'd say something like that."

Kelsea nodded and collected clothes to stay somewhere other than her house for a few days. She wasn't going to invade Jaymes, but maybe Jack would let her stay with him.

They left her house and headed toward campus. She told him where to park and promised to talk to campus police if there were any issues.

"I'm not leaving you here," Jack said, getting out with her.

"You can't come in. What are you going to do, follow me around all day?"

Jack studied his phone for a second, then nodded. "That's exactly what I'm going to do."

"No. No, I can't do this. You have more important things to do than watch me. I've never had trouble at school."

"Except for someone following you?"

"Well, yes, but—"

"No buts, Kels. Let me stay with you. We'll figure it out together, okay?"

Kelsea dragged in a breath and nodded. It felt good to know someone believed her.

She led Jack to her office and locked up the tests her students took the day before. She'd collect them before the end of the day, but she didn't want to carry around everything. She left one of her bags in her office and took the other bag and her purse to the classroom for her psych 101 class.

Kelsea loved teaching the entry level course. A lot of her fellow educators saw it as a lesson in futility, but she enjoyed it. Most of her students were freshman, but she occasionally picked up an older student. She had fun teaching them all about psychology and how the mind worked, and what happened when it didn't work as designed.

Her own psych 101 class, when she was in college, was the turning point for her college career. Before she took it, she was set to become a neurologist, but when she met Dr. Farr, she knew she had to learn more about the way the brain worked.

She took every psych course she could fit in her schedule around her pre-med classes and ended up loving it. She moved straight into grad school when she was done with her undergrad and hadn't looked back since.

Except when she had to tell her parents about her decision. That made her second-guess everything.

Kelsea spent her first three semesters teaching looking for a student like she was. A student whose eyes would light up when they talked about psych. Someone who would love the way the mind works and would devour everything he or she could on the subject.

So far, she'd only met one student who came close, but she wasn't giving up. She'd find that one who would tell her she made the right decision giving up everything she walked away from when she made the switch.

Jack stopped outside her classroom door with her. "I'll be right out here. You need anything, you just shout. I'll keep my eyes on you, but I'm not going to interrupt your class."

Kelsea shook her head. "This is a really big class. To be honest, you could sit in the top row and no one would ever know you were there."

"Would you feel better if I did that?"

She hesitated for a second, then nodded. She hated feeling weak, but better weak than dead.

Jack waited a beat, then nodded to the door and followed her inside.

Her classroom was empty, but it wouldn't be long before it filled up. Knowing Jack could hide told her someone else could also. Having him in there made her feel just a little safer.

He scanned the classroom, then nodded once at her and made his way up the stairs to the top of the theater. She watched him look from one side to the other and finally settle into a seat near the door.

Military Jack was very different from break-down-the-door Jack. This guy was serious and focused. He was not going to let anything happen to her. She knew that.

Just like she knew Jaymes was going to keep her safe. Except he handed her off to a SEAL. In most people's eyes, it was probably an upgrade, but she trusted Jaymes. With everything. She was sure Jack was fine, but he wasn't Jaymes.

She smiled at her students as they slowly filed into the classroom over the next ten minutes. As the theater filled up, her mind moved from her personal issues to the subject that she loved. By the time the theater was full, she was focused and ready to teach. The furthest things from her mind were her stalker and Jaymes.

JAYMES COULDN'T GET Kelsea out of his mind all day. He picked up the phone to call her a few times, but he realized he didn't have her number, and even if he did, it would be stupid because she didn't want him.

He couldn't help thinking about her, though. He searched her name online and found article after article about her. Everything from her research to her teaching syllabus came up. Jaymes read through her bio on the university website, then scanned her professor page. A few hidden pages came up that had old tests for her students to practice with, and a page on her research.

He clicked to the next page and found some papers she published in grad school. She was crazy smart, and really knew her stuff. She was only a couple years out of grad school, but she was a teaching at a higher level than most recent grads. She'd taken on a few independent study students during the last semester and told his mom she had more.

Jaymes kept searching, reading more about their research and checking each of her independent study students' social media profiles. Nothing alarming came up on any of them, so he kept digging into Kelsea.

The only social networking presence she had was on LinkedIn. Her profile detailed her research and had links to articles she'd written, including a few he hadn't gotten to from his first search.

He got lost digging in to Kelsea, and was ready to quit his search when he found something else. Something he wasn't expecting.

Shit. He needed to find her.

Jaymes left his office and went straight to Kelsea's house. Everything was dark and locked up tight. He could have picked the locks and let himself in, but he didn't want to be a criminal. He looked her up on the university website, but no one answered the phone number he found online. He thought about going there, but he wanted to change first. He was still wearing his khakis and button-down shirt for work.

An abundance of black SUVs filled the parking lot when Jaymes pulled in. He wasn't sure if he should be annoyed that Jack or Archer were getting together with everyone and didn't invite him, or relieved. He was not in the mood to deal with all of them.

He rushed past the second floor, hoping he wouldn't get caught up in their stuff. He wanted to find Kelsea, and the team would argue if he tried.

He knew he wasn't capable of handling something like a stalker on his own, but he was not about to let Kelsea try either.

Jaymes opened his door and groaned. Seven oversized men were huddled around his dining room table, all looking at something on English's computer. They looked up at him, then immediately turned back to the laptop.

He was inconsequential.

Jaymes ignored them right back and tried to move around them. Something smelled amazing in the kitchen. Lily. If Archer was there, Lily was there.

Jaymes looked and stopped dead in his tracks. Not just Lily, but Kelsea, too.

"What are you doing here?" he blurted.

She tilted her chin up at him and met his gaze with a pissed off one of her own. "Jack said I could stay with him, but they're all up here. He wouldn't let me be alone. I'll be out of your way as soon as possible."

Well, if that didn't put him in his place, nothing would.

He nodded once, then pushed past the bulk of muscle and headed to his room. He closed the door and sank onto his bed, dropping his head into his hands.

He sat like that for a long minute before someone knocked on the door.

"What?" he barked.

The knob turned, and the door opened, revealing Slade. He leaned against the doorframe, glaring and menacing all at once. "What the fuck is wrong with you?"

Jaymes rolled his eyes. Slade never minced words, but he wasn't Jaymes's boss or dad or anyone who could tell him what to do.

"She wants you, dude. All day she's been asking when you'll be back. And you just ignore her? What the fuck?"

Jaymes huffed an annoyed laugh. "She doesn't want me. Not when she has a man-candy-bar on display in front of her."

Slade grinned and waggled his eyebrows. "Well, I do have a pretty spectacular ass, and she'd be blind not to notice, but the only one of us she's spoken to is Jack."

"He can have her. She wants him, and I won't stand in the way. They always fall for the one who actually made it through training and has the trident to prove it. I can't compete."

Slade slammed his hand against the wall, the sound echoing through the hollow frame. "Shut up for a second, will you? She doesn't want Jack, dumbass. She wants you."

Jaymes rolled his eyes and stood. He ignored Slade and moved to change into clothes he could sit around his house in. The rest of them would save the world from his dining room, but he could camp out on the couch, watch Netflix, and ignore them all.

Slade was still standing in the doorway when Jaymes pulled his shirt over his head and moved to leave his bedroom. They stared at each other for a long minute.

Jaymes was starting to think of Slade as a friend. He showed up at Jaymes's door a week after they got him back and demanded Jaymes go with him. They ended up at a gym run by a former SEAL. It was quiet and low-key and perfect. Slade showed Jaymes what weights to lift, how to balance different muscle groups to maximize the effects of lifting, and how to do some of the exercises at home. Jaymes was getting stronger every week, and he felt more in control of himself and his fear.

"What do you want?" Jaymes finally asked, looking up at Slade.

"Your head out of your ass would be a good start. There's a beautiful woman in the kitchen who wants to be around you. She trusts you. She's being stalked, and she feels safe with you. At this moment, I don't give a shit if she's fucking half the guys on the team, you're going to be there for her."

Jaymes scoffed. "I'm not on the team. What do I have to do with any of this?"

"Son of a bitch. You know you're on the team. You're a part of us. Don't do this whole pity thing. It makes you look like a pussy."

"Fuck you, Slade."

He smirked. "That's better. Come out here and eat. Lily and Kelsea cooked for everyone. And English has a few thoughts." Slade waited a second, running a hand over his short hair, then locked onto Jaymes's gaze. "We're not going to let someone take her. Not again."

The familiar fear snuck up Jaymes's spine and wrapped tightly around his throat. He couldn't breathe for a few seconds, remembering how helpless he felt. The thought of Kelsea going through that nearly made him sick.

Slade slapped his arm for reassurance, then headed back to the living room.

It would all be okay. Kelsea would be okay. They would keep her safe. She had nothing to worry about, and Jaymes had no choice but to share her with the men who'd eventually steal her from him. Because just like last time, they were the real heroes. He just had the apartment they could all fit in.

5

———

Kelsea finally felt safer when Jaymes walked in the room. She couldn't explain it, but being around him settled her.

All the muscle and brains in the room were great, but they were doing a job. Those guys cared, as much as they could care about a client, but Jaymes was the one who made her feel safe. Who made her feel like she wasn't crazy. They had a connection, at least, she thought they did.

"He's been moody since he got back," Lily whispered when Jaymes stomped out of the kitchen.

"Got back?" Kelsea asked, staring after Jaymes's retreating back.

Lily nodded when Kelsea finally looked at her. "He was kidnapped a few months ago. I'm sorry. I know you probably don't want to think about that."

Kelsea shook her head. "I know. He told me."

"He did?"

Kelsea nodded. "Yeah, why? Was he not supposed to?"

Lily shook her head. "No, of course not. I'm just

surprised. He doesn't talk to anyone about it. Most of his coworkers just thought he took some time off."

"Do you work together?"

Lily shook her head again and stirred the chili she whipped together. Kelsea loved to cook, but she'd never cooked for a group like the one invading Jaymes's apartment. She never would have known what to do for them, but Lily definitely did.

"Jaymes and I went to college together. We've been best friends since then, and I've always been his plus-one at work events. He was mine, too, but Archer came with me this year. We met this summer. He came here to help when Jaymes was taken, and we fell in love."

When Kelsea and Jack got back to Jaymes's apartment earlier, it was full of oversized men and one curvy woman in the kitchen. She introduced herself as Lily, but Kelsea never made the connection. She was Lily. Jaymes's Lily, who was now Archer's Lily. The woman Cecelia alluded to at dinner the night before.

The whole thing finally made sense.

She was the woman Jaymes was in love with, but his brother was marrying her. Jaymes stepped back because he was a good guy.

It didn't take a psych professor to understand that there was a good bit of resentment and pain still there. Jaymes was still in love with Lily, and he walked into his house to find his brother and his best friend there together. And then she stuck her nose in the middle of it.

She was such an idiot.

"It makes sense that Jaymes would tell you, I guess. If he was trying to relate to you and make sure you knew he understood where you were coming from. He's a good guy like that. He understands people, and he's very caring, but he's private. He doesn't share a lot of himself with a lot of people. He's been even more closed off since his kidnapping, but that makes sense to me. I was only gone for a day, but he was gone for ten. I have no idea what he went through."

Kelsea nodded. Lily obviously cared a lot about Jaymes. She wasn't in love with him, but she cared. Jaymes had a room full of people who were there for him, and they were there for her because he asked them to be.

He was lucky, and he didn't even seem to know it.

Lily pulled a tray of garlic toast out of the oven and reached down bowls from a cabinet near the dishwasher. She knew her way around Jaymes's apartment like it was her own.

Kelsea stood back, trying not to be in the way. When Lily called everyone in to eat, Kelsea tried not to be jealous when Archer wrapped an arm around Lily's waist and kissed her hard.

"He's already taken her. I think you're out of luck. But there are plenty of other SEALs for you to drool over," Jaymes said from behind her.

The pain in his voice had her heart breaking for him. She wished Lily could see how amazing Jaymes was, and how much he loved her. Any woman would be lucky to have a man like Jaymes love her.

Kelsea shook her head. "I'm not interested. They look happy, that's all I was thinking. I hope they are."

Jaymes held her gaze for a minute, then nodded. He moved around her and fixed a bowl of chili, grabbed a piece of garlic bread, then headed into the living room to find a spot to sit and eat.

Kelsea waited until all the men had bowls before she grabbed one for herself. Every available seat was taken, but there was space on the floor near Jaymes. She felt his eyes on her as she worked her way closer, then lowered herself with a thump to the floor close to his feet.

"Do you want the couch?"

She shook her head and dug in to her dinner.

The men talked all around her. She didn't really listen to their conversation, choosing not to participate so she could clear her mind.

She was smart, educated, and quiet. She kept to herself. She never went to bars or dated men online. She was a nobody. Who the hell would stalk her?

None of it made any sense. She wasn't the kind of woman who normally attracted the attention of men. She'd dated here and there, but nothing had ever gotten serious. The closest she came in the last few years was Maxwell, and he clearly didn't want her if he thought she was fat.

So who was after her?

Maybe she was losing her mind.

JAYMES HATED that Kelsea sat on the floor. He nearly got up and physically deposited her on the couch, but he wasn't going to do that. Jack should, but Jaymes was keeping his hands to himself.

Everyone ate and talked, but it wasn't long before the conversation turned back to the reason they were all together in his apartment again. There was a new threat.

The team had spent months looking for Williams. Dunn made himself crazy with it. He felt guilty. He told Jaymes once that it was his fault Jaymes was kidnapped. It wasn't, but Dunn didn't listen when Jaymes told him so.

This time, none of them thought it was Williams, unlike

every other threat they'd dealt with over the last few months.

"There isn't much to go on," Dex said. "We have no description and no suspects. Where the hell do we even start?"

"With her history," Dunn said. "We always go back to the beginning."

"Yeah, but there isn't much. No offense, but I don't see any red flags. We have college, grad school, new job, but nothing much beyond that. Kelsea doesn't have much of a social life, and you're not on any social media. There isn't much out there."

Jaymes watched Kelsea while they all talked about her. He felt bad, like they were talking over and around her. She had a room full of people analyzing her life and breaking it down to a tiny piece to pinpoint one person who might have a reason to stalk and scare her.

Jaymes didn't even want to think about it, but he had to. It didn't matter if she wanted him or not, he was going to do everything he could to protect her.

"No social media?" Slade asked.

English shook his head. As the resident computer expert, he was always connected to something. He stuck his phone in his pocket and carried his bowl to the sink, then sat back down in front of his computer.

"I've checked everything. There's a LinkedIn account with a bunch of articles and some papers mentioned. She has a bunch of connections, but there isn't anything suspicious."

"What about her ex-boyfriend? From high school? Dane Lewis."

Kelsea met Jaymes's gaze with a questioning one. "Dane? What about Dane?"

Everyone watched the two of them, waiting for the answers that could lead them in a direction.

English tapped keys as Jaymes spoke. "He was your boyfriend, right? Grew up together, went to prom together, then you chose different schools, but you stayed together through it all."

Kelsea nodded. "Yes, to all of it. I'm trying to figure out what he could have to do with this. I haven't seen Dane in almost six years."

"Do you know what he's doing now?"

Kelsea shook her head, fear sneaking into her eyes.

"Dane Lewis, twenty-eight. He's a private investigator. An hour from here. He knows how to sneak around," English said.

"And he has a military background," Jaymes added.

"Definitely someone worth looking into. Why do you think he might have something to do with this?" Dunn asked.

"He was humiliated when she decided to give up med school. Her parents pulled all kinds of strings to get her into the best school in the country, him, too. And when she pulled out and decided to study psychology, he lost his opportunity also. Her parents cut the strings for Dane when Kelsea decided not to go to med school," Jaymes explained.

"Dane didn't want to be a doctor. He always wanted to do something with his hands. He had an amazing imagination and could see shapes in a block of wood or metal or ice. He was a sculptor. And he was incredibly talented." Kelsea smiled at a memory of Dane.

"It says here that he had to give up two dreams when you left. Being married to you and being a doctor. Are you sure he didn't want to go to med school?" English asked.

Kelsea nodded. "My parents are well known in the

medical world. They wanted me to follow in their footsteps, but I didn't love surgery the same way they did. I was fascinated with the way the brain worked, but in a different way. They didn't like that. They thought I was quitting, giving up. Taking the easy way out is what my father said. He was mad and hurt and he thought I'd change my mind when they said Dane couldn't go to medical school either. Dane is an amazing man, but he and I parted ways as friends. The story was for the benefit of our parents. I told him to do it."

The team exchanged glances before Dunn spoke. "It sounds like he's not doing what you thought he'd end up doing, so maybe there's something there. Definitely a good idea to look into him. Put him on the list."

"Great," English said sarcastically. "Now we can start a list."

"Kelsea," Dunn said, taking charge like he always did. "Do you have any idea who could be following you?"

Kelsea set her bowl on the floor and shook her head. "No. I wish I did."

"You told Jack it started about six weeks ago, right?"

She nodded.

"Did anything change in your life around then? Was there something going on around then?"

She thought for a second, then shook her head. "No. I was working, but I've been in this job for eighteen months. I didn't change jobs, I didn't even change what classes I was teaching."

"Someone you dated?"

"Dated?" she asked, going still.

Dunn focused on her, sensing there was something there. "Yes. A new person, or someone you broke up with. Someone who asked you out and you turned him down. Or... or her. Sorry. I don't mean to be disrespectful."

She was silent for a long moment. The entire room was still with her. No one even breathed as they all waited for her to answer Dunn's questions.

"I was seeing someone. We broke up around then," she finally whispered, looking at the floor.

"Why did you break up?"

Kelsea shook her head. "It doesn't matter. It's not him."

Dunn gave her a placating grin. "I know you want to believe that, Kelsea, but we never know why someone snaps. Did you break up with him?"

She nodded and tugged on her shirt. She chewed her lower lip.

"I know this is uncomfortable for you, but we need to know what happened. And we need to look into him. Maybe you can tell us his name and English can research him while you think about it."

She stood and went to the kitchen. She rinsed her bowl and put it in the dishwasher while the rest of them waited.

"Would you feel better talking to Jack alone? Or someone else?" Dunn asked when she walked back into the room.

She stood to the side, arms crossed, protecting herself. She stared at the floor and shook her head. "No, it's fine. I guess what he had to say won't come as a shock to any of you."

She finally looked up and met Jaymes's eyes, holding his gaze while she spoke. He couldn't look away from her if he wanted to. There was so much raw pain there that he wanted to tug her into his arms and take it all away, but he knew they needed to hear the story.

"I was dating a man named Maxwell Greene. He's a geneticist and teaches at Erie with me. We started dating a few months ago. Everything was fine, but he constantly tried to get me to go for runs with him or hit the gym. I always told him I worked too many hours for exercise, but he kept pushing. It frustrated me, and I finally called him on it and asked why he wanted me to work out with him all the time. He said because I'm too fat and he wanted to help me get healthy. So I broke up with him."

The men in the room busied themselves with other things. English tapped keys. Everyone else acted like they weren't really listening to her story. The only one who said anything was Lily.

"Well, he's not only an ass but an idiot. You did the right thing breaking up with him."

Kelsea struggled to smile. She broke eye contact with Jaymes and turned to Lily. "Thanks. I just can't imagine he'd be the one who's following me. I mean, why would he?"

"We're still going to put him on the list. There's no way for us to know, but we'll look into him just in case. Can you think of anyone else?"

She thought for a minute, then shook her head.

"I'm sorry I pushed, Kelsea. I didn't mean to upset you, but we needed to know," Dunn said softly.

She nodded but didn't move. Jaymes waited for Jack or one of the other guys to go to her, but they didn't.

Jaymes struggled with what to do. He wanted Kelsea to know she wasn't alone, but he didn't think she wanted him the way Slade said she did. He busied himself cleaning up the kitchen and tried to stay out of the way of the SEALs. He wasn't a part of their team. He was a former victim, and the brother of a teammate, but he wasn't one of them.

Time ticked by and they slowly realized they had no choice but to call it a night. Jaymes had no idea where Kelsea was staying. He wanted her to stay with him again, but if she wanted to be with Jack, he didn't want to put her in an awkward position.

Jaymes pulled Jack aside as the guys were packing up their stuff. "Is she going to stay with you?" Jaymes asked.

Jack shook his head. "She needs to stay here."

"Why? She likes you."

Jack grinned. "All women like me, but she trusts you. That matters a lot more."

Jaymes wasn't sure how to take that. "You'll keep her safe."

Jack nodded. "I will, and if you don't want her here, I'll take her to my place, but I think she'll be more comfortable here."

Jaymes looked up and found Kelsea watching them. Her eyes were fearful, but when they landed on him, something eased.

Jack was right.

"She can stay here. Just don't break down the door in the morning again."

Jack slapped Jaymes's back and nodded. "Deal."

6
______

It wasn't long before the apartment emptied out. No one said anything to Kelsea about staying with them, so she just stayed put, hoping Jaymes wouldn't kick her out.

He'd been distant all day, but he found out about Dane, which meant he was looking into her past. She wondered if that meant something.

"How was your day?" he asked when they were alone.

She nodded. "It was okay. Jack was a good bodyguard."

Jaymes grinned. "He's a good guy."

She nodded again, unsure what she should say.

"What do you have going on tomorrow?"

"I have a couple more classes, but Friday is usually an easy day for me."

Jaymes nodded. They were both being so polite. Kelsea confessed her most embarrassing moment in front of him. He knew how scared she was, and how crazy she felt. He told her about everything he'd been through. But they were acting like strangers. People who didn't know anything about each other.

In a way they were. In twenty-four hours, Kelsea had

gone from not recognizing the man who opened her friend's door to sleeping in his bed to dreaming about him joining her and wishing he was with her all day. She didn't know his middle name, if he had any pets growing up, how he felt about psychology, or anything.

But she still felt like she knew him.

"I usually volunteer at an animal shelter on the weekends. I can just head there tomorrow when I'm done with classes so I'm out of your way for the weekend. I mean, unless you want me to leave now. I can go—"

"I don't want you to go. I... No. I was going to ask if you wanted me to stay with you tomorrow, or if you'd rather have Jack again."

"Yes. I mean, no. I want you. With me. As my bodyguard. Jeez, I can't say anything. I'm sorry. Yes, I'd like you to stay with me tomorrow. That would be great. Unless I'm dragging you away from something." She was a mess.

Jaymes shook his head. "You wouldn't be pulling me away from anything someone else can't handle. I told them today that I might not be back in tomorrow. I'll just leave a message so they know why I don't show up."

She nodded, thinking back to what Lily said about him not telling his coworkers he was kidnapped. She wanted to ask him about it, but she didn't want to violate Lily's trust, or make Jaymes feel bad.

"What time do you need to go tomorrow?" he asked.

"My first class is at ten, but I have a couple of studies I'm working on. I have someone coming in for a test at eight."

Jaymes nodded. "Okay. I'll be ready."

She smiled. She wanted to stay up and talk to him, but she could tell he was dismissing her. Since she was sleeping in his room, she figured that meant she was the one who had to leave.

"Well, um, good night. I'll see you in the morning."

Jaymes nodded once. "Good night, Kelsea."

"Good night," she replied reluctantly and closed herself in his room.

JAYMES WOKE up in a shitty mood. He was horny and really in need of a run, or something. He had too much pent-up energy in him, and running every morning with Jack usually got rid of it. With Kelsea at his place, he skipped his run for the second day in a row.

He took a quick shower and fixed a pot of coffee. He had no idea what she liked for breakfast, or if she even liked breakfast, but he had to do something.

He'd just cracked a few eggs in a pan when the shower turned on. Just that fast, he was hard and frustrated again. He imagined her, water sluicing down her naked curves, using his shampoo to wash her hair, sliding soapy hands over her body...

"Fuck," he groaned to himself. If he had a second bathroom, he'd take care of the problem pressing against his zipper, but he was out of luck. He had to find a way to remove the problem before she finished her shower and joined him in the kitchen.

He stared so long at the wall that he burned the damn eggs and had to come up with plan b for breakfast.

He was out of eggs, but he had bagels and cream cheese, so he threw a couple of those in the toaster and hoped she was okay with it.

By the time the bagels popped up, he'd cleaned up the burnt eggs and his erection went away. He smeared cream cheese on one of the bagels, but left the other one in case she didn't like it.

"Is that for me?" she asked, surprising him.

He didn't hear her join him in the kitchen. He turned to face her and had to take a moment to just look at her. She wore a pair of black pants that clung to her curves without being tight. Her white sweater revealed nothing, but hugged her in all the right ways.

And he was right back to having a problem in his pants.

"Uh, yeah. Do you like cream cheese?"

She nodded. "I like everything. As my ex so kindly pointed out."

"He was a fucking idiot," Jaymes blurted, handing over the bagel. He painted cream cheese on the other bagel and joined her at the table.

Kelsea shrugged. "He was right, though. I do need to make better choices. I eat crappy food, never sleep enough, and live on caffeine most of the time."

"You just described everyone I know."

She laughed, as he hoped she would. "I know, but that just means we all need to do better. It doesn't mean it's okay. Some people don't carry the weight with them. You clearly have no issues with your weight. You're perfect." Her cheeks pinked, and he grinned. "I mean, you're very attractive, and you have the whole sexy nerd thing going on, and...I'm just going to shut up now."

He chuckled at her discomfort, his chest puffing with pride. He'd never been called sexy in his life. Not once. It was nice. No, better than nice. It was fucking awesome.

"Well, Maxwell was an idiot, and he had no idea how good he had it with you. If you want to get healthier, that's one thing, but if he thinks you need to lose weight just to lose weight, he's insane. You're perfect."

Her gaze snapped to his, and she grinned.

They ate their breakfast in silence and were out the door in enough time to meet her first test subject.

"You can park over there," she said, pointing to a spot in a faculty only parking lot. "My building is the one over here, so I try to park on this end of the lot."

He looked around before they got out, a new habit he'd picked up since getting kidnapped, and followed her into the large brick building she'd pointed to.

Kelsea unlocked an office on the ground floor. Jaymes followed her in, smiling when he looked around. Bookshelves lined the wall behind a large desk. The books ranged in subject from neuroscience to reading a functional MRI to advanced psychology topics. Jaymes didn't recognize a single title, but he instinctively knew Kelsea had not only read every single book in the room, but probably read them all more than once.

She locked her purse in a desk drawer and picked up the folder on top of her desk. The metal surface was neatly organized with only her computer set up and an inbox that was empty. A filing cabinet to the side and two chairs across from her desk filled in the rest of the small space.

"You're welcome to sit in here while I do this. I need to open the lab. Edward will be here soon."

"I don't think I should leave you alone," Jaymes said, his eyes tracking her as she moved to the other door in her office.

She shrugged. "We can ask Edward. These tests are supposed to be confidential, but he's pretty easy-going so I doubt he'll have a problem with you being there."

Jaymes nodded and followed her again, through the door into a small room full of equipment that made his tech-loving brain jump. He scanned the room, looking at the computers and monitors while Kelsea turned on lights in the attached lab and unlocked the door at the far side.

When she came back in, he was staring at a monitor that appeared to be showing a brain. "Is that what I think it is?"

Kelsea grinned. "I told you I had the best toys. This is a functional MRI. It measures brain activity. I show each test subject a series of pictures and blood flow increases to the area of the brain they are using. Between pictures, the subjects are asked to close their eyes to rest their brain and get a baseline reading."

"What do you learn from this?"

Kelsea clicked a few things on the computer and brought up two scans, side by side, on the screen in front of Jaymes.

"The one on the left is a test subject. This was a freshman in her first semester. She was feeling stress and this particular scan was taken when she saw one of the blue books. The ones that we use for exams?"

Jaymes nodded. He hated those things. He could figure out any math problem you could throw at him, but give him an essay and he'd start to panic.

"This area shows her anxiety at seeing the blue book. But in this second one, the same blue book is shown to a person with autism. This person has a much more dramatic reaction. This particular test subject was actually excited about the blue book because the person is high functioning and loves tests. He is a fabulous student, but stresses out in social situations."

She clicked another button, and a new screen popped up.

"For this test, we used audible responses. Here you see the results when the same subjects were scanned while a track of people talking was played. They weren't talking about anything in particular, and most of the talking was indistinguishable, but the first subject was invigorated by the idea of being around people. The second subject shut down, but fear took over."

"You can see all that?"

She nodded and pointed to a spot on the screen, but before she could explain, the door at the end of the lab opened.

"That's Edward. Sorry. Let me go talk to him."

Jaymes nodded but kept his eyes on her. Kelsea called out to Edward and smiled at him. When she reached him, they hugged for a quick second, then she started talking.

She turned and pointed to Jaymes. Edward's eyes followed her. Jaymes wasn't close enough to read the guy, but he shrugged and nodded. Kelsea waved him over.

Jaymes walked out of the smaller room and into the lab.

"Jaymes, this is Edward Bailey. He was one of my first students when I started teaching. Edward was gracious enough to step forward when I asked for test subjects. Edward, this is Jaymes. He's... a new friend."

Edward grinned and extended his hand. "Nice to meet you. Are you a neuropsychologist, too?"

Jaymes shook his head. "No, I'm a computer guy."

"Nice. I took a few computer classes over the years. I finally found my thing when I met Dr. Arnold, though."

"Oh, yeah?"

Edward nodded. "Yeah, I floundered for a while. I dropped out of school for a year after my parents died. I knew I wanted to finish, but when I came back, I didn't love what I was doing before. I changed majors and was basically starting over, but I didn't love sociology either. I took Dr. Arnold's 101 class and realized psych was for me. I've done almost every study you've had since then, haven't I?"

Kelsea grinned and nodded. "Edward is awesome. He's going to be great at all this one day."

Edward smiled at her. "Thanks, Doc. It's all because of you."

Jaymes took in the exchange and felt more than a little jealous. Edward was older for a college student, and it was obvious he and Kelsea had a connection. He made a mental note to ask her about him, and to mention him to Dunn and English. Just in case.

KELSEA GOT Edward set up in the machine and went over the ground rules with him. He nodded along, even though he'd heard it all many times before.

Kelsea and Jaymes left the lab and went into the control room. Kelsea clicked over to her scanning program and chose the program she was using that week. She leaned forward and pressed the button on her microphone, then said, "All right, Edward. We're going to get started. We'll start with thirty seconds of controlled breathing with your eyes closed. When that's done, we'll alternate pictures and eyes closed. Are you ready?"

"I'm good, Doc."

She smiled and started her timer. "Starting now."

Kelsea took her finger off the button and watched the brain activity on the monitor. She had another of Edward's scans up on another screen so she could watch them side by side. Just like before, his baseline was low and steady.

"Okay, first picture," she said into the mic after the timer went off.

Almost immediately, there was a spike in activity. Red

and yellow filled the occipital and parietal lobes, as she expected when she showed him a picture of a fire.

They cycled through more pictures, taking a break between each one. Edward's scans were always fascinating to Kelsea. He had an amazing brain, and he'd been a part of so many of her studies that he'd become almost like a baseline for her.

When they were finished, she went back into the lab to talk to him. Jaymes stayed behind in the control room.

"Thank you. You're amazing, as always."

He grinned. "It's fun. I'm always happy to help. And one of these years I'll be in the control room with you, so I figure it's good to be able to talk to my subjects from a place of knowledge. The first time I did this, I would have freaked out if you didn't calm me down."

She chuckled. The first time Edward did a scan, he was really nervous, like most subjects. She always scheduled first-timers for an hour, even though the scans took closer to twenty minutes. Edward almost ran over. "You got past it, though."

He nodded. "I did, thanks to you. Oh, damn. I had something for you. I've applied for an internship this summer and was hoping you'd be willing to be a reference for me. I forgot to bring the paperwork."

Kelsea shook her head. "Not a problem. You know I'll recommend you. I just wish I could hire you. Bring the paperwork by whenever you can. My office is always open."

"Thanks, Dr. Arnold. I really appreciate it."

"Any time, Edward. I'll see you later."

He nodded and hugged her one more time, then waved at Jaymes and headed out of the lab.

Kelsea walked back to the control room with a smile.

"Is something going on between you two?"

"Excuse me?" she asked.

Jaymes nodded to the empty lab. "You were pretty friendly with him. I thought professors and students sleeping together was frowned upon."

Pissed, she punched her fists into her hips. "It is. And I'm not sleeping with him. I've never slept with a student. Edward is older than the other students. When he took my class, he told me he had trouble connecting with his class-mates because they were all so much younger and innocent. He'd already lost both his parents and was completely on his own. I understood how he felt because I was the youngest professor by a decade. We bonded over the situa-tion we were both in, that's all. Nothing beyond that has ever happened."

Jaymes studied her. He obviously didn't believe her. "I think he needs to go on the list."

"The list? What... Wait, *the* list. You're kidding, right?"

He shook his head.

"Edward is not going on the list."

Jaymes stood up and faced her. "Yes, he is."

She rolled her eyes. "Whatever. If you want to look into him, fine. But you're wasting your time. He's as innocent as they come."

"We'll see about that. No one's innocent."

"Then maybe you should be on the list," she spat.

His eyes were dark. "I'm an open book, Kelsea. You can ask me anything."

She held his gaze for a minute. His eyes were blazing, dark with lust and passion that she'd never seen directed at her. "Why didn't you talk to me yesterday?"

He stared at her for a long moment, then cursed and walked away.

Open book, my ass.

7

JAYMES SULKED THE REST OF THE DAY. HE DIDN'T WANT TO tell Kelsea why he was acting like a child. She would just laugh at him. Not because it was ridiculous for him to be jealous, but because it was insane for him to think she wanted him.

It was better to just keep his distance, so he did exactly that. He stayed close, but he didn't hover. He made sure she knew he was there, and she was safe, but he stayed far enough away that she didn't feel smothered by him.

Her first class went off well. It was an upper level class and the entire discussion was way over his head. He sat in the back since it was one of her bigger classes, but he got a few looks. It was obvious her students knew each other, and they knew he wasn't one of them. He moved around for her next classes but still felt out of place and obvious.

For her last class of the day, Jaymes decided to sit in the hallway outside. He should have grabbed one of his laptops so he could get work done while he was there, but he expected to be in her classes and didn't want to be rude. Next time he'd know to bring something to do.

He scrolled through his phone while she taught. He checked all his emails and answered the ones that needed his response. He watched a few videos on YouTube and played a couple games. Mostly, he was bored.

He could hear Kelsea talking, and the sound of her voice hypnotized him. He missed talking to her all day, even though he barely knew her. She was right there, but she was so out of reach for him.

Movement down the hall drew his attention. Jaymes looked up and saw the student from the morning walking toward Kelsea's office, head down, not paying attention to anyone.

He let himself into her office, disappearing from Jaymes's view. He wasn't sure if the guy was as innocent as Kelsea wanted to believe he was or not, but Jaymes wasn't going to let someone hurt her.

He eased out of his seat and quietly walked down the hall. He heard movement in the office and peeked in.

Edward was standing behind Kelsea's desk looking at something. Jaymes couldn't tell what it was, but Edward was grinning.

"Can I help you with something?" Jaymes asked.

Edward jumped and dropped the piece of paper he was holding. "Man, you scared me."

Jaymes stepped into the office, blocking the escape if Edward tried to run. "Sorry. Just wondering if there's something you need."

Edward grinned and shook his head. "Nope. Just leaving an application for Dr. Arnold to fill out for me. I asked her about it this morning. I need a recommendation and she said she'd give me one. It looks like she already did, and I was peeking."

"Peeking?"

Edward shrugged, looking slightly embarrassed to be caught. "Yeah. She must have written this today. It was sitting here on top of her desk. I'll get anything I want with a letter like this." He smiled and set the recommendation down. "She's pretty great."

Jaymes nodded his agreement. "She is. Is something going on between you two?"

Edward scoffed and shook his head. "Me and Dr. Arnold? No. Of course not. I mean, I'll admit I had a bit of a crush on her when I was in her class, but she made it clear nothing was going to happen. I have a girlfriend. Dr. Arnold just taught me to love neuropsychology. I like to be a part of her research because it helps me learn."

Jaymes nodded, deciding he was wrong about Edward. The guy was an innocent student, and if having a crush on Kelsea meant he needed to be on the list, Kelsea was right and Jaymes needed to go on the list, too.

"I don't even understand what she's talking about in those classes," Jaymes admitted.

Edward chuckled. "The 101 class is easy to follow. She makes it simple enough to draw everyone in, but she keeps you learning. A lot of the results she gets from the scans are used in that class. You should check it out one day. It's a Tuesday / Thursday class."

Jaymes nodded. "Thanks. I might have to do that."

Edward grinned. "You won't be disappointed." He tapped the papers on Kelsea's desk. "Will you make sure she sees this? I'm not going to take the letter, but tell her thank you for me?"

Jaymes nodded. "Definitely."

"Thanks, man. I'll see you later."

Jaymes smiled and stepped out of the way for Edward to walk by. He followed him out into the hall and turned back toward the classroom, returning to his seat while he waited for Kelsea to finish teaching.

KELSEA DEBATED TELLING Jaymes they didn't need to go to the shelter, but he seemed interested in it. When she mentioned it the night before, she never thought he'd ask to join her.

She directed him to the shelter and smiled as they got closer. She loved her work and teaching, but working with the animals at the shelter always made her feel like she was actually doing good in the world.

Before they left school, Kelsea changed into old jeans and a sweatshirt, but Jaymes still wore the clothes he had on all day. She needed to make sure he didn't get the dirty jobs and ruin his clothes.

They walked inside, the silence between them making her crazy. She wanted to talk to him and soothe whatever hurt she caused, but she had no clue what she did. Dogs and cats were easier than men. The moment she walked in, the animals were happy to see her. She didn't have to guess if they liked her.

No one was at the front desk, but Mason called out from the back, "Be right with you."

"It's just me," Kelsea answered.

Mason turned the corner and smiled, wrapping her up in a big hug. Mason was a massive guy with arms the size of her thighs and a chest wide enough to need to turn sideways when he walked through doorways. His shaved head and 6'4" height intimidated her at first, but he was a big teddy bear.

As long as you didn't piss him off.

"I didn't know you were coming here tonight. Usually you wait until Saturday or Sunday. I thought Friday was your night to relax with a glass of wine in your pj's."

Kelsea's cheeks heated at Jaymes finding out her usual weekend plans. Men always found a woman more attractive when they knew other men wanted her. Finding out she was a loser who spent her Friday nights alone and her weekends with a bunch of unwanted animals was not going to score her any points in the desirable woman category.

Kelsea shrugged. "My friend wanted to come by."

Mason looked up at Jaymes, his smile slipping from his face. The two men studied each other silently. Kelsea had never seen Mason look so serious, or so pissed off. She'd heard about his temper, but to see it was downright scary.

"Um, Mason, this is Jaymes Ford. Jaymes, this is Mason O'Connor."

The men nodded at each other, keeping their distance. Neither offered to shake hands or said a word.

"Okay, so we're going to go back and see the dogs first. Is that fine, Mason?"

Mason spared a glance at Kelsea and nodded, then went right back to glaring at Jaymes.

Kelsea moved to the door, turning back when she realized Jaymes wasn't following her. She grabbed his arm and tugged him toward the door, finally separating the men.

They walked down a short hallway, the sound of barking getting louder and louder as they moved closer to the dogs. Kelsea's smile grew, but before they could push through the next door, Jaymes stopped her, spinning her to face him.

"Why the hell are you working with Mason O'Connor?"

Kelsea stepped back. "You know him?"

Jaymes's eyes went wide. "Everyone knows him, Kelsea. He's a murderer. He was all over the news a few years ago."

Kelsea shook her head. "He's paid for that. He went to jail, and he's a good person."

"Kelsea, he killed his wife."

She nodded. "I know. And he's sorry for what he did."

"How can you work with him? You're not safe here. And why didn't you tell us about him?"

"Because he's not dangerous!"

"Except for the fact that he killed someone."

"It was an accident," she said quietly.

Jaymes scoffed. "He has you fooled. Why didn't you put him on the list?"

She laughed. "You're kidding, right? Why would Mason go on the list?"

"Uh, because he's a murderer, and you're being stalked. You don't see where the two of them might go hand-in-hand?"

Kelsea rolled her eyes and turned away. She was not going to defend Mason to Jaymes. Mason was a good person. He served his time, and he was sorry for what he did. Yeah, he could be dangerous, but he was always kind to Kelsea, and he loved the animals they worked with.

Kelsea pushed through the door and into the chaos of the dog zone. Cages lined both sides of the walkway with dogs barking excitedly when they saw her.

Kelsea stopped at each cage, talking to every dog. She gave them each a biscuit and smiled when the treats were devoured. When she made it to the end of the line, she opened the back door, letting the cool air in.

The room fell silent.

"What good dogs you all are!" Kelsea said. She'd been training the dogs to be quiet when she opened the door. The ones that were quiet would get to go outside first.

She went back to the beginning of the line and opened

one cage after another. The last cage she opened was Howler's cage. They believed he was close to five, but he hadn't been chosen in the six months he'd been at Best Friends Forever because of his deficiencies instead of his age. His back legs struggled to keep up with his front legs, making him fall every few steps. He ran full out and ended up with scrapes down his legs where they dragged on the ground. Not only that, he was a hound dog with no sense of smell. None of them knew what happened to him, but the vet said it was likely a serious trauma. Kelsea hated to think of him hurt. He was a sweet dog who always stopped to nuzzle against her leg when he went by. Kelsea bent down and wrapped her arms around his neck, enjoying the feel of his soft fur. She knew she'd regret it in a few seconds when her allergies kicked in, but for the moment, snuggling up to the sweet dog was worth it.

Howler fought her after a second. Kelsea released him and smiled as he followed the rest of the dogs outside into the snow. Only five were allowed out together, so when Howler made it out, she turned to Jaymes.

"Will you go out with them and make sure they're playing nicely together?"

He flinched. "Seriously? It's fucking freezing out there."

Kelsea nodded. "I know, and I'm sorry. I need to clean out their cages while they're outside. You can stand at the door and watch them if you'd rather."

Jaymes took a deep breath and headed for the door.

Kelsea breathed a sigh of relief and got to work. She pulled out the beds, food, and water from each cage. She swept them clean, getting the dust, dirt, and anything else her broom picked up out of the way. When she was done, she moved the dog's supplies back into the cage and moved on to the next one.

She worked her way around the room, letting five dogs at a time outside and cleaning their cages until all of them were done. She'd just let the last group of dogs out when Mason walked into the room.

"You didn't have to do that, Kelsea."

She shook her head. "I like to. It makes me feel like I actually accomplished something today."

"You teach classes, help students with their projects, and do your own research. You accomplish a lot every day."

She shrugged. "I don't see those jobs as finished. They take months, or years. With this, it's done. For today at least."

Mason laughed with her for a second, then spotted Jaymes. "Are you okay with this guy?"

Kelsea nodded, watching Jaymes and Mason glare at each other.

"You seeing him now?"

Kelsea shook her head. "No. He's just a friend. Well, his mom is a friend. I don't really know what he is."

Mason glared at Jaymes for another moment, then swung his gaze to Kelsea. "Be careful with him. I don't trust him."

Kelsea smiled and nodded. If Mason knew why Jaymes was there, he wouldn't say that, but Kelsea didn't want to tell him. He'd lose it if he found out someone was threatening her.

"Are you ready to head out? I have somewhere I need to be tonight," Mason said.

Kelsea nodded and whistled for the dogs to come back inside. They all returned to their clean cages and settled on their beds, ready for the night.

Kelsea, Mason, and Jaymes walked outside together.

Kelsea hugged Mason after he locked up and said she'd see him soon. The men just glared at each other.

Kelsea got in with Jaymes and stared out the window on the drive to her house.

Jaymes parked in her driveway, then followed her inside. Kelsea went straight to her room and grabbed clothes for the weekend. She hated the thought of staying with Jaymes any longer, but she hated the idea of staying home alone even more.

When she collected everything she needed, she met Jaymes in her living room.

"I don't think you should volunteer at the shelter anymore," he said.

She laughed, but he wasn't smiling. "You're insane."

Jaymes shook his head. "I'm not. You are. You're working with a known felon."

She groaned. "Mason is harmless."

"Do you know his story? Have you bothered to read about it?"

She sighed because no, she didn't want to know what happened. She didn't want to read about him and associate the man she knew with the monster he was before. He admitted that he made a mistake. He told her once before that he was ashamed of himself, but he couldn't take it back. He served his time, and he was set free. Kelsea never wanted his past to taint her picture of him. He was a good man, and she wanted to always think of him like that.

"His wife—"

"No," she said firmly. "I don't want to know. I know you're trying to help me, but I can't. Please, Jaymes."

He stared at her for a minute longer, then finally nodded. He picked up her bag and headed for the door, waiting for her to follow him and lock up behind them.

He tossed her bag into the backseat and pulled out, heading toward his apartment in silence.

Great, more silence.

He sat in his car and watched her drive away with the new guy. He didn't know where this guy came from. He was going to need to do some digging. She couldn't be with someone else. She was supposed to be with him.

He followed them, taking a picture of the license plate so he could run it later.

They got close quickly, which pissed him off. He got rid of the last guy easily enough, but she was never with him like she was the new guy. He drove her to work, stayed all day, and went home with her.

Then again, she was with someone else the day before, so maybe she was just fucking them all.

They pulled into an apartment complex and went into one of the buildings. They all looked alike. He couldn't imagine living in a place like that. Why would she go there when she had a perfectly good house?

What did she see in him? He wondered what she saw in all of them that she missed in him. He was the best one. He was perfect for her. She would learn it soon enough. Until then, he had the videos of her in the bathtub and her in bed with the other guy to keep him entertained.

She'd be his one day. Then he'd have the real thing instead of replays. Forever.

8

———

Kᴇʟsᴇᴀ ғᴏʟʟᴏᴡᴇᴅ Jᴀʏᴍᴇs ᴜᴘ ᴛʜᴇ sᴛᴀɪʀs ᴛᴏ ʜɪs ᴀᴘᴀʀᴛᴍᴇɴᴛ and wondered what they'd find inside. When she got back with Jack the day before, the place was a zoo.

No voices spilled out the door, making her wonder if they actually had the place to themselves.

The apartment was dark when Jaymes let them in. He stopped for a second, before he went in, and felt for the light switch. Light flooded the place, then he stepped inside, holding the door for her to follow him in.

He went straight to his room, leaving her in the living room to feel like she was waiting for her punishment. Things with him were more than awkward. She didn't like shutting him out, but she really didn't want to know what happened with Mason and his wife, or anything else. She was already scared enough, and hearing that she'd been alone with a felon was not going to take her fear away.

Instead of sitting around doing nothing, Kelsea went to the kitchen. The least she could do was make dinner. She didn't have Lily's skills in the kitchen, but she could make something.

Except his kitchen was pretty pathetic. His fridge looked more like it belonged in a frat house after a party with two beers, bottles of condiments in the door, and a gallon of milk. The shelving unit he used for his pantry didn't offer much more in the way of inspiration. He had a box of spaghetti, cereal, and a few slices of bread. She found redemption in the freezer when she unearthed a pizza buried under a large bag of ravioli.

Kelsea put the pizza in the oven, hoping Jaymes wouldn't mind, and went back to the couch with her laptop. She wanted to analyze the latest round of tests she'd done.

She pulled up the scans and got lost in the data, reviewing the different results for each of the tests she conducted. Some subjects had increased reaction the further they went into the test, and some activated different areas of their mind.

She went back to her initial notes where she did interviews with the subjects. Four of the subjects had a family history of depression but didn't show any signs themselves. Two were undergoing treatment for depression. And the rest of her subjects were in the control group.

She was so lost in her research that she didn't hear Jaymes walk in until the pan she set the pizza on slammed onto the top of the stove.

"Oh, shit. I forgot all about it," she said, setting her computer aside and going into the kitchen.

He shook his head. "It's fine. I could smell it and didn't want to disturb you."

"I was trying to do something nice for you and cook dinner, and I forgot. Jaymes, I'm so sorry. I've invaded your life and taken over your apartment. I'm not doing anything for you, and you're doing all this for me."

He took a breath and smiled at her. "You're safe. That's what matters to me right now."

She looked up at him. "Why do you believe me?"

He gave her a sad smile. "Because I didn't believe myself when I thought someone was watching me. And I was too proud to tell anyone. You reached out. You went to my mom. You tried to be safe. I'm not going to let anything happen to you."

Kelsea knew psychology. She understood how people were attracted to a person they wouldn't normally be when they were in high-stress or crisis situations. Her brain said that was what was happening, but her body said she didn't care. Jaymes stared at her with such understanding and compassion that she couldn't just stand there. She had to kiss him.

She reached for him and pulled him down to her. Their lips were a breath apart when someone pounded on the door.

"I'm going to kill him," Jaymes said, sucking in a ragged breath.

"Who is it?"

He shook his head and stepped back. "I don't fucking care. I'm going to kill him."

She laughed softly and tried to squash her disappointment.

Jaymes opened the door to Dunn, whose eyes scanned the apartment, quickly landing on her. "Can we talk?" Dunn asked.

Jaymes nodded and stepped back to let the other man inside. "Did you find something?"

Dunn glanced at Kelsea and shook his head. "No."

"I have a couple new leads for you—"

Dunn shook his head. "The two guys you told English

about? He already dug into them. O'Connor has a shady past, but there's nothing to connect him to Kelsea outside the shelter. And the student is just a student."

"So now what?" Jaymes asked.

Dunn shuffled his feet and avoided eye contact.

"There's nothing they can do," Kelsea filled in for him. "They don't have anything to go on, and they're not even sure there is a threat, so they're done looking."

Jaymes started to argue, but she put a hand on his arm to stop him.

"I get it. I don't have a name. I can't even describe a face. I have nothing to point them in the direction of anyone. All the people in my life are people that I have very casual rela-tionships with. I don't get attached to people, and they don't get attached to me. I sound paranoid, and they can't afford to throw resources at something that isn't really anything. Does that about cover it?"

Dunn had the decency to look ashamed, but he nodded.

"You can't," Jaymes said. "I saw the footprints. I saw the circles outside her house where he was standing, watching her. Someone was there, Dunn."

Dunn shrugged. "Look, I believe you, but I have nothing to go on. I can't throw resources at a case that isn't even a case. We have other cases we're working on, and we're still trying to track down Williams. If you get me a name, I'll have English run it down, and we'll do anything we can to help, but I can't have the whole team focused on this any longer. I'm sorry."

Kelsea nodded. She got it, but she was disappointed. And terrified. She never thought she'd get any help, but when Jaymes and the rest of the team took her in, she thought she'd finally get rid of the feeling she had. Instead, she wasted their time, probably a lot of money, and she was no closer to finding out who was watching her.

Dunn left, but the damage was done. Kelsea was on borrowed time, and she wasn't going to get a reprieve.

JAYMES WORKED HARD to erase the depressing news Dunn brought. He wasn't surprised, but it pissed him off. Kelsea was being followed. He didn't know if she was in danger, but it didn't matter. Someone was following her, and that was bad enough.

Jaymes cut up the pizza and asked her about her work. She obviously loved what she did, so he figured that was a safe enough topic.

She jumped into an explanation of the research she was doing to help people with depression. She was passionate about making a difference for people who were frequently misunderstood.

"Depression isn't seen, so people think all you need to do is cheer up, but it's so much more than that. The newest research shows that there is something in the brain chemistry that affects your ability to control your mood. Depression isn't something people should be ashamed of, but they are. We can't control depression any more than we can control cancer, but we feel bad for people with cancer and criticize and lecture people with depression."

"You're doing great work," Jaymes said. "How do you find your subjects?"

"I put up flyers. I mention it in all my classes, too. Most of my subjects are my students. They all have to sign contracts that they agree to let me use their scans in whatever way I see fit, and that they will not share the details of the study. None of the subjects know who else in involved. It can make it tough because I discourage word of mouth. I know some of them talk, but none of them have access to anyone else's scans so it's not like they're violating anyone's privacy."

"How many subjects do you have in each study?"

She bobbed her head from side to side. "It depends. Some I have up to a hundred. Most are closer to thirty. I offer extra credit for my undergrad classes to any student that is willing to be a part of my research, so I get more students when I have those classes to tap into."

Jaymes grinned. "That's a great idea. I wish I could do things like that. With my job, if I need to roll something new out, I have to send it to the management first. They're the worst ones about it because they don't have time to test out any new programs. Maybe I should look into teaching instead."

Kelsea laughed and shook her head. "Students are not easy to work with. They're moody and temperamental. And don't get me started on the ones who get dumped and how they're so heartbroken and damaged. They think they're depressed, but they have no idea."

Jaymes laughed. He had a few coworkers who fit the bill. They were young and thought their world was over when things didn't go their way, with women and work and life in general. They were so dramatic, like the world was ending.

"They get better as they get older," Jaymes said. "We all do. At least, I hope we do."

Kelsea nodded. "Me, too. Do we ever really know if we're smarter, though? Maybe the things that bother us don't disappear but change as we get older. Maybe something new becomes more important. Something new becomes the thing that we get all worked up over."

Jaymes thought about it. "That's true. So for you, instead of boys, you get worked up over your research?"

She thought for a minute, then nodded, a smile on her face. "I can agree with that. Although I never worried about boys all that much."

"No?"

She shook her head. "No. There were a lot more important things for me to worry about back then."

Jaymes nodded. "Not me. I was always worried about girls. It drove my dad crazy, but I didn't really care."

"You don't seem like the girl-crazy type to me."

He shrugged. "It's the nerdy look, isn't it? Girls didn't go for it in high school, and things haven't changed much. Didn't stop me from wanting them."

Kelsea grinned. "I always liked the nerdy look. They were the boys that were smart and kind. They didn't get into trouble. I liked those boys."

Jaymes wanted to dig into that subject a little more, but he just grinned and asked to see some of her research.

"Are you sure? I mean, you don't have to ask just to be nice."

He shook his head and pushed his glasses back up. "It was really interesting to see that test this morning. I'd love to learn more."

She tilted her head, then got up and grabbed her laptop.

They spent the next hour going over her tests and all the results she'd gathered. She practically vibrated in her seat, telling him all about the research she'd been doing.

Jaymes leaned back and smiled. She was cute. She didn't want to be cute, but she was. He liked it. He liked her, too. More than he expected. She was funny and smart and drove him a little crazy.

"So, here, you can see where everything came together.

It was beautiful. Almost poetic, if I believed in that kind of thing."

"You don't?" he asked, unable to resist learning more about her. All the time they'd spent together and he didn't really know her. He knew she was scared, and she was strong. But he didn't know much else. He wanted to.

She shook her head, her dark hair spilling from the high ponytail she'd tried to corral it all into. She blew a wisp from her face, but it fell right back into her eyes. She swiped a hand back, tucking the hair into the thick nest.

"I believe in working hard and doing my best. I believe in helping people and being good to people. I believe in the good in people. Or at least, I used to. Now?" She shrugged.

Jaymes wanted to drag her into his arms and make her forget everything that was going on. Everything that happened. He wanted to kiss it all away and love her until she felt safe, but he knew that wasn't possible. He was just as damaged as she was. He was taken, actually kidnapped, by someone who needed his skills to exact his revenge. And the bastard was still out there. After the torture Jaymes went through, the son of a bitch got away.

There was no such thing as safe. Not when someone was after you.

"Not everyone is bad," he forced himself to say. Was it wrong to lie to her? The words tasted bitter. He wanted to believe people were good, but he'd seen the bad in too many of them. Not just the men who took him and held him captive, but in people since. People who thought he was hiding something. People who believed he wasn't who he said. People who saw Jaymes as damaged goods instead of the normal guy he used to be.

Normal no longer existed.

"No one is all good either," Kelsea argued. "I liked things better when I thought some people were all good."

"What about me?" he asked, attempting to change the subject. He flashed her a grin that always put the people around him at ease. It was a variation of the grin he flashed his brother and the other SEALs who'd invaded his world over the last few months. The one that made them all believe he was okay.

Kelsea huffed a laugh. "You're definitely not all good."

His eyes went wide with shock. He was protecting her. Taking care of her. How could she trust him and think he wasn't good? Did she trust him? "Are you afraid of me?"

She licked her lips and nodded.

Jaymes got up from his chair and paced away from her. He knew how it felt to be a prisoner. He never wanted her to feel that way when she was with him. "You know you can leave any time you want, Kelsea. I'm not keeping you here. I thought it would be easier, but if you don't feel safe—"

"No," she interrupted. "It's not that. It's…"

"What?" he asked. He needed to know.

She licked her lips again. She drew in a deep breath, then stood. Her hands smoothed a line over her rounded belly to her wide hips.

Her curves drove him crazy, but he couldn't tell her that. He was trying to make sure she was safe. That was it. His mother was trusting him to take care of her friend. He wasn't going to take advantage of that.

Kelsea closed her eyes for a second, then took a step toward him. Her gaze met his, and the realization of what she meant finally sunk in.

His pulse kicked up, and his heart pounded. His cock rose as his gaze dipped down to appreciate the curves he was finally allowed to look at.

When she was close enough that he had to meet her gaze, she stared up at him with vulnerability and desire painted all over her face. She thought he was going to turn her down. The knowledge nearly knocked him on his ass. How could any man say no to her? She was beautiful, sexy, and every fantasy he'd ever had come to life. Any man who resisted her was a saint. Or a fool.

Jaymes was a lot of things, but he wasn't either of those.

9
———

Kelsea stared up at him. She'd never been all that shy with the men she dated, but she rarely made the first move. As she stood there, looking up at him, she remembered why.

It sucked getting shot down.

The longer he looked at her, the more she realized the emotions and desire swirling around the room were all coming from her. He didn't want her. He wanted to keep her safe, but that had nothing to do with wanting her.

She felt so stupid.

She ducked her head and swallowed the hurt. She went to step back, but he grabbed her arms. Lightly, but enough to get her to look up at him again.

"Don't."

"Don't what?"

"Don't walk away. Let me see you. All of you, Kelsea. Just let me look at you for a minute."

The deep, rough, lust-filled tone of his voice sent a delicious shiver down her spine. She held his eyes for another second, then he tore his gaze away and scanned her body. Every inch of her felt his appraisal like a sensitive caress, a brush of him over her. It lit her up from the inside out and made her want him that much more. If that were possible.

He stepped closer to her, bringing his gaze back to hers. Lust burned in his dark chocolate eyes, making her as hungry for him as she usually was for the treat.

Oh, he'd be an even better treat. Maxwell was an adequate lover, but he never looked at her with the desire Jaymes pointed at her.

His hands rose slowly, cupping her jaw and tilting her head up. He swallowed, his Adam's apple bobbing in his throat. He drew in a deep breath, his chest brushing hers. Then he leaned down, dragging out everything until she was vibrating with need.

His lips finally touched hers, and everything inside Kelsea burst into flames.

His kiss was gentle and sweet, but it made her want more. He tasted her like he wanted to spend all night learning exactly how she liked to be kissed.

She could get behind that plan.

Kelsea wrapped her arms around his waist, drawing him closer. His hard length pressed against her stomach, telling her he wasn't able to resist whatever was happening between them any more than she was.

His lips continued to tease hers, pecking her, moving around her lips, torturing her with his sweet movements. His hands never strayed from her face, keeping their kiss chaste.

Kelsea didn't want chaste. She wanted to feel desired. She wanted to know someone wanted her. She doubted, still, that what was happening was real, but she had to know.

"Touch me," she whispered between kisses.

He let out a strangled growl and slanted his mouth over hers, thrusting his tongue between her lips. She gasped, surprised by the aggressive move. She recovered quickly and toyed with him, stroking his tongue with hers and slipping her hands under the back of his shirt.

He tore his lips from hers, dragging them across her cheek and nipping at her earlobe. "I won't be able to stop if you keep touching me, Kelsea."

"Then don't," she breathed.

"Kelsea," he warned.

She took a step back, clearing her head of the lust-fog he put her in. "If you don't want me, then just tell me. I'm a big girl, I can handle it. But if you think you're protecting me or something, then stop."

"This isn't a normal situation."

She scoffed. "What's normal? We meet in a bar and have a one-night stand? Or friends introduce us and when we split, they have to pick sides. How about online dating? Is anything normal anymore?"

"I feel like I'm taking advantage of you."

She laughed. "And I feel like I'm forcing you. Maybe I should just go. Get out of your way."

"Don't you dare," he growled. "You're not forcing anything. I wanted you here. I invited you here. And I want you so bad I'm about to come in my pants, Kelsea. Trust me, you're not the only one worried about the other one regretting this tomorrow."

"Will you?" she whispered. She had to know, even if she doubted he'd tell her the truth.

He moved closer to her again, so close that she either stared at his chest or met his gaze. She picked chest.

A finger tipped her chin up, changing her mind for her.

He smirked, just enough that she could tell he knew what she was thinking. He shook his head and whispered, "Not a chance in hell."

He stripped his glasses off and tossed them on the table, then yanked her against him with a strong arm around her waist. She gasped, giving him access at the exact right moment. His tongue filled her mouth, stealing her next breath and making her dizzy.

God, she wanted him.

"Tell me to stop, Kelsea," he whispered between kisses.

She shook her head and dragged her hands through his hair. "Please, don't stop."

He lifted her, wrapping her legs around his waist, and carried her from the kitchen toward the bedroom. When he reached the hallway, he stopped and pressed her back to the wall. He ground against her, igniting a fire between her thighs that she wasn't sure would ever go out.

"Oh, God," she groaned, dropping her head back.

"I'm taking you to bed, Kelsea. I want to kiss and touch and fuck you. If you aren't up for this, tell me now, because once I get you naked, I'm going to lose my fucking mind."

"Please, Jaymes. Please."

"Tell me what you want, Kelsea. Say the words."

She met his gaze, holding it for a second before she spoke. "I want to feel you inside me, Jaymes. All over me. Your hands on my body. Please."

He barely waited for her to finish speaking before he turned them and was headed into his bedroom. He flipped on the light, then lowered her slowly, dragging every inch of her skin over his. The second her feet hit the ground, he released her and stripped his shirt off. His hands went to his jeans, then stopped.

"You're not taking your clothes off."

She shook her head. "I was enjoying the show."

"You want a show?"

She grinned and nodded.

He popped the button on his jeans, then looked up at her, his gaze hooded. He reached for the hem of her shirt and eased it up, exposing her fleshy stomach. "I want a show, too."

He dropped to his knees in front of her and kissed her belly, nosing her shirt higher and higher so he could kiss more skin. When he reached the edge of her bra, he pushed her shirt up and she helped him take it off.

"So beautiful," he whispered against her flesh. "So soft. I knew your skin would be soft."

"More, Jaymes," she said softly, clutching his head to her breast.

He obliged, tugging one cup to the side and wrapping his tongue around her nipple.

She sighed happily, then gasped when he nipped at her.

"You're wearing far too many clothes," he said, reaching around to unhook her bra. It went with her shirt to the floor and he cupped her breasts together, taking both nipples into his mouth at once.

He flicked one, then the other, teasing both as he held them up with his hands. She looked down at him, his eyes closed in bliss as he worked to pleasure her.

"You're so beautiful," she whispered, stroking his hair.

His eyes snapped open and immediately found hers. The lust staring back at her soaked her panties.

Kelsea knew how to take care of herself. She had plenty of options in her bedroom at home, but staring into the eyes of a man who wanted her was better than any fantasy could ever be.

He stood, keeping her nipples in his mouth until the last

possible second. Her mouth watered just looking at him. Dark hair circled his flat nipples, then worked its way toward his belly. A small trail led the way below the waistband of his jeans, where he was tugging down his zipper with a very impressive bulge. She watched him, waiting for him to show her what she ached to see.

He left his jeans on his hips, but the gray briefs he wore hid nothing from her imagination. She licked her lips, wanting to circle him. She nibbled her lower lip and he growled.

"I'm not gonna last if you keep looking at me like that, Kelsea."

"I want to see you. I want to taste you."

"Me, too, beautiful."

He dragged her back in, a rough slap of their bodies together. His chest hair rubbed her nipples, making her squirm. His body was warm and hard, a perfect match to her soft curves. He speared his tongue into her mouth, catching the breath she lost.

He kissed her hard, demanding she pay attention to everything he was doing. His tongue stroked along hers, stirring her brain and making her want more than she had any business wanting from a man who was in love with someone else.

The thought made her pause for a second. She'd forgotten all about Lily. Jaymes loved her, thought of her as his, until Archer stole her away. That was something she needed to keep telling herself. Jaymes wasn't completely available. He was in love with his brother's fiancée, which meant she didn't need to get attached.

Jaymes kissed his way down her throat to her breasts, teasing her flesh with his lips and tongue. She moaned, pushing Lily and Archer and the rest of the world from her mind. At that moment, who Jaymes loved didn't matter. Kelsea wanted sex, not love. She wasn't looking for a relationship. Which meant Jaymes was perfect. He'd take the edge off, and before long, they'd go their separate ways.

There was no reason to think it would be more.

JAYMES LOST himself in Kelsea's soft curves. She smelled like him, like his soap. The thought of her naked in his shower turned him on even more.

He wanted everything with her to be slow. He needed to savor every second. At first, he wanted to go slow so she had plenty of time to change her mind, but once he had a taste of her, he knew he needed to taste every inch of her, and planned to take his time doing so.

Her breasts were perfect. Round and full and over-flowing in his hands. He loved getting both his hands and mouth on them together. And the noises she made when he stroked his tongue over her nipples had him so close to coming it was like she was toying with his nipples.

His cock ached in his briefs. He wanted to let it out and just sink into her, but waiting, giving her a few more minutes to be really ready, was going to make it even better when he finally slid inside her.

He kneeled in front of her, loving the way her skin pinked at his touch. He brushed his cheek against one breast. She moaned, holding his head in place. She was enjoying the feel, but Jaymes liked marking her skin. Knowing he'd be the only one who would see what he did to her.

He couldn't wait to do the same thing to her thighs.

Jaymes worked the button and zipper on her jeans free and helped her slide them down her curvy legs and off. She stood in front of him in just her blue panties. They were cotton, basic. Nothing most women wore when they were trying to get laid. Not that Kelsea was trying to get laid. She was just being her amazing self. And if she did plan to turn him inside out and upside down, he loved it even more. A woman who didn't feel the need to dress up for him was a woman he wanted to spend more time with.

He kissed the top of her mound, tracing his tongue across the top band of her panties. She moaned softly and leaned into him. He could smell how much she wanted him, and it spurred him on.

"Lie down, Kelsea."

"What? Why?"

"Because I want to taste you."

She sucked in a ragged breath and closed her eyes. Her entire body shivered, then she did as he asked.

He took a few seconds to appreciate the beautiful woman stretched out on his bed. Her dark hair circled her head, spilling over her shoulders and melting into his sheets. Her breasts pointed to the sky, her nipples dark and erect. He could spend all day kissing and sucking them, but he was hard as fuck and needed to make her come.

She lifted her hips to help him slide her panties off. He refused to look at her until her panties were on the ground, then he lifted his eyes.

She was beautiful. A patch of dark curls sat right above her slit. The rest of her was smooth. Her muscles were tense, her thighs pressing together. He wanted to look at her more, but he needed to get her to relax.

He stood, drawing her attention. He kicked his jeans off

with her eyes locked on him. Her thighs relaxed with the distraction, letting him see the beautiful pussy she was hiding from him.

His briefs went next, exposing his cock to her gaze. A drop of pre-cum clung to the tip. She licked her lips, her hungry gaze locked on his cock, and he jerked. Sinking into her mouth was going to be heaven.

She reached for him, but he lowered to his knees again, not letting her get a hand on him.

"Jaymes," she groaned.

"You first, Kels. We have all night."

She made some kind of frustrated noise, but it turned into a moan when he spread her thighs and dragged his tongue from one end of her pussy to the other.

"Oh, God, yes."

He was thinking the same fucking thing. She tasted like heaven, sweet and smooth. A smart man would bottle that taste and sell it. It was better than beer for making a man drunk. And Jaymes planned to get wasted on her.

He licked her again, flicking her clit with the tip of his tongue. Her hips jerked and her stomach muscles fluttered. He spread her wide with his hands, using his thumbs to open her folds and see everything.

He blew on her wet flesh, enjoying the tremor that shook her. He slid his tongue into her, pulsing in and out. She moaned and circled her hips. He licked his way up and sucked hard on her clit at the same moment he pressed a finger into her.

She clamped down hard on him, coming instantly. He'd never been with a woman who was so responsive. His experience in the bedroom had been somewhat limited over the last few years, but Kelsea made him forget every woman he'd ever been with. It was just her, all her. He took his cues from her, learning exactly how to touch her and making her come apart.

He kissed and teased her flesh, waiting for her to come back to him. When her breathing slowed and she managed a deep breath, he set about making her lose her mind again.

"No, Jaymes. I can't. I've never come more than once."

He looked up at her, loving the view he had from her wet pussy, over her soft belly, between her sexy tits, and to her beautiful face. "Then you haven't been with the right men."

He lowered his face to her before she could protest again. He added a second finger and curled them to press against her g-spot. He teased her clit with the tip of his tongue, and she fell back to the bed.

He smiled against her skin and dug in. One wasn't enough for him. He was ready to explode, but he had to taste more of her.

He brought her up slowly, alternating hard strokes of his fingers into her with quick flicks of his tongue. She panted his name, begging him to make her come.

Jaymes teased her more, backing off when her pussy pulsed around his fingers.

"Oh, God. Please. Jaymes, please."

"Please what?" he asked against her flesh.

"Make me come, Jaymes. I need to come."

"I thought you couldn't come more than once."

"Oh, fuck. You. Only you. I've never... You, Jaymes."

Hearing her beg and praise him sent him right up to the edge with her. He sucked hard on her clit and crooked his fingers, letting her fly.

She came hard, soaking his hand and flooding down his throat. She screamed his name, clawing at his sheets, then holding his face to her as she rode it out.

When she released his head, he eased back and grabbed

a condom from his nightstand. Before she opened her eyes, he positioned himself at her entrance. He slid his cock up and down her slit, making her jump every time he brushed her clit. But he didn't enter her. He wanted to see her eyes as he filled her body.

10

"Oh, God. More, Jaymes. More," Kelsea begged shamelessly. She'd never come that hard in her life, and feeling his hard cock against her again made her greedy. She wasn't done.

"Open your eyes, Kels. Look at me."

She pried her eyes open and met his gaze.

"You're so beautiful."

Her throat closed up at the sweet words. She wasn't supposed to like him. She wasn't allowed. He wasn't really available, but when he said things like that, he made her think he was just as lost as she was.

Instead of replying, she wrapped her legs around his hips and urged him into her.

He stopped his forward progress and repositioned, lining them up again. He held his cock still and locked his eyes on hers again. Slowly, he eased into her, stretching her and filling her up.

When he was fully seated, they both closed their eyes and took a deep breath. Kelsea had never been with a man as big as Jaymes. The feel of him inside her was like nothing she'd ever felt before. It was like he was made to stretch her, to push her, to challenge her. She'd never had someone in her life who took care of her first and pushed her beyond her comfort zone into a place that made her feel better than she ever imagined.

But Jaymes did exactly that.

And she fucking loved it.

She blinked her eyes open and found him watching her. His expression no longer held the overwhelming lust that he directed at her all night. Instead, there was more there. Something softer. Something deeper. Something far scarier.

Then he started to move. A long stroke out, and a smooth stroke back in. Her body knew what to do, stretching to welcome him deeper with each slide. Her eyes drifted shut again, the emotion in his gaze and the need inside her requiring she shut herself off from him.

She was not going to let herself fall for him. She couldn't. He didn't want her, he wanted his brother's fiancée. She was just a replacement for Lily. Falling for a man who was thinking of someone else topped the stupid list. And Kelsea was not stupid.

"Look at me, Kels. I need to know you're with me."

She opened her eyes, but only because he said her name. If he called her some ridiculous pet name, she wasn't going to look at him.

His lips quirked up in a grin and he slammed into her harder.

"Oh, God," she murmured, her eyes shutting again.

"Kelsea," he demanded.

She opened her eyes once more, locking on to his gaze. He hovered over her, his body rippled with damp muscles as he slammed his cock into her over and over again.

"Let me feel you, Kels. I want you to come again."

She shook her head. "I can't."

"Yes, you can. Please, Kelsea. Come for me."

The need in his voice ratcheted up her desire. He needed her. He wanted her. He was there with her, not thinking about someone else. It was *her* in his bed. It was her that made him beg. Her that had him hard and so close to coming that he was clenching his jaw.

"Touch me," she whispered.

He lifted up on one hand, reaching the other between them. He found her clit quickly and stroked over it.

Her eyes slammed closed again.

"Look at me."

She yanked her eyes open and watched him. His eyes drilled into hers, monitoring every twitch she made. When she gasped, he pressed hard on her clit again. When she pulled in a short, ragged breath, he pinched her clit again. And when she moaned, he stroked hard into her and sent her flying again.

"Jaymes. Oh, fuck. Yes. Jaymes!" she cried out, trying her hardest to keep her eyes open.

He reared back and slammed hard into her again. "More, Kelsea. One more."

"No," she cried. "I can't."

Even as she said it, she knew he'd send her over the edge within seconds.

He fucked her harder, his thumb sliding over her clit so fast she wasn't sure how he was doing it. His jaw tightened, pulsing every time he stroked into her.

"Let me," she said, pushing his hand out of the way and replacing it with her own. She was soaked, her skin slippery where he entered her.

His hands went to her hips as she slid two fingers over her clit. She was close, so close she saw stars. The whole bed shook with his hard strokes, slamming them together. She brushed his cock with her fingertips, then moved back to her clit.

"Kelsea," he said, his voice raw and needy. "Look at me, Kels."

She met his gaze and instantly went flying. The desire, lust, need in his eyes sent her over the edge.

"Jaymes! Yes! Fuck, oh, God. Jaymes, Jaymes, Jaymes!"

He thrust into her once more, hard and deep. With his gaze locked on hers, he tensed and pulsed inside her, then shouted her name. "Oh, God. Kelsea."

He collapsed onto her seconds later, his entire body still twitching.

Their breath came in rapid pants. Kelsea laid there, pinned to the bed by a man she never saw coming, and wondered how she was ever going to go back to her life.

One night in his bed and she made the biggest mistake of her life. She was falling for the sweet, sexy man who took her in and made her feel safe. The man who trusted her when no one else did. The man who was in love with someone else.

What the fuck was she thinking?

JAYMES FORCED himself off Kelsea and headed straight to the bathroom. She would think he was taking care of the condom, but he needed a minute.

He never should have let himself sleep with her. She was vulnerable, and she trusted him. He violated that by fucking her. He wanted her so badly that he could barely see straight, but he was smart enough to know that what she was feeling was more due to the situation than him.

He glared at himself in the mirror for a long moment, hating himself for dragging her into his life in the first place. She thought the person watching her was a threat, but she had no idea who he was. Jaymes would hurt her more than anyone else out there. Just ask any woman he'd ever dated.

Jaymes had never been good with relationships. Every one of his exes would tell anyone who would listen that he wasn't worth the trouble of getting involved. He was obsessed with his computer and figuring out the puzzles in his world, which left very little time for whatever woman he was supposed to be dating. It wouldn't be long before Kelsea was saying the same things about him.

There was only one woman Jaymes had ever put everything in his life aside for, and she was downstairs in bed with his brother.

Kelsea was curled up on her side when Jaymes went back into the bedroom. He knew he should save her from the pain and walk away, but he couldn't bring himself to do it. He drew back the covers and slid in behind her, wrapping his body around hers.

She hummed in her sleep and nuzzled her perfect ass against his cock. He wrapped an arm around her waist and kissed her shoulder. He fell asleep with only one woman on his mind. The same one who was in his arms.

A buzzing woke Jaymes a few hours later. He stirred slowly, not wanting to leave the warmth of Kelsea. When the buzzing didn't stop, he turned and grabbed his phone from the nightstand.

You running today?

Jack. Jaymes looked at Kelsea sleeping peacefully. He would have much preferred her to wake him up instead of

Jack, but he needed to run. It had been days since he'd been out with Jack, and he had to keep himself going or he'd be an easy victim again.

He texted back that he'd be down in five and scribbled a quick note to Kelsea that he was going out for a run with Jack and would be home soon. Then he kissed her bare shoulder and dragged on warm clothes.

Jack was bouncing up and down on his toes when Jaymes met him outside. They shared a glance, went through their stretches in silence, then took off.

Jaymes let Jack lead the way for the start of their run. He needed to clear his mind, and having Jack in the lead meant Jaymes didn't have to think about where they were going. He just had to follow the footsteps in front of him.

They ran for a solid thirty minutes before they were back in the neighborhood. Jack slowed to a jog for the last stretch, giving Jaymes a chance to catch up to him.

"You doing okay?" Jack asked.

Jaymes nodded.

"Have you heard from Kelsea?"

Jaymes spared his friend a glance.

"Ah. She's still with you. Is she okay?"

Jaymes nodded.

"Did you sleep with her?"

"I don't know how that's any of your business."

"So, yes. Wow. I really didn't think you had it in you."

"What, a dick?" Jaymes demanded. He needed to find a new running partner. A few days ago Jack told him he was slow, and now he's pissed off that Jaymes slept with someone. What. The. Fuck?

"Yeah, it kind of was a dick move. She's scared out of her damn mind, we can't find anything, which means whoever is after her is smart and slick, and you're up there fucking her? Yeah, you're a dick."

"Oh, fuck you, Jack. You're just jealous because you want her."

Jack laughed mirthlessly. "I wish it were that simple. She's a nice woman. And you're fucked in the head right now. Does she really need to be dragged in to your world?"

"Fuck you." Just because Jack was right didn't mean Jaymes had to like it.

Jack shrugged. "Have you talked to Archer? Or anyone? You were kidnapped, held captive for days. You can't just go back to normal after that."

Jaymes spun on Jack. "You think I don't know that? Why do you think I'm running with you? Or shooting with Dunn? Or lifting with Slade? I'm trying to survive. That son of a bitch is still out there. He already took me once. I was an easy target, a weak link. And he's still out there. I refuse to be taken again. But I don't need to talk to any of you about it. None of you fucking get it. You don't know what it's like to feel weak."

Jack scoffed and shook his head. "You'd know that isn't true if you asked."

"Yeah, right. All of you made it through BUD/S. I didn't. I wasn't strong enough then, and I wasn't strong enough six months ago."

"We've all made mistakes. Half of us have been taken. And all of us were fooled by Williams. We all blame ourselves for what happened to you because we were to blame. We didn't see who he was. And you paid for it."

Jaymes shook his head, the emotion that threatened to choke him more than once filling his throat. Fear. Anger. Hatred. He'd never felt any of them as strongly as he did after Williams ruined his life and destroyed his world.

"Kelsea is a nice woman. She's kind and smart and scared out of her mind. You want to protect her. I get that. I do, too. But sleeping with her is only going to end up with one or both of you hurt."

Jaymes shook his head. "You're wrong, Jack. It's just sex. She initiated it last night, and I couldn't say no to her. I didn't want to. She's beautiful and strong and amazing. And if I can help her feel safe, why shouldn't I?"

"Because it's a facade. You're not helping her feel safe, you're taking advantage of her. And you're using her to get over Lily."

Jaymes glared at Jack. "I repeat. Fuck you, Jack."

Jaymes didn't wait for a response that time. He let himself into the building and up the stairs to his apartment. He checked the dark room before he entered, then locked everything behind him and went straight to his room.

Kelsea was still sound asleep, stretched out on his bed naked. Jack's repeated warnings rang in his mind, but Jaymes ignored them all and coaxed Kelsea awake with a few kisses, then dragged her into the shower with him and gave them both a hell of a wake-up.

HE SAT in his car on the far side of the parking lot and grinned. Not only did the two idiots not see him, but they had no idea how much they revealed.

So Kelsea was fucking the new guy, and the other guy wasn't happy about it.

He filed that information away for later, knowing he could use it. He needed to find out who Lily was, and how she figured in to the whole situation. She was obviously someone important to Jaymes, which meant he could use her.

He did a quick search and found a Lily in another one of the apartments in the big building. No one else was listed on her lease, so she could be an easy target for him. If he got her away, Jaymes might be distracted enough to leave Kelsea alone. Then he could make his move.

But he had to be smart about the whole thing. Kelsea wasn't stupid. She'd proven that time and again. She always knew when he was there, which only proved that their connection was deep. He just needed to get her alone so he could convince her that they were perfect together. She'd listen to him eventually.

He started his car and went to his next stop. Maxwell wasn't a threat anymore, but no one was going to tell the perfect woman that she was fat. He was going to pay for what he said. Kelsea would appreciate that. He hurt her, so he was going to be hurt. Except he wouldn't be around long enough to apologize. Maybe they could make a video together. Then she would know the lengths he would go for her.

Right on time, a light came on in the front of Maxwell's house. The man was even more predictable than Kelsea or her new fuck buddy.

He grabbed his bag from the front seat and got out of the car. It was time to pay Maxwell a visit.

11

KELSEA STUCK A BITE OF PASTA IN HER MOUTH AND LAUGHED. She and Jaymes spent the day together, in and out of bed. It had been a long time since she let herself be that free with a man, but it felt natural with Jaymes. He made her feel beautiful, so walking around naked wasn't an issue for her.

"I wish I'd known you when you were younger," she told Jaymes.

He shook his head. "Oh, no. That wouldn't have been good. I never would have gotten my degrees if I had a woman like you around when I was younger. I spent most of my sex life alone. That worked well for me."

"Yeah, right. A guy like you can't possibly go unnoticed. The glasses give you a sexy, nerdy vibe. And these muscles. You're seriously hot, Jaymes."

He went silent on her for a minute. When he met her gaze, there was something unreadable in his. "I started working out after I was taken. And the glasses are new, too. I was kept in a basement. It was so dark and I stared at a computer screen for so long that it strained my eyes and I need glasses now."

Well, shit. "I'll just chew on my foot in silence for now."

He shook his head and gave her a tight grin. "You didn't know."

She shrugged. "No, but I should have. You said something before, and I just forgot. Is that bad? That I forgot you were taken."

He shook his head. "It's not. It's good. It means you see more of me than the victim I am."

Someone pounded on the door, startling both of them.

Kelsea swung terrified eyes to Jaymes, waiting for him to tell her what to do. She hated being weak and scared, but she'd come to depend on him. She liked knowing she wasn't alone.

"It's me," Archer's voice said from the other side of the door.

Kelsea breathed a sigh of relief, adrenaline still racing through her veins. Her hands shook.

Jaymes wrapped an arm around her shoulders and kissed the top of her head. "Go change. Or at least put on some shorts. I'm not sharing you with my brother, too."

The reminder that she was second was a slap to the face. She nodded and turned to go to his room where her clothes were. One day, she needed to go home. Playing house with Jaymes was fun, but it couldn't last forever.

She heard their voices but ignored them. She found a pair of yoga pants in her bag and tugged them on under Jaymes's oversized t-shirt. She tied her hair back into a loose ponytail and checked her phone for something to do. She needed a minute before she went back out to face Jaymes and Archer, and probably Lily, too.

There was a video message from Maxwell. It had been months since she heard from him. Curious, she clicked on it.

"Oh, my God," she gasped, falling to the bed.

The camera was in tight on Maxwell's face, bloody and bruised. One eye couldn't focus on the camera. He barely kept his head up.

"Do you have something to say?" a muffled voice prodded.

"I'm sorry," Maxwell choked out.

Tears ran down Kelsea's cheeks. Maxwell's good eye flipped from the camera to whoever was behind it. Pain and fear filled the tiny screen. Kelsea was going to be sick.

"About what?" the voice said again.

"Kelsea," Maxwell said softly. He choked, coughing up blood. "Kelsea, I'm sorry. You're not fat. You're perfect. I was an idiot to ever say there was something wrong with you. I hope you can forgive me."

She nodded, tears pouring down her cheeks.

The muffled voice drew Maxwell's attention again, his eyes flicking past the camera to whoever was behind it. "Make a wish, Maxwell. Before you die."

The screen went black, cutting Kelsea off from him. She whispered, "No."

She shook her screen, then pressed play again. A sob broke free when she saw his face again. Again, he apologized to her at the demand of whoever was there. She strained to hear the voice, to understand it. But she had no idea who it was.

She started to watch it a third time when a new video popped up from Maxwell. She hit play on that one, praying it would be him in a hospital bed, saying he was fine. Or maybe him laughing his ass off, saying it was all a joke.

The video opened on a shot of Maxwell's house. Sunlight streamed toward the camera, the front of the house in shadows. Morning it looked like. There was no sound, just picture. The house was still. Kelsea strained to see something, looking closely at the house she'd been to more times than she could count. She zoomed into one of the windows, thinking she saw movement inside, then...

Boom!

The house exploded. Right there on her screen. She screamed, crying harder. She watched the video again, zooming in where she thought she saw movement the first time. She was so focused on the video, she didn't realize Jaymes was there until he put a hand on her shoulder.

She jumped, screaming and spinning on him. She nearly hit him, but he caught her fist.

"Kelsea."

"He's dead, Jaymes. Someone killed him."

"I know, Kels. I'm so sorry," Jaymes said, pulling her into his arms.

Shock had her jumping up, examining the man she trusted. "You know? How do you know?"

"Dunn got a call from local PD. They knew he was looking into Maxwell and told him about the explosion. He was inside."

Kelsea shook her head. "No. Maybe he's still alive. Maybe he got out."

Jaymes smiled softly at her. "I'm sorry, but he didn't. They told Dunn they found a body inside. They're going to confirm his identity, but they think it was him."

"Who would do this?"

"It was whoever has been after you."

"What?" she asked. His words took the wind out of her sails. Her stalker did that? "Why?"

Jaymes held her gaze. "To punish him for saying... for what he said about you. He wanted him to pay for hurting you."

"How do you know that's what he said in the video?"

"Whoever this was left Maxwell's phone at the scene. The police have it. They sent the videos to Dunn. Dunn sent Archer and Jack up here until the rest of the team can get here. You're now officially a case."

All the fight left Kelsea and fear took over. She shook, hard, and the desire to run away filled her. She had one dead ex-boyfriend, and a whole slew of people who were going to protect her. She didn't deserve it.

Her stalker proved he was a psycho. He would kill anyone who hurt her. Which meant none of them were safe.

"You should go," Kelsea said quietly. "You won't be safe around me. You need to leave."

Jaymes stepped toward her. "I'm not leaving you, Kelsea."

She looked up at him, her expression dialed to determined. "I will not let you get killed because of me. Maxwell did. He didn't deserve this, Jaymes." She slapped her phone.

He nodded. "I know, Kels. I know. But neither do you."

She shrugged and huffed a laugh. "Maybe I do. I have no idea who this is. I didn't recognize his voice. But there's some reason he's following me. And now he's killing people. Because of me. It's my fault Maxwell is dead."

Jaymes shook his head and moved around the bed. He dragged her into his arms and held her tight. "It's not your fault. None of this is your fault. This is because of that son of a bitch who thinks he can do whatever he wants. You're not to blame here."

"But—"

"No," Jaymes said fiercely. "No. He's sick. He's obsessed

with you, and that isn't your fault. You have done nothing wrong. And don't you dare tell me you have. Dunn and the rest of them are going to make sure you're safe. You will be with one of them from now on, until this bastard is caught."

"What about you?" she murmured against his chest.

"What about me?"

"If he's after Maxwell, he might come after you. Are you going to be with one of them?"

Jaymes swallowed the hurt. She didn't think he was strong enough either. He wasn't her protector, he needed protection.

"We'll see. For right now, you're the most important one."

She pulled back and looked up at him. "I can't get another video, Jaymes. I can't watch you die. Please."

He nodded and wrapped her up again. For her, he'd swallow his pride.

It wasn't long before Jaymes's apartment became stalker central. English took over the table with his computers. He searched for traffic cams, but nothing was in the neighborhood where Maxwell lived. The police already canvased the residents to see if anyone had a security system that showed anything, but none of them did. It was a quiet, safe neighborhood.

Was being the key.

Jaymes wasn't around for the activity last time. Usually the team worked out of an office they had downtown, but since Kelsea was staying with Jaymes, Dunn had them all there.

Kelsea was in the kitchen with Lily so Jaymes stayed out of the way. Lily would help take Kelsea's mind off everything. As much as was possible.

Jaymes leaned against the wall and watched everything

swirl around him. Dunn barked orders to everyone, like he always did. The others liked and respected him as their leader. When they were SEALs, Dunn wasn't in charge, but with Williams in the wind, and a psycho, Dunn took on the leadership role for the group. He was level-headed and objective. Two good qualities for a leader to have.

Jack and Archer sat on the floor and cleaned their guns on the coffee table, ready for a firefight. Jack was the class clown of the group, but he was deadly as a sniper. He hadn't shared any stories with Jaymes, but the secrets in his eyes said there was definitely some shit in his past. Archer... well, Jaymes still didn't know his brother well, but Archer was definitely the muscle. The guys called him "Hulk" when they wanted to piss him off. It worked, too. No one liked Archer when he was angry, but he got the job done.

Dex and English sat at the table with their laptops, digging into everything about Maxwell, watching the videos, and analyzing everything. Dex, code for Poindexter, was crazy smart. He saw things in new ways, a skill set that came in handy more than a few times. He was almost as good with computers as Jaymes and English, but not quite.

Rocky, whose real name was Adrian, stood near the door, guarding it even though none of them thought anyone would get in. They weren't taking any chances. Rocky was a medic and could have gone to work just about anywhere he wanted, but he stuck with the team when they all settled in Niagara Falls. He talked about going some place warmer, but so did everyone else in Western New York in the winter.

Slade, the last member of the team, stood in front of Jaymes and looked him up and down. Slade was a beast of a man with the steadiest hands of anyone Jaymes had ever met. It made sense since he made a name for himself disabling, and occasionally setting, explosives. He told

Jaymes once that he was just glad he actually had all his fingers. "You good?"

Jaymes shrugged.

"We'll get him."

Jaymes leveled Slade with a look. "Like last time?"

Slade had the decency to look ashamed.

Jaymes knew it was a low-blow, but he was pissed off. None of them believed Kelsea when she said someone was following her. They dismissed her claims and stopped checking into her background and the people around her. They ruled out the handful of people they saw as suspicious, but there were tons of people in her life.

And one of them killed someone.

"We'll get Williams, too. And whoever this is, we have the best guys on it."

"If you'd listened to her, this might not have happened."

Slade nodded. He stood with his feet as wide as his shoulders, arms crossed over his chest. Even though he'd been out of the SEALs for six months, he still wore his hair military short. His dark eyes gave him a menacing look. They swung around the room, taking in everything.

"I know you care about her, but we need to move forward."

"Yeah, well, she wants to leave. She doesn't want to stay here and risk anyone else getting killed."

"Meaning you?" Slade asked pointedly.

Jaymes took a deep breath and nodded. "Yep. I'm still the wimp who can't protect himself. Except now I have Kelsea telling me so."

Slade glared at him for a long second. "You know that's not true. If the threat were on any of us, we'd have someone on our six at all times. That's the way it works. I'm staying here for the night, assuming the rest of them leave."

Jaymes shook his head, but Slade cut him off.

"Don't. Just don't. It's already been decided. This is what we do. We're here to keep people safe. And when there's a psycho running around blowing up houses, people aren't safe. Now stop acting like a fucking pussy and accept it."

Jaymes held Slade's gaze for a long minute, then nodded. He didn't like the thought of having a babysitter, but Kelsea needed someone with her. If she was there, Slade needed to be, too.

"You haven't shown up at the gym lately," Slade said quietly, eyeing the rest of the room.

Jaymes nodded. "I haven't wanted to leave Kelsea here alone."

Slade shrugged. "Maybe you should bring her."

Jaymes snorted. "Why? So she can see what a pussy I really am? You lift what... two hundred pounds? And I'm pushing to get to seventy-five?"

Slade turned and glared at Jaymes. "That woman can't take her eyes off you. I know you think the rest of us are eye-candy, but as far as she's concerned, you're the only sugar in the room. And regardless of that, what about protecting her? Pull your head out of your ass and think about her. Would it help her to go to the gym? Did it help you? Make you feel more in control? Are you so desperate for attention from a hot woman that you want to keep her locked up in here and scared, or do you want to help her have the confidence to fight back?"

Jaymes hated the implication that he was no better than his own kidnappers. By keeping Kelsea from the gym, and whatever else she enjoyed doing, he was locking her up. It wasn't fair to her.

"Sometimes I really hate you," Jaymes said.

Slade nodded. "You're not the first person to tell me that."

Jaymes snorted. "That doesn't surprise me a bit."

Slade slapped him on the shoulder, nearly knocking him down. "After your run, we can go to the gym? Maybe she'll want to run with you."

"How do you know I run?"

Slade smirked and nodded toward Jack. "He was pissed off the other day when he found out he wasn't the only one you went to for help. Thought he was special."

Jaymes chuckled. "I didn't want you all to know what I was doing."

Slade nodded, his smile replaced by seriousness. "I get it. It's not easy being taken. Feeling like you were the easy target. The one on your team that was the weakest." He met Jaymes's gaze. "I've been there."

Jaymes drew back. He never would have thought Slade was one of the ones who were taken. When Jack mentioned it, he almost thought it was lip-service to make Jaymes feel better. There was no humor in Slade's eyes. Only fear, determination, and full truth.

"I didn't know."

Slade nodded. "I don't talk about it. Officially, it never happened."

Jaymes understood those words. All too well. He hid his disappearance from his coworkers, but that was his choice. Slade's kidnapping, and whatever happened when he was gone, was likely done by a group the government and the SEALs by extension didn't acknowledge existed. Which meant not only could he not talk about it, but no one was allowed to know. At all.

"That fear will always be there," Slade said. "It fades, but it's there. All the time. Help Kelsea find her strength."

Jaymes nodded. "I will. I'll talk to her about going on our run, and to the gym. After all that, think we can go to the shelter? She volunteers there on the weekend, and we didn't make it out there today."

Slade smirked again. "More important things to do?"

Jaymes chuckled and nodded. "Definitely."

Slade grinned. "Yeah, we can do that. Maybe I'll get a dog while we're there."

"You? A dog?"

Slade nodded. "I used to have one. I think it's time for another. Something tells me Kelsea will know which dog is right for me."

Jaymes looked across the room to where Kelsea stood talking to Lily and nodded. "You're probably right. She seems to have a sixth sense about some things."

Just then, she looked up and met his gaze. She smiled at him and he realized he'd do anything to keep her safe.

Anything.

12

Kelsea completely understood why Jaymes was in love with Lily. She was sweet and funny and had the ability to make her forget she was in danger.

She wasn't all fluff, but she understood Kelsea needed a break from all the serious men in the other room.

"I can't believe he said that," Kelsea said on a laugh. "What did you do?"

Lily shrugged and tossed her brown hair over her shoulder. "What other response was there? I told him exactly what to do."

Kelsea laughed again. She'd never had a girlfriend like Lily. She knew they weren't really friends, but it felt like it. She was the one person in the room who wanted to know how she was feeling.

Except Jaymes. She glanced up at him and found him watching them again. He met her gaze and smiled. She smiled back, feeling the warmth of his attention all over her body.

"He's a really good guy, you know," Lily said, turning her back to the group of men and focusing on the stove. She stirred the large pot of spaghetti sauce and tapped the spoon on the edge before setting it down. She glanced at Kelsea, waiting for a response.

Kelsea nodded. "He is. I know that. Any man who would take me in like he did is amazing."

"I don't just mean that."

Kelsea tilted her head in question.

"He's had shitty luck with women, but he's a pretty great boyfriend from what I've heard."

"You two never dated?"

Lily laughed and shook her head. "No. He's like my brother. Always has been. I love him, but it's not like that."

"I think it might be for him," Kelsea mumbled.

Lily shook her head again. "I'm not the one he keeps looking at over here."

Kelsea glanced again and caught Jaymes watching her. The look of raw desire in his gaze stole her breath.

"He really likes you, Kelsea."

She nodded. She didn't know what to say, especially not to Jaymes's best friend and the woman he loved. Lily put her hand on Kelsea's arm, drawing her attention. Kelsea looked up and met Lily's worried gaze.

"He had a really rough year. I don't think he really liked that I got together with Archer. They weren't close before. Archer carried a lot of guilt from when they were kids. But he's trying to make up for lost time. I think Jaymes is, too, but he and I don't talk the way we used to. Jaymes is distant and withdrawn, but since you've been here, I see my best friend again."

Kelsea shook her head. "I'm not doing anything."

Lily smiled. "You're helping him live again. He hasn't let anyone in since before. He's kept to himself. But with you... he's the person he used to be."

Kelsea looked back at him. He was talking to English, studying something on the computer. He pushed his glasses up the bridge of his nose and leaned in closer to the screen. Finally, he nodded, then straightened. He rolled his wrist and rubbed his forehead.

He looked tired. Kelsea smiled when she thought back to how he got so tired. Sex did that to a person. Not that she had a lot of experience with all day sex marathons after all night ones. She wouldn't pass up the chance to have another, but with the invasion of Jack and the rest of the team, she wasn't sure she'd have the option.

She was a scientist. She knew things weren't always what they seemed. What was happening between her and Jaymes was purely based on the situation they were in. She thought she could be falling for him, but it would end as soon as the threat to her life was over. When they caught whoever was after her, she'd go home, back to her quiet, boring life, and Jaymes would continue to heal and fall in love with someone else. It was the only way their story could end.

"I know what you're thinking right now," Lily said with a smirk. "You wish we'd all leave so you can take him back to bed."

Kelsea gawked but didn't answer.

"I get it. I felt the same way when Archer and I met."

"How did you know...?"

"That you were sleeping together?"

Kelsea nodded.

Lily shrugged. "I know him. He's happy. And when he smiles like he has been whenever he looks at you, it's because he's getting lucky."

Kelsea processed, trying to decide how she felt about Lily and Jaymes and the whole situation. If Lily knew they were sleeping together, the rest of the team probably did, too. But Lily knew Jaymes. She could tell he was smiling a certain way. And she saw Jaymes, really saw him.

If Kelsea let herself get more attached to him, she'd only end up hurt. Jaymes was in lust with her, but she wasn't the woman he really wanted. That woman was standing in his kitchen, as comfortable as could be, making dinner for the entire group of men who'd invaded Kelsea's life in the last few days.

She didn't belong there. She wasn't a part of their group. She was the outsider. The one everyone was trying to analyze. She was the job. And when the job was done, they'd all go back to their lives. Never to be seen again.

WHEN ALL THE activity died down and the team headed out the door, Jaymes turned to Kelsea for the first time since Archer and Jack showed up at his door. She was tucked into the corner of the couch, her feet pulled up, her chin on her knees. She looked small and scared, and he didn't blame her a bit.

Slade cleared his throat and nodded toward the bathroom. Jaymes nodded and moved to Kelsea.

"I don't know what I'm doing here," he admitted. "I was gone last time we went through all this, so talk to me. What are you thinking?"

She lifted her gaze to him and smiled sadly. "I wish I met you under different circumstances. Without a psycho chasing me."

Jaymes nodded. "I wish that, too." He paused to see if she said anything else. When she didn't, he continued. "Where do you want to sleep tonight? Slade has his eye on the couch, but that doesn't mean we have to share my bed."

Her eyebrows drew together. "You, um..." She took a deep breath and dropped her feet to the ground. "It's fine. I can sleep out here. You shouldn't have to give up your bed all the time."

She stood, avoiding his gaze. She moved past him, skirting him so he couldn't touch her.

He moved into her path. He screwed up again. "What did I say?"

She shook her head and forced a grin. "Nothing. Today was great, but it's over now, so I'll do my best to stay out of your way."

"Today was more than great," he argued. "And I don't want you to stay out of my way. I want you in my bed again. I want to hold you and know you're safe all night. I want to wake up next to you and kiss you and slide into you and know everything is right with the world, even if it's just for a few minutes."

She pulled in a shaky breath and wrapped her arms around herself. "You do?"

He nodded and stepped closer to her. He felt centered when she was in his arms, like she was the reason he was okay. Like he had to be okay for her.

He almost reached her when Slade cleared his throat behind them. "Excuse me," he said, walking past them.

Slade changed into a tight muscle shirt and a pair of gym shorts. His clothes from the day were folded neatly in his hand, his Glock on top of the pile.

Kelsea looked at him for a second, then focused back on Jaymes. His chest puffed up. She had a perfect male specimen on display in front of her and she was watching him.

"Let's go to bed," Jaymes whispered, wrapping his arm around her and tugging her toward his room. He didn't stop until they were inside with the door closed and locked behind them.

Kelsea reached for him as he tugged her closer. Her arms went around his neck, his around her waist. She lifted up on her toes to kiss him, and he backed them up toward the bed. He hadn't had enough of her, and he was starting to think he never would.

Her legs hit the edge of his bed, and he finally stopped. He grabbed the edge of her shirt, his shirt really, and slid a hand underneath. Her skin was soft and warm and so tempting he couldn't see straight.

He ripped his glasses off and yanked his shirt over his head. Her hands went to his chest, teasing him from his belly button to his nipples and back. Her light touch made him even harder than he already was. Then she pinched his nipple, and he groaned.

He tore her shirt off, throwing it to the ground before he went for her bra. He needed her naked as quickly as possible. After spending the day with her, then being invaded and unable to touch her, he was dying to be inside her again.

She pulled at his clothes with the same urgency, then stretched out on his bed, naked and ready for him.

"Inside me, Jaymes. Please."

He shook his head. "Not yet, Kels. I need more than a quick fuck right now."

"More later. Fuck now."

He smiled and shook his head again. He kneeled on the floor and dragged her to him, dropping her knees over the edge of the bed.

She started to protest, but he didn't want to hear it. He sucked hard on her clit and her arguments died on her lips.

He added a finger, then two, and she sank back to the bed and moaned.

She gasped and sat up. "I forgot Slade's here." She pushed him away. "Jaymes, you can't."

He pressed her to the bed and teased her with his fingers. She groaned and squirmed, trying to get him to stop.

"Kels, Slade knows what's going on. He doesn't care. He probably has headphones on so he doesn't hear anything. And even if he does, it's not like we're doing something wrong in here."

"But—"

Jaymes shook his head. "No buts, Kels. If you don't want me, then I'll stop. Now. And I'll walk out of this room naked and deal with Slade seeing me like this. But if you're saying no because you're worried about what he's going to think, then put him out of your mind and come for me."

She hesitated for a second. His fingers were still inside her, his thumb on her clit. One brush and he knew which option she'd pick, but he wasn't going to manipulate her like that. He wanted everything that happened between them to be a mutual choice, not something she agreed to because her hormones took over.

She reached for him, pulling his face to hers. Her tongue pressed into his mouth, hot and wet and commanding. He had no problem with her taking over for a few seconds and followed her lead with the kiss.

She stroked her tongue alongside his, then nipped at his lip. She clutched him to her, so tight together their bodies met from shoulder to hip. She tipped her head back, and he took full advantage of her position by running his tongue down her throat. Her arms eased their tight grip around his neck, letting him go lower. She dropped her elbows to the bed, and he sucked one nipple into his mouth.

Her eyes tracked his movements. He stared up at her, watching her watch him. Her pupils dilated when he circled her nipple with his tongue, then blew on it. She tugged her lip between her teeth when he moved to the other breast. She sucked in a breath as he moved down, closer and closer to where his hand still disappeared into her.

He hadn't moved his hand, trying to stay as still as possible. When she spread her thighs and stared between them, holding his gaze as he kissed his way to his thumb, he couldn't hold out any longer.

He slowly withdrew his fingers, enjoying her full body shiver. Her eyes rolled back in her head, and he bent to lick her.

She missed tasting her all evening. Her sweetness faded from his tongue hours ago. He needed more of her. Her hips rose to meet his face. He licked her again, timing the thrust of his finger so he circled her clit the same moment his fingers hit her g-spot.

She gasped, then moaned. "Oh, God. Jaymes. Don't stop."

He had no intention of doing so. He licked and sucked and teased until she was begging him to let her come. Her pussy rippled around his fingers. He drew her clit into his mouth and sucked hard, pressing his fingers deep inside her, and she lost it.

"Yes! Oh, Jaymes, yes! More. Oh, God, more!"

He didn't let up on her, thrusting deep and hard and teasing her just enough for one orgasm to slow before he nipped and sucked and flicked her clit for another one.

He only stopped when she begged him to. "No more. I can't breathe. Inside. Now."

He wasn't ready to stop, but he wanted her breathing when he buried himself in her. He rolled on a condom while she panted and recovered her breath. When she finally looked up at him with a satisfied grin, he lined up and sank into her tight pussy.

"Oh, God, you feel so good," she groaned.

"Thinking... same thing," he grunted.

He took a minute to breathe, not willing to come on his first stroke into her. She was tight and soaked and perfect. The way they fit together overwhelmed him. Like she was made for him to be inside of. She could take all of him, and she wrapped around him perfectly. None of the other women he'd been with were such a perfect fit.

When he thought he could move without coming instantly, he pulled out. She moaned with him, then lifted her legs and set her feet on his hips, dropping her knees to the side. The move opened her wider so he sank in deeper. He didn't think it was possible.

"Oh, God," she groaned when he thrust in again.

"You okay?"

She nodded. "Might come again. Oh, God."

Fuck yeah.

He clenched his teeth and stroked harder into her. With every stroke inside, she moaned and thrust up to meet him. He held her hips, matching their rhythms to maximize her pleasure.

A few strokes later and she was moaning loudly, begging him to make her come once more.

He slid his hand between them and found her clit. One touch and her pussy clamped down hard on him, her scream a choked moan. She bucked hard, taking what she needed from him.

He took right back, thrusting hard into her pulsing body

until she pulled him right over the edge with her. He screamed her name, emptying himself into her.

Jaymes trembled. His body felt like it had been wrung out. He gave her everything he had, everything he was. He wasn't sure if it was enough, but she had him. All of him.

He'd never been so wrapped up in another woman, so willing to expose himself. With Lily, he fell for her slowly, over time. She was his best friend, the one woman in his life who was a constant. She was someone he saw every day, so it felt natural to love her.

Everything was different with Kelsea. Their relationship, if he could call it that, started a few days ago. Fear was the primary emotion at work, but he wanted to keep her safe the second he saw her. The thought of anything happening to Kelsea made him sick.

Being with her, talking to her during sex and letting himself lose control and fuck her the way he did, it was different. He'd always held himself back with the other women he dated. He wasn't even dating Kelsea, but he showed her more of who he was than anyone else he'd ever known. Even Lily.

Jaymes didn't want to think about what it meant. A part of him knew, but he wasn't willing to let the thought fully form. Because then he might be tempted to tell her. And that would be a huge mistake.

13

———

Kelsea groaned and rolled over. Every inch of her ached. She hadn't felt so good in... maybe ever. It was sad, really. She was a grown woman with a healthy sex drive, but Jaymes was the first man who had any interest in trying to fill it.

Boy, did he fill it. And her. Her thighs tingled with the memory of him stretching her as he entered her from behind.

She'd never felt so cherished as she did with Jaymes. He constantly asked how she felt, and not in the way Maxwell did where he wasn't sure of himself, but in a sexy way where he was trying to make it as good for her as possible.

Maxwell.

Her heart hurt thinking about him. She didn't love him, but she didn't like the idea of someone hurting him, killing him, because of her. It wasn't fair. And it wasn't right.

Jaymes stirred beside her, rolling over. His hand slapped her side, and he jerked up.

"It's me. Kelsea," she whispered in the darkness.

He laid back down and moved closer until his front was

tight against her back. He wrapped his arm around her middle and cupped her breast. Just that fast, she was ready for him again.

She laid still, her thoughts bouncing between Jaymes's cock growing against her ass and who would hurt Maxwell. When Jaymes brushed his thumb over her nipple, she forgot all about Maxwell and moaned.

Jaymes kissed her shoulder and pressed his cock against her. She spread her thighs, encouraging him to slide into her. He teased her other nipple, then slid his hand down her body to her soaked pussy. He nipped her shoulder and groaned.

It didn't take him long to have her whimpering. She came quietly, as quietly as she could. He grabbed a condom and was inside her before she stopped quivering.

His fingers toyed with her clit as he pumped long, slow strokes inside her. Her body, already primed, wasn't willing to wait for him to tease her into another orgasm.

She whined and pressed back into him. He got the picture and set out to make her scream. He pulled out, then flipped her onto her back and was over her, plunging into her in seconds.

He slammed hard into her, and she forgot to be quiet. She screamed her release, loving the fact that he was right behind her, grunting and pulsing in her.

He collapsed onto her a second later. She wrapped her arms around him, enjoying the feel of him pressing her to the mattress. He breathed hard in her ear, his heart pounding against her chest. She could lay there forever, surrounded and protected by him.

Far too soon, he rolled over and left the room. He was back a few seconds later, pulling back the covers and dragging her into his arms again. "That was a hell of a good morning."

She smiled and nodded against his chest.

"Much better than Jack pounding on my door."

Kelsea chuckled. He told her the night before that he and Jack might go for a run in the morning. Kelsea had never been a runner. Not only did she fear giving herself two black eyes, but she hated exercise. She never had time for it. She preferred to spend her time in her lab or playing with animals.

"Are you going to join me this morning?" Jaymes asked, the sexy rumble of his morning voice vibrating through all her good parts.

She found herself nodding, not really paying attention to what she was agreeing to. A shower for two? Another round before the sun tried to wake up? Breakfast in bed? She could go for any of those.

But Jaymes leapt out of bed and got dressed, and she remembered what she was agreeing to.

"I'm not a runner," she said. "I hate it."

Jaymes shrugged. "Then we walk."

She shook her head. "I should probably just stay here. I'll be fine."

Jaymes gave her a look that left little room to argue. "You're not staying here alone."

Kelsea was scared. Someone was following her and had already killed her ex. But no one told her what to do. Not since she decided she didn't want to go to medical school and cut ties with her parents. Or rather, they cut ties with her.

"You're not keeping me prisoner here. I refuse to let whoever this is steal my life from me."

"And I refuse to let you get taken. You're not staying here

alone. You're not going anywhere alone. Not until we know what's going on."

She climbed out of his bed, her argument weakened by the fact that she was completely naked. She searched for clothes and found his t-shirt tossed over the edge of the bed near her. She snatched it and pulled it on, feeling marginally better.

"I'm not going to stop living my life. I should have gone home days ago, but..." she glanced at the bed.

"We started sleeping together. And I wanted to keep you safe," Jaymes provided.

Her eyebrows shot sky high. He was fucking her so she'd stay, and she thought she was falling in love. Well, the joke was definitely on her.

"Do you screw all the women you vow to protect, or am I special?"

His eyes went hard. He finished getting dressed with jerky movements. When he left the room without looking at her again, she almost felt bad.

Almost.

The apartment was silent within minutes. It was time to leave. She couldn't stay there any longer. She wasn't stupid, and she wasn't going to sleep with someone who didn't really want her. She stripped off his t-shirt, then found her own clothes. She packed up the rest of her stuff and threw her bag over her shoulder.

Before she left his room, she called for an Uber. Her car was still at her house, and she needed to get back to her life. Hiding wasn't going to fix anything, and hiding behind Jaymes was only going to hurt more in the long run.

Kelsea moved out into the living room and checked to see how long before her ride got there. She was about to head outside when a voice stopped her.

"I know you're not leaving."

Kelsea screamed.

A light in the living room flipped on.

Slade. On the couch. Rumpled and clearly still half asleep.

"You can't leave, Kelsea."

She stiffened her spine even though her heart still pounded, trying to break free. "I can't stay here."

"Why not? It sounded like you had a pretty great night."

She glared at him, her cheeks heating. "Yeah, well, Jaymes was only sleeping with me so I'd stay here."

Slade scoffed. "Yeah, right."

She shook her head. "He said he was. He said he wanted to keep me safe."

"That doesn't mean he fucked you to keep you here. It means he wanted to keep you safe. And he wanted to sleep with you."

Kelsea shook her head, her hair catching on her lashes. She set her bag down and tied her hair back into a ponytail. "He's in love with Lily. I don't know if you know that, but I'm just a substitute."

Slade took a deep breath and stood. He towered over her, easily topping her by six or more inches. His shoulders were as wide as her hips, and his arms rivaled Mason's in size. If she was into beefcake instead of sexy nerds, she'd be all over Slade. He was probably the smarter choice.

"You've only just met Jaymes, so you don't really know him. It sounds like you're well aware he was taken a few months ago, right?"

She nodded.

"Do you know he hasn't gone on a date since then?"

She shook her head.

"Or that he hasn't slept with anyone?"

She shook her head again.

"Or that he's happy for Lily and Archer?"

"He's not. I've seen the way he looks at her."

Slade chuckled. "Me, too. And I've seen the way he looks at you. You two may have met under strange circumstance, but that doesn't mean he doesn't want you. In the six months I've known Jaymes, he's never once asked for my help."

"You lift weights together."

Slade nodded. "Because I asked him to come with me. Told him I needed a spotter and the other guys were busy."

"He bought that?"

Slade shrugged. "No clue, but he didn't argue about it. We've been going ever since. He's told you things he's never told me. Never told any of us. Jack was pissed as hell when he found out he wasn't the only one trying to help Jaymes. He's the one who wants to fix everyone else and won't admit how fucked up he is."

"Jaymes?"

"No, Jack. He thinks he's good, but he's not. None of us are. But we have a job to do. I'm here to keep you safe. I'm here because I'm being paid for it. But Jaymes? Jaymes is here, and has you in his bed, because he cares. That's the kind of guy he is. Not the kind who fucks a woman for the hell of it. That asshole designation belongs to me."

Kelsea smiled softly at Slade. "You're not an asshole. You're a nice guy."

He snorted. "You only think that because I'm not trying to get into your pants. Trust me, you'd have a different opinion of me if Jaymes hadn't gotten to you first."

She smiled at him. "Maybe so, but I don't think you give yourself enough credit."

Slade shrugged and didn't argue.

Kelsea chewed her lip, thinking about Slade's assessment of Jaymes. Was he right? Did Jaymes really like her? And did she screw it all up by getting an attitude with him?

She really should not be allowed to interact with other humans. The brain was easier to figure out than the people the brains were inside.

JAYMES HALF WONDERED if Kelsea would still be there when he got back from his run with Jack. He woke Slade up before he left and told him to make sure she didn't leave.

Yeah, he was pissed that she thought he was sleeping with her for the wrong reasons. He spent his entire run trying to decide exactly why he was sleeping with her.

She was gorgeous, that was an easy one. But she was also funny and smart and sexy. When she let her guard down, he felt like he could do anything. And that was a shitty reason to sleep with her. She deserved better. Which meant he needed to hand off her protection to one of the other guys. One of the guys who was actually trained and could keep her safe. Without screwing her. He hoped.

"You okay?" Jack asked when they slowed to walk through the neighborhood.

Jaymes nodded. "Yeah. You need to take Kelsea."

"Take her where?"

"No, you need to be her personal bodyguard from now on. I can't do it anymore."

"Why not? She trusts you."

Jaymes shook his head. "No, she doesn't. She thinks I'm sleeping with her to keep her from leaving. To keep her safe."

"Are you?"

Jaymes shrugged. "Maybe partly. And also because it was nice to feel like I could keep her safe."

"You know what happened with Williams wasn't your fault."

Jaymes shrugged again. "Feels like it was. And all I'm doing with Kelsea is keeping her locked inside my apartment so she can't go out and get snatched. It's not fair to her. I need you to watch her."

Jack slid him a look but finally nodded. Jaymes felt better knowing Kelsea would be safe. And he wouldn't be taking advantage of her any longer.

"Slade wanted to go lift. You going to join us?"

Jack nodded. "Yeah, I could use it. But, um, Kelsea?"

Jaymes sighed. "You can ask her. It's up to the two of you."

Jack nodded and followed Jaymes up the stairs to his apartment. He let them in, stopping short when he heard Kelsea and Slade laughing.

"Don't tell Lily, but this is better than hers," Slade said.

Kelsea laughed. "I don't think I can hold a candle to Lily on pretty much any front, but thank you for the confidence boost."

Jaymes walked inside, bypassing the kitchen and heading straight to the back of the apartment. He noticed Kelsea's bag by the couch, clearly full and zipped, and told himself it was for the best that she was ready to go.

KELSEA SAW JAYMES RUSH BY, and her smile fell. She wanted to talk to him, but he obviously didn't want to see her.

"His brother is engaged to the last woman he had a thing for. We walked in here and he saw you with this muscle head and thinks you're going to ditch him for Slade," Jack said with far more insight than Kelsea was comfortable with.

She looked at him, but he just stared at her with his hands on his hips.

"He asked me to move you to my place. He thinks you don't want to be here. Yeah, he's acting like a pussy, but don't hold that against him. He needs to know you're not going to screw him over. Lily had no clue Jaymes liked her, but you do. Shit is still messed up in his head. He's not going to get over it and move on, especially when your situation is so close to his."

"How so?"

"Someone watching you. Someone following you. Someone waiting to grab you when you're vulnerable. Jaymes was taken for different reasons, but at the end of the day, it doesn't matter why someone gets snatched, just that they did. He's fucked up. If you don't care about him, we can leave now. Your bag's ready to go, which he also noticed. If you care, go kiss and make up."

Kelsea didn't have to think long about how she felt. The confusing part for her was how Jaymes felt. The hot and cold was frustrating. But she understood how the brain worked. She knew how a traumatic situation could mess with someone. Throw their sense of security off, make them doubt everyone in their lives, and even make them question themselves.

She didn't want to make things worse for Jaymes. She cared about him, could even love him if she let herself, but she wasn't going to force him to be with her. If he felt anywhere close to how she felt, they could give whatever was going on a shot.

She walked out of the kitchen and straight to the

bedroom. The door was closed, but she took a deep breath and let herself in. Jaymes was sitting on the bed with his head in his hands.

"I'm not in the fucking mood, Jack."

She stepped in and closed the door behind herself.

Jaymes finally looked up and saw her. He closed his eyes again. "Here to say goodbye?"

"You're a real pain in the ass, you know that?"

"Excuse me?" he snapped.

"You. You're a pain in the ass. You let me in one moment, then shut me out the next. You hold me all night and make love to me, then tell me it's all in the name of keeping me safe. I've never met a man who was so hot and cold all the time. I don't know how to take you."

He glared at her. "Well, it looks as though you're not taking me. You're leaving. Jack will keep you safe. Or maybe you're going to stay with Slade now. Whatever. I don't care."

"See, that. That's what I'm talking about. You say you don't care, but I know you do. You're looking at me like you'd do anything for me. What the hell is going on?"

He shrugged. "Nothing. I just happened to be in the right place at the right time. Now the real heroes are taking over. You'll be safer with them. They have actual skills when it comes to this kind of stuff. I just hide. Like I've been doing for months."

"I know, Jaymes," she said softly, sitting down next to him.

He sighed. "I can't keep you safe, Kelsea."

"Nothing has happened to me since I met you."

Jaymes shrugged. "Because we're hiding."

She shook her head. "You believed me when I said someone was following me. You didn't tell me I was crazy. You trusted me and you kept me safe."

He sucked in a breath. "Slade or Jack would be better."

"I don't want one of them. I want you, Jaymes."

He finally met her gaze. She let him see all the ways she meant those words. She chewed on her lip, hoping he'd understand. If not, she didn't know what she was going to do.

14

———

Jaymes stared at Kelsea, wondering if she was saying what he thought she was saying. "Spell it out for me, Kels."

She turned to him, lifting up on her knees and straddling him. His hands automatically went to her hips. She lowered herself down until her hot center lined up with his cock. The greedy bastard stood up and took notice.

"I have a thing for sexy nerds. For smart guys who can hold an intelligent conversation with me. For guys who wear glasses and have dinner with their mothers. For guys who take in strange women because they're more concerned about the safety of a perfect stranger than anything else."

She ground against his cock, making his eyes roll back in his head.

"And I have a really big thing for you, Jaymes. So stop pawning me off onto all your friends. Sure, they can stay here and carry the big guns and all that, but I'm not thinking of any of them when you slide into me. It's all you that makes me so wet, Jaymes. The sexy nerd who took me home and kept me safe. The gorgeous guy who looked into my past to try to keep me protected. The smart, kind man who gets jealous when I'm talking to one of his friends because he thinks I'd rather be with one of them. Spoiler alert. I wouldn't. I. Want. You. Only you, Jaymes. Is that spelled out enough for you?"

He flipped them, making her gasp, then laugh. He kissed her, hard, stealing her laughter and replacing it with a moan. He flexed his hips into her, dying to strip away the thin layers that separated them and sink into her.

Before he could take action on that, someone pounded on the door. "Let's go lovebirds. I want to hit the gym early, then we'll have plenty of time to get to the shelter this afternoon."

Jaymes pulled back and looked at Kelsea. Her dark hair was spread out on his bed, her cheeks flushed. Her chest rose and fell with each breath she sucked in. She was stunning.

"I don't want to get up," she whimpered.

"Stay here. Jack said he'll stay with you."

She shook her head. "And miss a chance to see you get all sweaty? Not a chance."

His eyebrows went up. "Yeah?"

She nodded and ran a hand through his hair. "Oh, yeah. That's a real turn-on for me."

Jaymes wasn't sure he'd survive the gym if she was going to watch him, but he'd put on the show of his damn life if it made her hot.

"Let's go," he said, jumping up and dragging her with him. He grabbed his glasses from the nightstand and practically dragged her out of the room.

They all rode to the gym together with Jaymes and Kelsea in the back. He held her hand the entire time, stroking his thumb over her knuckles. She chatted with Jack and Slade on the drive, but Jaymes was quiet. He admired her. Not only was she willing to walk away from him for a damn good reason, but she was willing to fight him to stay for an even better one.

When he got her back to his place, he was going to show her just how much he appreciated that.

HE WAITED until the apartment was empty, then let himself into the building. He hated that he didn't know more about the guy. There was a lot of activity, and he was sure the others were there for her protection. They would fail, of course, but it was nice of them to try.

He took the stairs slowly so he didn't draw any attention to himself. The last thing he needed was someone to notice him. He started up the second staircase when a door below him opened. He kept going, not looking back. If he was lucky, and he always was, whoever was leaving their unit would leave the building without even noticing he was there.

"I'm worried about Jaymes, babe," a woman's voice said. "It's fast for him to get involved with her. She's nice, but I don't really know if he should be getting involved with someone. He's still not himself."

He paused on the stairs to listen to the conversation below him. If he could learn more about Jaymes, it would help him figure out how to get to the guy.

"You're overreacting. I think it's a good thing he's getting laid. He's been less than thrilled about us being together."

She scoffed, her voice drifting as the outside door opened. "He shouldn't just get laid. He needs to find someone who..."

He peeked out the window to get a look at them. The

guy was tall with bulk that was visible through his jacket. The woman had plenty of curves and an ass that made him hard. She stopped and tipped her chin up, her dark hair slipping down her back as she got a kiss from the guy.

He needed to check into them, too. She could be Lily. More people who were between him and Kelsea. No one would be between them when he was done.

He continued up the stairs and quickly unlocked the door to apartment seventeen. Everything was dark inside, but stillness told him no one else was there. He closed the door behind himself and flipped the lock. He walked through, turning on lights as he went. He was careful to only touch what he needed to touch, making sure he didn't move anything.

He took pictures of the place, especially the bed. It was clear two people shared it the night before. So she was definitely fucking him. He thought about setting up a camera in there so he could watch them, but he didn't bring all his equipment.

His plan was only to make sure he could get in and learn more about Jaymes. Between the medical bills and files he downloaded, he had plenty of information about Jaymes Ford. And his mother and brother.

KELSEA NEVER ENJOYED a trip to the gym as much as she did spending the time with Jack. He was funny and kept her laughing instead of reminding her why he was hanging around her. She noticed all the women checking him out and tossing dirty looks her way, but she was beyond the point of caring. None of them were good enough for Jack if they were that nasty. Jack needed a sweet woman, one who would understand he flirted with everyone and didn't get upset by it. Basically, a saint.

After the gym, they all went back to shower and get dressed. She hoped to save some water and shower with Jaymes, but Slade followed them into his apartment and blew that plan out of the water.

An hour later, the four of them piled back into Slade's SUV and headed for Best Friends Forever. Kelsea was excited to get there. If she made it there during the week, she spent most of her time with the dogs, cleaning cages and letting them out. On the weekends, they had extra volunteers, which meant she got to play with the cats.

She practically jumped out of the SUV when Slade put it in park. Jaymes was right with her, with Jack and Slade close behind. The parking lot was almost full, which was a great thing. It meant animals were getting adopted.

Kelsea opened the door and smiled at all the excitement. Two people were at the counter with dogs on leashes, signing the last of the paperwork to take home their new pets. A third person stood to the side with a cat carrier. Kelsea wasn't sure if it was empty or occupied. If it wasn't occupied, it definitely didn't have Moby in it.

The two dogs spotted her and pulled at their leashes. She went to both of them and rubbed their fur until they slumped to the ground for full body rubs. Since it was likely she'd never see either of them again, she obliged, smiling up at the new owners.

"You picked great ones. Both are such sweet dogs. Aren't you?"

The dogs jumped up and licked her. She laughed, wrapping her arms around both their necks. The dogs barked an answering laugh, then trotted between Kelsea and their new owners, one of whom had a pair of kids nearby.

"Hi Kelsea," Jeremy said from behind the counter.

"Hey Kels," said his wife, Amanda. They owned Best Friends Forever. Kelsea had been volunteering there for so long they'd become like family to her, except better because they didn't try to control her life.

"Hi guys. Good day?"

They both nodded. "Did you bring some new volunteers or new owners?" Amanda asked, glancing behind Kelsea to Jaymes, Jack, and Slade.

"Volunteers," Kelsea said.

"Maybe a new owner," Slade added, stepping up next to her. "I was going to check out the dogs and see if I find one that's a good match for me."

Amanda met Kelsea's eye for a second, then focused on Slade. Her customer thanked her and headed for the door with her new best friend. Amanda asked Jeremy if he could handle things out front for a minute and nodded toward the back.

The four of them followed Amanda down the hall. Slade walked right behind her, listening to what Amanda was saying.

"We have a lot of great animals here. Our dogs get outside play time daily, rain, snow, or shine. Most dogs come here from bad situations. Whether it was abandonment or abuse or neglect, they didn't get here because they were well loved. Some have behavioral issues. Some are still just happy dogs, but with obvious trauma. We use soft voices so the ones who have abuse in their background don't get scared of us. Kelsea put us in touch with a dog psychologist who helps us to see what each of the dogs might need."

"A dog psychologist?" Slade asked skeptically.

Amanda nodded. "I thought it was crazy, too, but it's helped some of our dogs. We can't ask them what's wrong, so having someone come in once a week and try to work with the dogs that are the most volatile is helpful. Our goal is to adopt every dog we have at some point. We're a no kill shelter, so the ones who aren't ready to be adopted just stay here until we feel they can handle it."

Slade shrugged. "Sounds perfect."

Amanda opened the door and stepped inside. The dogs barked excitedly when they saw all of them there. "Have a look around. Kelsea can help you out with any of them you want to spend some time with. We have a few pens in the back where you can play if you want."

Amanda rested her hand on Kelsea's arm as she headed back toward the front. Kelsea nodded, understanding that she was in charge.

The three of them watched Slade walk by the cages and talk to the dogs. It didn't take long for Kelsea to get antsy. She went over to Howler's cage and waited for him to drag himself to the door so she could pet him.

Slade walked around, then came back to where Kelsea was. "There's a cool one over there. Who's this?"

Kelsea smiled. "This is Howler. He likes to make noise." She patted Howler's head. "Who did you want to see?"

Slade led her to the cage he spotted and she let Bob out. Slade and Bob went into the play pen, which still sounded so dirty to Kelsea. She laughed as she closed the door behind them.

"What do you do here?" Jack asked.

Kelsea shrugged. "Whatever needs to be done. Clean out cages, play with the animals outside, scoop cat litter."

"Seriously?"

She nodded. "I always wanted pets growing up, but my parents never had time for them. I'm allergic to dogs so I can't get one, but I'm a cat person. I'm gone so much that I don't think it would be fair to a cat. They're independent and all, but I'd feel guilty getting one and then never being home."

"You should get two. Then they can play together," Jack said.

Kelsea grinned. "And destroy my house. Moby is not a gentle cat."

"Moby?"

Kelsea nodded. "There's a cat here I'd love to adopt, but he's a little crazy. He would definitely be hanging from the drapes when I get home. And if I got a second one, I have a feeling Moby would teach him bad habits instead of the other one being a good influence on Moby."

"Kelsea," Slade called. "He's afraid of me."

Kelsea went back to the playpen. Bob was in the far corner, hiding from Slade. He tried calling the dog, but Bob wasn't interested at all.

Kelsea chuckled. "He's very skittish. We think he was abused. He just got cleared last week to be adopted. I'll make a note on his chart that he was afraid of you. How tall are you?"

"Six-four."

Kelsea nodded. "Thanks. Sometimes dogs who are abused are fearful of people who are significantly bigger than them. It could be your boots or your clothes or even your scent, but my guess is your height because of the way he's looking up at you."

"Wow. Poor thing. I can't imagine who would hurt an animal."

Kelsea nodded. "Me either."

"What about the one you were petting? How's that one?"

Kelsea opened the cage for Slade and Bob to get out. She walked Bob back to his cage, giving him a biscuit for being so good. She rubbed his back and smiled when he circled his bed, then flopped in the middle and munched on his biscuit.

"Howler's a good dog. He's... he's one of the ones Amanda mentioned. He's been through some trauma."

"Is he available to adopt?"

Kelsea nodded.

"Can I meet him?"

Kelsea went to Howler's cage and opened it. Howler smiled up at her, his tongue falling to one side. "Come on," she said, patting her leg.

Howler tried to jump up, but his back legs gave out and his ass flopped to the ground again. He didn't give up and tried again, saving it right before he landed again. He walked beside her, half prancing and half falling, to the playpen. Slade followed them in. Kelsea patted Howler's head and left, closing the door behind the boys.

And Howler lived up to his name.

Slade clamped his hands over his ears. "Holy shit, he's loud."

Kelsea laughed. "He's Howler for a reason. Here, give him a treat. It usually gets him to quiet down."

She passed a biscuit through the chainlink to Slade. He held it out to Howler, calling his name. He stopped howling and tried to get over to Slade, but fell again. Slade tossed the biscuit onto the floor near him, but Howler got up and ran toward Slade, nearly knocking him down as Howler skidded to his side.

"Dude, the biscuit is over there," Slade said with a laugh.

Howler just looked up at him, then barked.

"He can't smell either," Kelsea shared. "If he didn't see you throw it, he'll never find it."

"Seriously?" Slade asked.

Kelsea smiled at him and nodded. "He's a great dog, but no one wants to deal with his struggles."

Slade muttered something that sounded like, "I can relate." He went over and grabbed the biscuit, then turned and held it out for Howler. The dog rushed over, giving up on running and just dragging his feet behind him. He gently took the biscuit from Slade's hand.

Slade looked up at Kelsea. "I thought he was going to eat my hand."

Kelsea shook her head. "He's a really sweet dog. He'd never hurt anyone on purpose. He's never bit any of us, or any of the dogs."

Slade lowered himself to the floor and let Howler crawl all over him for a few minutes before he announced that he was going to adopt Howler.

"Really?" Kelsea asked. She wasn't entirely sure Slade was serious. "Are you sure you want a dog? Especially him?"

Slade met her gaze with his own hard one. "He's a great dog. And I don't care that he can't move his legs or smell. He deserves a good home."

Kelsea nodded. "He does. I was just starting to doubt he'd find one."

Slade shrugged. "I like dogs."

There was definitely more to it, but Kelsea wasn't going to get it out of Slade. Instead, she grabbed a clipboard and handed it to Slade. "Fill all this out. Amanda and Jeremy will go over it with you, but he's all yours."

Slade jumped to his feet and rubbed Howler's back until he flopped to the side for a belly rub. Slade laughed and rubbed his new best friend until Howler let out a loud fart. And scared himself.

"He's going to be a lot of fun," Kelsea said.

Slade just shook his head.

15

———

As soon as they walked into the cat room, Kelsea was smiling. The excitement on her face had Jaymes grinning. He swore someone said hello, but the room was empty besides them.

"Hello, Moby," Kelsea cooed, going straight to the cage on the end. A large black cat was climbing the cage, upside down, and yowling at Kelsea.

"Hello," the cat said.

Jaymes swore to God the cat talked.

"What the hell?" Jack said.

Kelsea laughed. "Yeah, he says hello. It's really funny. He's a weird cat."

"What else can he say?" Jack asked, moving closer.

Kelsea shook her head. "Nothing. Just hello. He always says it when I walk in. He doesn't say hello to Amanda or Jeremy. Only me."

"I want a cat that says hello to me when I walk in. How fucking cool is that?" Jack laughed.

"This is the cat you want to adopt?" Jaymes asked.

Kelsea nodded and let Moby crawl from the cage door

into her arms, then up onto her shoulder. He perched there and wrapped his tail around her neck. She groaned. "He's twenty pounds of love."

"Twenty pounds?"

Kelsea nodded.

"That's a big fucking cat," Jack said. "How are you holding him up there?"

She shrugged. "I'm used to it by now. He's been doing this since he first came here."

"How long has he been here?" Jaymes asked.

"Three months. He was dropped off in a box outside the shelter. Amanda found him in the morning."

Jaymes had a hard time believing people could be so cruel. Or he did before he witnessed firsthand how fucked up people were.

"People suck," Slade said.

Everyone nodded in agreement.

"What do you have to do in here?" Jaymes asked.

"Scoop the litter, refill the food and water, and play with the cats. That's about it. Moby's wild, but he plays well with others so he hangs out with me while I work."

"How can we help?"

Kelsea turned a satisfied smirk their way and ordered them all around. She definitely enjoyed being in charge. Jaymes grinned at the thought, and all the ways she could tell him what to do.

When Jaymes finished scooping the cat litter, he walked over and stroked Moby's back. The cat purred and nuzzled into Kelsea's throat. "He really likes you."

Kelsea nodded. "I'm going to be so heartbroken when he gets adopted. I wish I could have him."

"Why can't you?"

She shrugged. "It wouldn't be fair to him. I'm gone so

much with school and research and projects. I'm almost always the last one to leave campus."

Jaymes nodded. He understood being too busy for anything else. He'd never had a burning desire to adopt a pet, but he definitely kept himself occupied all the time. It was worse since his best friend and brother got together. His downtime used to include Lily, but since Archer moved in with her, Jaymes stopped calling. They were still friends, but Jaymes didn't talk to her like he used to. He missed it, but he was happy for Lily. She deserved love, and for some reason, she loved his brother.

"I should get a cat," Jack said. "I like cats." He held a tiny orange cat above his head. The cat looked down at him, meowing loudly. Jack lowered it to his shoulder and the cat snuggled up against him. "See? Cats are awesome."

Slade shook his head. "Nah, dogs all the way. Howler is cool as shit. He's going to get so many women for me."

"Tell me you didn't adopt that dog so women would sleep with you," Kelsea said, glaring at Slade.

Slade grinned. "Okay, I won't."

"Seriously? First, if you need a dog's help getting women to sleep with you, you're doing something very wrong because you have all that," she waved her hand in the direction of his body, "going for you."

Slade grinned and puffed his chest up.

"And second, I'll kick your ass myself if you're a shitty owner. I might not know you, but I doubt you'd hit me back. Howler's had a rough life. And if you just intend to use him to get into a woman's pants, leave him here until someone who actually wants him comes along."

Slade smirked at her, arms crossed, waiting patiently for her to finish talking. "You done?"

She heaved a breath and nodded.

"Good. First, I don't need a dog's help to get laid. Thanks for the compliment, by the way. All of this," he gestured to himself, "works well. And second, you should kick my ass if I'm a shitty owner, but I'm not going to be. I love dogs. I had one overseas, but he didn't retire with us, so he's still there. I grew up with animals, and I know how to treat them. Howler will be fine."

Kelsea narrowed her eyes at him. Jaymes wanted to laugh, but he knew better. Kelsea finally nodded. "Fine, but I reserve the right to check in whenever I want."

"As long as you call first," Slade countered.

"Why? So you can hide whatever you don't want me to see?"

Slade waited a beat, then nodded. "Hell, yeah. I can't have you walking in when I've got a woman halfway to heaven."

Kelsea rolled her eyes and turned away, but not before Jaymes saw the smile on her lips.

They all worked together to clean up after all the cats. Jack was fairly useless, but he kept the cats entertained while everyone else cleaned up. When they were done, Kelsea plucked Moby off her shoulder.

"I've got to go, buddy," she cooed to him.

He reached out and ran his paw down her cheek. She nuzzled into him, squeezing him to her chest and stroking his fur. He purred loudly enough that Jaymes heard it from a few feet away.

"See," Jack said, nudging Slade, "cats are awesome."

"That one is, but the rest?" Slade glanced around the room and shook his head. "You can have them."

Jack rolled his eyes and headed for the door. Kelsea set Moby back in his cage with a final pat and closed the door. Jaymes reached for her, wrapping his arm around her shoulder and guiding her out of the room. He wasn't sure what to say to her. It was obvious she was upset, but he'd only known her a few days. It would take a while for him to understand what she needed.

They went back down the hallway to the dog room to grab Howler before going up front and leaving for the day. In the dog room, they ran in to Mason.

"Hey, Mace," Kelsea said.

"You just left Moby?" Mason asked.

Kelsea nodded.

Mason reached out for her and she went to him, leaving Jaymes's side. "I'm sorry, Kels. I wish you'd just adopt him already."

She shook her head. "I can't. Maybe one day I'll be able to get a cat, but my schedule is too unpredictable right now."

Mason looked at the three men surrounding him and nodded. "I can see that. Juggling three guys?"

Kelsea laughed and slapped his arm lightly. "They're friends. They all wanted to see what we do here. And Slade is adopting Howler."

Mason's brows went up. He looked to Kelsea to point out Slade to him. The two men eyed each other, each trying to get a read on the other man.

Slade was tall, almost as tall as Dunn, but he was a few inches shy of Mason. Both had shaved heads and wide bodies with muscles to spare. If the two of them ever fought, Jaymes really didn't know who would come out on top.

Although with Mason's history, he'd probably fight dirty.

"Mason O'Connor."

Slade nodded. "I know who you are."

Mason nodded, his eyes going dark. He obviously didn't like Kelsea's friends being aware of his past.

Kelsea stepped between them and put a hand on each

man's chest. "Stop it. Both of you. No posturing here. It's not the time or place for it."

"I don't like these men coming in here and making it seem like I'm doing something wrong," Mason said, his eyes never leaving Slade.

"And I don't like Kelsea working with a felon," Slade countered.

"I served my time."

Slade nodded. "Duly noted. And if you can kill your own wife, what's to stop you from going after a woman like Kelsea? Maybe you have a thing for her and she's next on your list."

Mason's body went rigid. He took half a step back. "I don't have a list. And I don't have a thing for Kelsea. She's like a little sister to me, so tell me why I shouldn't be worried about the three of you with her."

"Because we're the ones who are keeping her safe," Jaymes blurted. As soon as the words were out of his mouth, he knew it was a mistake.

Mason's eyes swung to Kelsea. "What is he talking about?"

"Nothing," Slade said, stepping between Mason and Kelsea.

Mason glared at Slade, but Slade wasn't backing down. "Get out of my way."

"No."

Mason glared, then slid his gaze to Jaymes. "What did you mean?"

Jack stepped up, blocking Mason from Jaymes. "Where does Kelsea live?"

Mason looked at him, his face a blank. "How the hell would I know?"

"Where does she work?"

"The college."

"Which one?"

"Erie, I think. Why? What the hell is going on?"

"How you ever been to her house?"

Mason crossed his arms and rocked back on his heels. He glared at Jack, narrowing his eyes. "I'm not a man who can be intimidated easily. Why don't you tell me what the fuck is going on?"

Slade stepped forward. "No can do. You're a suspect."

"In what?"

"Did you know a man named Maxwell Greene?" Jack asked.

Mason thought for a second, then shook his head. "Not that I can think of. Who is he?"

"He was Kelsea's ex," Slade said with zero inflection.

Mason shrugged. "And?"

"And his house was blown up yesterday by a man who's been following Kelsea. Where were you between nine am and noon yesterday?"

Mason's brows went sky high. He looked around Slade to Kelsea. Her entire body shook during the exchange.

Jaymes wanted to go to her, but she didn't need him to protect her. The longer they talked to Mason, the less of a threat Jaymes thought he was. He was protective of Kelsea. His face said he was worried about her, not worried he was going to get caught.

Mason met Slade's gaze. "I was here all day yesterday. Amanda saw me come in at eight. I didn't leave until after five last night."

"And she can corroborate that?" Jack asked.

Mason nodded. "Absolutely. I saw her or Jeremy every twenty minutes or so. They're in and out of the pet rooms all day."

"And you didn't leave once?"

Mason shook his head. "No. I bring my lunch with me and eat in the office. All three of us ate together because it was quiet for once. I spent the morning with the dogs and we had a lot of people come through. I was with the cats a little in the afternoon, then back with the dogs until the end of the day."

"Why are you being so agreeable?" Jack asked.

Mason looked him dead in the eye. "I know how being questioned works. Been there, done that. I'm not hiding anything. Kelsea is a friend. She reminds me of my wife. And I'd never hurt her, just like I didn't mean to kill my wife. I made a mistake that night. I've wished every day since that I could go back and recognize her when she walked into our bedroom, but I can't change my past. I was only home for a few weeks, and I was still fucked up, but that isn't an excuse. I couldn't save my wife, but I can help protect Kelsea."

"We've got a handle on it," Slade said.

"I was a SEAL also. I'm happy to help."

Slade and Jack traded a look and nodded. "We'll keep you posted."

Mason nodded, and everyone in the room seemed to take a collective breath. He reached for Kelsea, and she went to him, letting him wrap her in his big arms.

"Are you okay?" he asked with concern.

She nodded. "I am. These guys have been taking good care of me. Especially Jaymes."

Mason swung his gaze to Jaymes. "That's why you were here the other day."

Jaymes nodded in agreement.

"You should have told me," Mason chastised Kelsea.

She shrugged. "I didn't think it was a big deal for a while.

I convinced myself I was losing my mind. The night I met Jaymes, someone was outside my bedroom window."

"Tell me you aren't staying there alone," Mason said with a glare around the room.

Kelsea shook her head. "I've been staying with Jaymes since."

"Good." Mason glanced between them. "Oh." He leveled Jaymes with a hard stare. "You hurt her, and I'll kill you."

Jaymes crossed his arms and stared down the bigger man. "Same goes."

Mason nodded once.

Guess they were all on the same team.

AFTER THEIR DAY at the shelter, Jack and Slade invaded Jaymes's apartment for dinner. Kelsea enjoyed spending time with them, but it had been a long day and she was hoping for a quiet night with Jaymes.

The other two men and Howler were a firm reminder that the relationship she had with Jaymes was nowhere near conventional. They weren't spending time together because they were in the middle of a whirlwind romance that was going to end with a marriage proposal and a happily ever after. She was with Jaymes because he was protecting her. And when the threat was gone, he would be, too. Maybe not entirely, but in the capacity he was at the moment.

Howler snuggled up to Kelsea on the couch, his big head on her lap. It wasn't long before he was snoring, the loud rumble nearly rattling the windows. Kelsea smiled. She'd worked at the shelter for years, but she'd never had the chance to see one of the adopted animals in his or her new home. Howler would eventually go to Slade's, but having him out of his cage and happy was close enough for Kelsea. Her heart squeezed. These adorable animals all deserved great homes. Maybe she would adopt Moby. *When all this is over.*

She'd spent enough of her life following everyone else's rules. If she had Moby, and a reason to go home at night, maybe she'd work a little less. She'd give herself a reason to leave work, and she'd change her life and the life of her favorite cat.

She slid her hand down Howler's back, smiling when he sighed peacefully, then farted.

Slade turned to her. "Tell me that was you."

She snorted and shook her head. "Nope. That was all Howler. Maybe I should have warned you about him before."

Slade looked down at his new dog affectionately and shook his head. He sat on the other end of the couch, near the dog's feet, and scratched his back. "Wouldn't have mattered. I'd still have taken him."

Kelsea grinned, her throat tightening with emotion. She liked to believe there was a reason for everything. It was what drove her in her work. To be able to assign a reason to behaviors. She didn't like believing people couldn't control themselves and that they committed suicide or hurt themselves because they were incapable of stopping. She had to believe there was a way to help them, and she studied constantly to prove her theories and help as many people as she could.

Over the last few days, she tried to find the reason for her own personal hell. She wasn't the perfect model type who had men chasing her. She was curvy and didn't care enough to change or hide it. She barely had men looking in her direction, which was part of why she brushed off the odd feeling for so long. Who would ever stalk her?

Now, she knew it was true but didn't know why. But looking at Slade and Howler together made her believe that maybe, just maybe, all this was happening to her to bring the new people in her life together with the old people, and animals, in her life.

Howler never would have been adopted. She knew that with every fiber of her being. She hated it, but people didn't see the sweet dog that she adored. They saw a broken dog. One who couldn't control half of his body. But Slade saw Howler for who he was, and loved him for it.

If Kelsea didn't have a stalker, she never would have met Slade, and Slade never would have adopted Howler. That right there was enough of a reason for her. People were twisted, but good always won in the end. She knew that, and she wouldn't stop believing it. No matter what.

16

Jaymes answered the door for the pizza guy. Jack called on their way home and gave his credit card over the phone, so all Jaymes had to do was sign. Just opening the door was terrifying for him, but knowing Slade and Jack were behind him, protecting Kelsea if need be, gave him courage.

He hated worrying about the pizza guy, and everyone else in his life. He never thought twice about ordering food in before, but he hadn't done it in months. He was slowly teaching himself to cook. He still burned more than his fair share of dinners, but he was trying. Fear was a hell of a motivator. So was hunger.

Jaymes thanked the pizza guy and closed the door behind him, double checking that it was locked. It wouldn't stop many people, but it made Jaymes feel ever so slightly better.

He set the pizza on the stove and opened the lid. He grabbed a slice just as his phone vibrated in his pocket. He pulled it out and smiled when he saw his mom's face looking up at him. "Hey Ma."

"Hi, Mrs. Ford!" Slade and Jack said in chorus as they rushed into the kitchen for dinner.

"Save me a couple slices," Jaymes called as he headed for his room and some quiet. "How are you?"

"Is everyone over there tonight?" his mom asked.

Jaymes shook his head. "Just Jack and Slade. They said hi if you couldn't hear them."

Cecelia laughed. "I definitely heard them. You all should have come here for dinner. You know I always have enough food."

Jaymes winced. He hadn't spoken to his mother since he was there for dinner and met Kelsea. He'd more or less forgotten about his own mother.

"Sorry, Ma. I didn't think. We were out all day and Jack ordered a pizza on our way home."

"Next time," she said agreeably.

Jaymes was definitely on alert after that. His mother rarely gave in. She specialized in guilt trips and passive aggression. Not in letting you off the hook. Something was up.

"I haven't seen Kelsea since you took her home the other night. You should call and check on her."

And there it was. The fix-up. His mom had no idea that he and Kelsea took care of that on their own, or that Kelsea was in danger. The second part he wasn't willing to fill her in on, just in case, but the first? That was inevitable.

"She's fine, Ma."

"How do you know? You should call her. She's a nice girl. And she works too much. I invite her over all the time, but she's busy. Always working that one. She reminds me of you."

"I know, Mom. I love my job, though."

"Yeah, I know, honey," she said, her voice going soft.

"After everything you've been through, you need something good in your life. Maybe Kelsea can be that for you."

"She is, Mom," he admitted.

"She's a...Wait. Did you say 'is?' What does that mean?"

Jaymes grinned. "It means Kelsea's here right now. She's been staying with me for a couple days."

"Jaymes Matthew Ford! I didn't raise you to take advantage of women. Why is she staying with you? That woman works too many hours. And you need to let her out of the bedroom."

Jaymes snorted a laugh, which only prompted an annoyed sound from his mother. He smothered the grin on his face and apologized. "I know, Mom. It's a long story. I promise you, Kelsea can leave any time she wants. We're getting to know each other. She's in the living room with Jack and Slade right now. Not trapped in my bedroom."

"Where is she sleeping?" Cecelia demanded.

"My room. I wouldn't let her sleep on the couch."

"So you are?"

"Uh, well..."

Cecelia groaned. "What is with my boys? First, your brother snatches up Lily when you're kidnapped, and now, you take advantage of my friend. It's like you weren't raised right."

"We were raised just fine, Mom."

"Then tell me what possessed you to sleep with my friend a day after you met her. And why she's been staying with you for the last four days."

Jaymes couldn't believe it had only been a few days since he'd met Kelsea. It felt like forever since he met her at his mother's house. He was smart enough to know that stressful situations changed the way people thought about everything. He'd convinced himself when he was gone to tell Lily he loved her if he ever saw her again. And he did, but she didn't know he meant he loved her the way his brother did. She thought he meant as friends.

It hurt, but over the last few months, Jaymes realized it was for the best. Archer and Lily were happy. They worked together. It stung that she fell for his brother, especially when he was being held captive, but Jaymes knew things with him and Lily would never have worked out. If it was possible, it would have happened long before Archer showed up. He still loved her, but he knew he wasn't in love with Lily. He just missed his best friend.

Kelsea, though? Jaymes was still trying to figure that one out. It had been a few days, but he would protect her with his life if he had to. He'd die before he'd let anything happen to her. He wasn't sure what that meant, but he knew it meant something.

"That's between Kelsea and me, Mom. We're both adults, and consenting adults. You don't get to tell me what to do."

She sighed loudly. "She's been hurt, Jaymes. I know you have, too, but don't use Kelsea to get over Lily. Or to get back at Lily. Or anything because of Lily. If you're still hung up on her, cut Kelsea loose. She deserves better."

The fact that his mother thought he was using Kelsea stung. A lot. "Kelsea has nothing to do with Lily, Mom. I like Kelsea. She's an amazing woman. Strong and smart and funny. She's beautiful and passionate and I really like her."

His mom was silent for a few moments. "Well, good. You two should come over for dinner again sometime. Maybe this week. I have Bible study Wednesday, but how about Thursday night?"

Jaymes ran a hand down his face and resisted the urge to take a deep breath. He hated lying to his mother, but he couldn't tell her about the stalker. If he agreed to dinner and they had to cancel, she would demand an answer. If he refused now, she'd press for a different date. He was stuck. "I'll check with Kelsea and let you know, but we'll figure something out."

His mom agreed, although reluctantly, and they were off the phone before long. Jaymes went back to the kitchen and found half a pizza left. He grabbed two slices and joined the others in the living room.

Where Slade's new dog was taking up half the seating.

"How is it you got a dog and I have to sit on the floor?" he asked Slade.

Slade shrugged. "Kelsea helped him up here."

Jaymes swung his gaze to Kelsea but found he couldn't be upset with her. She was too adorable in her stretchy pants and oversized t-shirt with the dog sleeping on her thigh. Jaymes wanted that spot for himself.

The four of them watched TV for a couple hours, enjoying the comedy that distracted them from the reason they were all together. Jaymes knew English and Dunn were working on the case and in touch with the police department about Maxwell. He tried to forget about all of it, but it lingered in the back of his mind. Kelsea wasn't safe. And they had no idea who was after her.

When the pizza was demolished, the dog was walked, and Kelsea started to fade, Jack finally left. Slade stretched and yawned. Jaymes wasn't tired yet, but his internal clock had always been off. He was a night owl without question.

Jaymes got Kelsea up and helped her to his room, saying goodnight to Slade and Howler. Kelsea stripped out of her clothes and crawled into bed naked, making Jaymes hard in an instant.

Her curves drove him crazy. Most of the women he dated

were curvy, but there was something about Kelsea that had him losing his mind every time he looked at her. Maybe it was her creamy skin and dark hair. Or her eyes that drew him in. It could have been her smile. All he knew was that it was something only Kelsea had. Something about her that made him want to say and do things that he'd never said or done before.

He slipped into bed with her. She immediately snuggled up to him and slid her hand between them. "Why are you wearing clothes?" she groaned.

He shrugged. "You're half-asleep."

She huffed a laugh. "I was counting on you to wake me up a little bit."

He flipped her to her back and pressed her to the mattress, fitting himself between her thighs. "With pleasure."

KELSEA FELT bad keeping Jaymes away from his work, but she had to admit she felt safer with him hanging around. He sat in the back of the classroom with his laptop during her big classes and camped out in her office during her small classes. But he was around, which was nice. He cared. He wanted to be there with her, even though Slade and Dunn were lingering, too.

She just finished up her psych two-oh-one class and her stomach growled. She was definitely ready for lunch. Jaymes had been working her out harder than she'd ever done in her life. Her clothes were already fitting looser, which wasn't her intention, but fear and lots of sex had that effect on her body, even after a couple of days.

Maxwell's words still rung in her ears, both his initial

assessment that she was too fat, and his apology before he died. She shivered.

"Are you okay?" a voice said from behind her.

Kelsea spun and smiled when she saw Edward standing there. He was in the class across the hall and almost always stopped to see how her research was going. He was the kind of student she'd always hoped for. Someone who loved the brain as much as she did. He was smart and had an amazing way of looking at her research. She'd gained a lot of insight from the work they'd done together.

"Yeah. Just tired. And hungry."

Edward scanned her figure quickly, then returned his gaze to hers with a smile. It wasn't creepy, but Kelsea was fairly certain it wasn't innocent either. Edward asked her out once, but she told him she didn't date students. Ever.

"Can I buy you lunch?" he asked.

Kelsea glanced up to where Jaymes was packing up his stuff. She smiled, catching his gaze. The heated look he sent her was far different from Edward's, both in intent and what it did to her.

"Thanks, but Jaymes is here."

Edward looked up and scowled when he saw Jaymes. "He's been hanging around a lot. Does he not work?"

Kelsea was surprised at Edward's sharp tone. "He does, but he's able to work from anywhere he wants. He's just... spending time with me."

Edward stared at her for a long moment, long enough that she dropped her gaze to the paperwork on her desk. "He's not good enough for you," Edward finally said.

Kelsea met his stare with her own sharp one. "Edward, we're not doing this. Who I date is none of your business."

He held her gaze, letting her see the pain in his. Kelsea felt guilty. Was she leading him on? Did she create this? He obviously had feelings for her, and he was hurting. He was dating someone else, but she knew he still had a thing for her. She wasn't going to put her life on hold until he completely moved, but it also wasn't kind of her to parade Jaymes around in front of Edward.

"You're right," he finally said. "I'm sorry. I just worry about you. Do you really know this guy?"

She nodded. "I know enough. His mom has been a friend of mine for a while. And Jaymes is a good man."

Edward spared him one last glance and nodded. "I hope he's good to you then. Enjoy your lunch."

Edward was out the door before Jaymes made his way down the stadium seats to her side. Kelsea was still staring after Edward when Jaymes asked if she was okay.

"That's what he asked, too."

"What did he want?"

Kelsea shrugged. "Nothing really. He asked if I wanted to go to lunch."

"Is something going on with you two?" Jaymes asked softly.

Kelsea shook her head. "No. He has a crush on me, but nothing has ever happened. He's one of my students and I don't think that's appropriate."

"If he wasn't one of your students, would you date him?"

She thought about it for a second, then shook her head again. "No. He's a nice enough guy, but moving him from being one of my students to being a guy I'd date is not a leap I'd be able to make. I've always thought of him as someone I should teach."

Jaymes wrapped his arms around her waist and pulled her flush against him. "You can teach me anything you want," he whispered, nipping her earlobe and nuzzling behind her ear.

She shivered and moaned softly. He turned her on instantly. She'd never been with a man who made her think of sex so often. Not that she wasn't a sexual person, but with Jaymes, it felt like if she didn't have him all the time, she'd burst into flames.

"I can't wait to get you home tonight," he growled. "I want to unbutton you, one by one, until I strip away your teacher look and leave only the sexy woman underneath. Then I'm going to tease you until you beg me to let you come. And when you think you can't take any more, I'm going to fuck you until you can't remember either of our names."

She trembled in his arms, her panties soaked through and her heart throbbing in time with her core. "Maybe we should go home for lunch," she whispered.

He pressed his cock hard to her, sinking into the soft flesh of her belly. "I'm definitely up for that, but Dunn wouldn't let us out of his sight."

Her body went cold, like someone doused her in icy water. She'd forgotten why Jaymes was there. Why he was really there. Dunn was a quick reminder that their lives weren't their own. Not until whoever was out there was no longer a threat.

Kelsea stepped back. "You're right. I'm sorry."

Jaymes reached for her, but she sidestepped him.

"Kels. I'm sorry. I shouldn't have said that."

She met his gaze and shook her head. "It's fine. I just forgot for a minute."

"Forgot what?"

She shrugged and gestured around the room. "All of it. Maxwell. The footsteps. Dunn and Slade and living with you because someone is after me. I forgot."

Jaymes sighed heavily and reached for her again. She

didn't resist that time and let him pull her in. One hand went into her hair, gently cupping her head. The other rested low on her hip.

She clung to him, absorbing his strength. She used all hers up over the last week, and she needed some of his. She trembled in his arms, for a very different reason than moments ago.

"I'm glad I could make you forget for a few minutes," he whispered in her ear. "I hate that you're going through this. I'm not going to let anything happen to you."

She nodded against his chest. "I know."

They stayed like that for a few minutes, until Dunn walked into the room and told them it was time for lunch. Kelsea reluctantly pulled back and nodded at her new protector.

She followed Dunn down the hall to where Slade was waiting for them. Jaymes walked just behind her, close enough to her side that they could be walking together. She felt silly with three large men surrounding her, but Dunn insisted.

She wasn't sure what to make of him. He was more than a bit standoffish, but she knew he would keep her safe. Jaymes trusted him, which was enough for her. If it were up to her, though, she'd take Jack over Dunn any day.

They ate lunch together, then went back to Kelsea's office so she could get her things for her afternoon classes. The men scanned her office while she was teaching, setting up bugs and motion sensors and more technology than she ever knew existed.

If anything happened in her office, English would see it. She just hoped his job was very, very boring.

17

WHEN KELSEA'S LAST CLASS OF THE DAY WAS OVER, DUNN said they needed to go to the office. All Jaymes wanted to do was get Kelsea home, but he couldn't argue. If Dunn thought it was important, they were going to the office.

Dunn pulled in to a nondescript office building in downtown Niagara Falls. They were close enough to the Rainbow Bridge that they could assist at the border if there was an issue, but far enough away that it wasn't obvious that's why they were there. Dunn didn't want anyone to know about their operation unless they had to know.

Like Kelsea.

Dunn showed Jaymes and Kelsea into the conference room and nodded for Slade to follow him out of the room. Jaymes felt like they were there for questioning. He had no idea what was going on, but he didn't like it.

"Well, this is intimidating," Kelsea said when they were alone.

Jaymes laughed softly. "Yeah, to say the least."

"Did we do something wrong?"

Jaymes shrugged. "Not that I know of, but who knows. Dunn doesn't like people wandering the halls around here."

Kelsea glanced at the solid walls surrounding them and nodded. "Definitely nothing to see in here. I'd never know where we were if I hadn't seen it on the way in. What's this place called anyway?"

Jaymes shook his head. "I don't know. F-BOMB headquarters, I guess. I've only been here once before when they first got the space."

Kelsea sank onto a chair, her flop making it spin. She grabbed the table and steadied herself, staring around the room absently.

"Are you okay?"

She nodded without meeting his eyes. "That's the third time I've been asked that. The truth is, I don't know."

"What do you mean?" Jaymes asked, taking the seat next to hers.

She shrugged. "I'm in a secret hideout for a government contractor, or something, hiding from someone who already killed my ex. Someone who's been watching me for months. This isn't my life. How did I get here? I'm not the beautiful woman who gets attention from men. I'm the fat friend who gets dismissed. I've always been that person."

"Don't," Jaymes said firmly. "You're not fat, and you need to stop believing that about yourself. Maxwell was wrong about you. He never should have said that."

"But he did. And he was right. I've always been overweight. Too much junk food and not enough exercise. It makes no sense that I have a stalker. Who the hell would obsess over me?"

"That's what we're trying to figure out," Dunn said, letting himself into the room. "Your background is limited, and the people in your life are innocent on first glance."

"On first glance?" Kelsea squeaked.

Jaymes reached for her hand, squeezing it when she slid her small palm into his.

Dunn nodded. "Yes. We haven't found anything, but we're digging deeper. Into everyone you know now, or have known in the last few years. Or earlier, in some cases."

"Why?" Kelsea asked.

Dunn sighed and set the folder in his hands on the table. He took a seat, with Jack and Slade filling in the seats next to him. English came in a second later and sat next to Jaymes.

"After Maxwell Greene was killed, we had no choice. The local PD is investigating this also, but they're working with us. They want to catch whoever it was that killed Greene, but we're more concerned with stopping him before he hurts someone else."

"You know it's a male?" Kelsea asked.

Dunn paused for a second, then shook his head. "No, but most stalker cases are. Especially when it's a woman and her ex is one of the targets. It speaks to a jilted lover or someone with an unhealthy obsession with you. Someone who knows you personally, and intimately. Someone who thinks he should be the one you love."

"I don't know anyone like that," Kelsea said. "I work constantly. I barely socialize. I don't have friends. That's why I'm here, why I'm staying with Jaymes. I had nowhere else to go. I'm pretty pathetic."

Dunn shook his head. "It isn't always someone you know, or someone you're aware of being there. It could be a former student, or a server at your favorite restaurant. Your ex's best friend or brother. Someone who knows just enough to know you, but not enough to be on your radar."

Kelsea stared at the table. She clenched her lip in her teeth, her eyes looking dangerously glassy.

"So how are you going to find this person?" Jaymes asked, taking some of the heat off Kelsea.

"We've already started digging deeper into the people we were looking at before. At the top of our list right now is Dane Lewis. He's a PI, and he has access to all kinds of things that the general population doesn't. Plus, he obviously knows how to stay out of sight and sneak around."

"Dane? Seriously? We haven't been in touch in years."

Dunn shook his head. "That doesn't always matter. If he blames you for his life not turning out the way he planned, or if he thinks you owe him something, his obsession with you could turn into something dark and deadly."

"I just can't see him going there. He was always such a nice guy."

Dunn shrugged. "The person that tortured and killed Greene was not a nice person. The preliminary autopsy was completed today. He had multiple broken bones, not to mention internal injuries that would have killed him if the blast didn't."

Tears spilled down Kelsea's cheeks.

"How do you know the injuries weren't from the explosion?" Jaymes asked.

"Some were, and the ME is going to look at everything, but there's no way all the injuries came from the bomb. Whoever did this was smart, in a sick and twisted way. He made sure Greene wasn't sitting on top of the bomb. That way his death was slower. He was likely knocked out by the blast, but he was buried under rubble and never would have survived, even if someone was there when the blast happened."

Kelsea sobbed softly. "This is my fault. He died because of me."

Jaymes shook his head and wrapped an arm around her. "You didn't do anything. The sick bastard who killed Maxwell is to blame for his death, not you."

"But he died because of me."

"Because of what he said to you. Not because of you. There was no way for you to know that whoever you told would tell someone else and this sicko would find out," Jaymes insisted.

"Wait," Kelsea said, sitting up and looking around the room. "I never told anyone."

"What do you mean you never told anyone?" Dunn asked, his voice going hard.

She shook her head, staring at the wall. "I was too embarrassed by what Maxwell said to me to tell anyone that was why we broke up. No one knew it was because he thought I was fat. No one." She glanced at Jaymes. "Not even your mom. I told her we broke up, but I didn't tell her why. I didn't tell anyone why."

The SEALs in the room exchanged a meaningful glance.

"Kelsea, where were you when he... um, when you..." Dunn stammered.

"He wants to know where you two broke up," Slade provided. "Where were you when the douchebag said you were too fat?"

Kelsea shrugged. "I was at home."

"Was he there with you or were you on the phone?"

Kelsea stared off. "He was there. Why?"

The men exchanged another glance, and Jaymes understood what was going on. He filled in the blanks for her. "Your house is bugged. Someone's been watching what happens inside as well as outside."

"Oh. My. God," she whispered. Then passed out.

JAYMES RUSHED to catch Kelsea before she hit the ground, but he wasn't quick enough. Her head flopped to the side after her eyes rolled back in her head and she dropped. She crumpled to the ground at his feet, and laid there, helpless, while everyone in the room stared at her for a few seconds.

Jaymes lifted her off the ground and maneuvered her into the chair Jack vacated. English shouted down the hallway for Rocky, the team medic. He was there in seconds, in Kelsea's face, snapping his fingers and trying to wake her up.

After a few long, painful minutes where the rest of the team made a plan to sweep Kelsea's house, Rocky managed to bring her back. She blinked her eyes open, first looking at him, then swinging her gaze up to Jaymes. Her face collapsed when she met his gaze.

"Someone's been watching me?" she whispered.

Rocky moved to the side, and Jaymes kneeled in front of her. "I'm sorry. They're going to go search for everything and see what they can find out. We're going to stay here until they get back."

"Kelsea. I'm sorry to do this to you, but do we have permission to search your home?" Dunn asked.

Kelsea nodded.

"I need you to say the word, Kelsea. We need verbal confirmation that you are giving us permission."

"Yes. Please, go search my house and find all the bugs this son of a bitch planted."

Dunn nodded sharply and turned back to the team. Jaymes stayed focused on Kelsea, but was aware of them moving around, checking the weapons hidden in pockets and boots and anywhere else that most people would never think to look for a weapon.

Rocky and Dex hung back while the rest of the team got ready to go. Dex grabbed Kelsea a bottle of water while Rocky paced nearby, waiting to get a good look at her.

"Are you okay?" Jaymes asked, blocking the others out.

She shook her head. "Someone hasn't just been following me, but has been watching me inside my house, outside my house. This is terrifying, Jaymes. How am I ever supposed to go back there?" She looked up at him with emerald puppy eyes, pleading with him to answer her question and tell her what to do.

Jaymes wanted to be able to tell her something. It wasn't fair that she was being watched. That someone not only followed her, but invaded her privacy and bugged her home.

"I'm going with you," he said, standing up and facing Dunn.

Dunn immediately shook his head. "No. You're a civilian. You can't walk into her house with us."

"You're a civilian, too. And I'm going, dammit. You're not going to keep me out of this."

Dunn started to argue again, but Archer, who ran in with Rocky, stepped forward and put a hand on his friend's arm. "Let him," Archer said, staring Dunn down.

Dunn finally heaved a sigh and nodded. "We're not giving you weapons. You have your own to carry, but that's it."

Jaymes nodded. He was still getting used to the weapons he kept on himself at all times. He knew he wasn't likely to be targeted again, but he wasn't willing to take the chance. He felt safer having a way to defend himself at all times. A knife in his boot and a gun in his pocket helped him. He felt in control, even though he hoped to never need to use either of them.

He knelt in front of Kelsea once more. "We're going to find whoever this is. You will be safe in your home again."

She nodded, her eyes locked on his. Jaymes leaned down and kissed her quickly, then followed the rest of the guys out the door.

He rode with Archer and Dunn to Kelsea's house, sitting silently in the backseat of the SUV. The others took the SUV that followed them. It felt like overkill, but Jaymes had no clue what they were going to encounter when they got there.

Dunn parked in the driveway with Jack right behind him. They all filed out and let themselves into Kelsea's home with her keys. Everyone took a room, looking around for anything suspicious. Jaymes ended up in the bedroom.

Since none of them knew Kelsea that well, or had been to her place, they had no way of knowing what items would be out of place or new. It was up to their devices to catch whoever was watching and listening to her.

He hated the thought of someone having a camera in there, but he knew it was the most likely. English gave Jaymes the infrared scanner to look for cameras in the bedroom and attached master bathroom while he scanned the rest of the place for other bugs.

Jaymes pointed the device at the wall next to the bedroom door first. He planned to work his way around the room slowly and carefully so he didn't miss anything. The display showed no activity until he reached the first corner, then it jumped.

Jaymes moved the device up and down the wall until the signal grew and he spotted a tony dot near the ceiling. If it was a camera, it was pointed directly at Kelsea's bed.

He kept going and found another camera behind the

bedroom door, again high up near the ceiling, and also pointing at her bed. Another was in her closet, and two more in her bathroom, one pointed at the shower and the other right outside.

In his mind, Jaymes could see the path she took when she got up in the morning from her bed to the closet where she stripped off her clothes and left them in the hamper just inside the door, then to the bathroom for her shower and returning to the closet for her outfit for the day.

The disgusting son of a bitch could watch her the entire time.

"Find anything?" English asked, walking into the bedroom.

Jaymes nodded. "Five cameras from what I can tell. Two in here watching the bed, two in the bathroom at the shower, and one in the closet."

"Fuck," English breathed. He looked up at the cameras Jaymes pointed out and shook his head. "This is one sick fucker. He also had two in the living room and another pair in the kitchen."

"Why two? It seems as though one would be enough."

English shrugged. "I don't know either. It feels like overkill to me, too, but I'm not a psychotic stalker."

"Is there a way to see where the feed is going?"

English nodded. "Yeah, but the question is, do we want to cut it first?"

Dunn joined them in Kelsea's bedroom and said, "No. We need the line open so we can find whoever this is."

Jaymes nodded. "I think so, too."

"Won't they know we were here? We're all over the apartment."

English shook his head. "I set up a signal jammer when we walked in. They might have heard something when we first got here, but it's likely they're going to think there's something wrong with the cameras. Unless they know who we are and are watching us."

"Are the feeds still live?" Jaymes asked.

English nodded. "Everything is still live."

"Then let's find this bag of dicks and cut him off."

"Hooyah!"

18

———

Kelsea tried to stay calm while the guys were gone. Rocky checked her out and said she was fine. Stress caused her to pass out.

Gee, really?

The guys didn't say much when they got back, but someone was definitely watching her. Actually had cameras and bugs inside her house. They were following her when she wasn't home and watching her every move when she was.

A part of Kelsea wanted to laugh because she really wasn't that interesting of a person. Who the hell would want to watch her sit on the couch and watch TV? Or cook dinner? Or sleep?

The cameras in her closet and bathroom were a little creepier because it said someone knew her enough to know she stripped in her closet, and they were watching her walk around her room naked.

Which almost made her laugh, too. She got dumped for being too fat and some creeper was out there watching her walk around buck-ass naked. She obviously picked the wrong guy to date.

Not that she wanted to date her stalker. That was disturbing on so many levels.

Jaymes and English were side-by-side in the conference room, both tapping so fast on the keys that Kelsea wasn't sure how the keyboards weren't broken. She felt so useless just sitting there, but she didn't have the same skills they had.

Dunn walked over and sat next to her with Archer taking her other side and Dex next to him. "Can we ask you a few questions?" Dunn asked.

She nodded, glancing at all the men surrounding her. "Am I in trouble?"

Dunn grinned and shook his head. "We all hear things differently. Something you say might mean nothing to me but trigger a thought for Archer or Dex, so I asked them to sit with me while we talk. If you're okay with it."

She nodded.

"Okay, good. We want to know more about the people on the list and see if there's anyone else that should go on it. So far, we've looked into Edward Bailey, Dane Lewis, and Mason O'Connor. Nothing has come up on any of them. English is running another check on each of them, more detailed, to see if we find something that was buried, but we want to know more about each of them. And about Maxwell."

"Maxwell? Why? He was killed because of all this. He's obviously not the person behind it."

Dunn nodded. "We know that. And the initial autopsy report confirmed it was him that they found inside the house, but we still need to look into his friends and family and see if anything comes up."

"I really don't think any of them would be stalking me. I didn't know his friends or family well. And the others... I haven't spoken to Dane in years. Edward is a student of mine, but there's never been anything else. And Mason is just a friend and coworker. He's a good guy. Slade and Jack agreed that he's not a threat."

"Actually," Dunn said, "they both said they don't think he's a threat, but everyone's a threat. We need to look into all of them. And we need to figure out if we're missing anyone."

Kelsea sighed. She hated that she wasn't able to help more. If she had any clue who could be watching her, she'd definitely tell them, but the thought of someone she knew following her, putting cameras inside her house, and then killing her ex-boyfriend was too much to even consider.

"Let's start with Maxwell."

Her heart clenched. She didn't still have feelings for him, but he died because of her. She'd carry that guilt with her forever.

"What about Maxwell?"

"Where did you meet him?"

"Online," she mumbled. She was hoping not to have to tell the room full of attractive men that she was so pathetic that she turned to online dating to find a guy. Even worse, Jaymes looked up when she said it, clearly listening to the conversation. Kelsea couldn't meet his gaze. She wasn't sure what she'd see.

"What website?" Dunn asked.

"Smart Singles."

Dunn glanced at English. He nodded back and took over.

"Login ID and password."

She told him and waited, but he didn't look at her again

as he typed in her information and started scrolling through her profile.

Kelsea hadn't been back on the site since she and Maxwell got together. She ignored all the messages that came through her email and seriously considered deleting her account.

"It looks like you haven't been in here in a while," English said. "You have a lot of unread messages."

Kelsea nodded. "I don't date more than one guy at a time, and I was seeing Maxwell. When we broke up... Let's just say I wasn't in the right frame of mind to date anyone else."

"Why didn't you delete your profile?" Dunn asked.

She shrugged. "I don't know." How pathetic would it make her to admit that she still hoped she would meet someone, a good someone? She didn't entirely believe in The One, but she liked the thought that maybe there was a person out there who would love her for who she was, lumps and all. She hadn't met him in real life, so she tried online dating before giving up completely on men. She was only twenty-nine, breathing down the neck of thirty in a few weeks, assuming her stalker didn't give her the same treatment he gave Maxwell.

She shivered at the thought.

"When did you start dating Maxwell?" Dunn asked, bringing her back to the conversation.

"Over the summer. All the conversations we had before we actually met are still in there. We finally met in person in early July."

"Nothing here that raises any flags," English said. "Started talking in March. He asked to meet early on, but she said no. They traded messages for months."

He paused and met Kelsea's eyes for a second, then

returned his gaze to the computer. Kelsea's cheeks flared with heat remembering some of the racier conversations they had. It was freeing to be so open with someone, to tell him about her fantasies and know he wasn't judging her. But to have English reading the personal messages they shared was more than a little humiliating.

"Their messages got more and more... intimate over time until Kelsea finally asked to meet him. They set up a date and the conversations on here stopped. Everything beyond that point is one-way inbound. No replies from Kelsea to any of the men who reached out."

"Any of them suspicious?"

English shook his head. "Nope. I'll have Jaymes check it all out, too, but not that I'm picking up on. Mostly one and done since she didn't reply."

Her chest constricted at the thought of Jaymes reading her personal messages. English reading them was bad enough, but Jaymes reading them was even weirder. She wanted to tell Jaymes her thoughts and fantasies and goals for her life on her own, not through a third party during an investigation into her past.

"Okay, so that is probably a dead-end, but they'll keep digging a little bit. What about people you met through him? Did Maxwell have a group of friends?"

She nodded. "Yeah, but I didn't spend a lot of time with them. We met in July and went out a few times, maybe once or twice a week through most of summer. School started back up in the middle of August so I got even busier. After that, we mostly spent the night together, one of us grabbing dinner on our way to the other's place. We didn't go out as much. That lasted for about three months, then we broke up right before Thanksgiving."

"And that's right around the time you noticed someone following you?"

Kelsea nodded, that fear sneaking back into her. She knew she was safe in that building, but she couldn't help but be afraid.

"Obviously, someone was watching you long before that. If he wasn't, he wouldn't have heard what Maxwell said when you two split up."

Kelsea nodded.

"Let's talk about his friends. Did any of them stand out to you?"

Kelsea thought back and shook her head, then she stopped. "He did have one friend who gave me a little bit of a creepy feeling."

"Creepy how?" Archer asked.

Kelsea shrugged. "I don't know. He was just watching me all the time when we were together. I thought it was because he said I was taking Maxwell away from them, but I don't know. We never talked much."

"What's his name?"

"Patrick Anderson."

English typed as Dunn continued asking her questions.

"Did he have any other friends that gave off a weird vibe? Men or women?"

Kelsea shook her head. "No. He had a group of friends that were really close, but for the most part, they were nice. About half of them were married, some to each other. His ex was a part of the group, which was always really weird to me. I sort of figured they would get back together one day. She was dating some other guy, but she was the perfect, skinny woman. I always wondered if he was with me because I was nothing like her."

Dunn, Archer, and Dex traded a look. Archer said,

"Okay, um, thanks. What about your students? You do a lot of experiments and run tests on them? Do any of them get angry if they aren't selected or when you share the results?"

Kelsea shook her head. "I offer it to all my students so none of them are ever left out. The results are never shared with them individually, just used in class and in papers I write."

"Did any of them ever ask to see their results?" Dex asked.

Kelsea shook her head. "No."

"What is your relationship with Edward Bailey?"

"He's a student of mine. He was in one of my classes last year and we developed a friendship of sorts."

"What kind of friendship? Do you get together and do things?"

"No, of course not. That wouldn't be okay with me. There are clear boundaries with professors and students, and I'm not interested in crossing them. Edward is a nice guy, and we talk sometimes when he comes in to participate in one of my experiments or when he has a class close to one of mine, but that's it."

"So there's never been anything romantic between the two of you?"

"No. Not on my side at least."

"What does that mean?" Dex asked.

Kelsea shrugged. "It means I don't have a thing for Edward. He asked me out last year, but I turned him down. He understands that I'm not going to date a student."

"He asked you out?" Archer asked.

Kelsea leaned back and crossed her arms. "Is that so hard to believe?"

Archer's confident look vanished, and he floundered. "I didn't mean it like that."

"He was confirming what you said. We haven't heard this before from you. It's new information, and any new information involves looking into the person more intently," Dunn explained.

"Edward isn't like that. He has a girlfriend. Why would he be stalking me?"

"Some men don't know how to hear the word no, Kelsea," Dunn said, slowly and carefully, as though there was a lot more to the story than she was aware of.

"It's not Edward."

Dunn slid a look to English who nodded and went back to work. They weren't listening to her at all.

"When was the last time you had any contact with Dane Lewis?"

Kelsea shook her head. "You're definitely off base with him. I don't even know when I talked to him last. We split up years ago... seven years I think, maybe eight. We stayed in touch a little after that, but we drifted apart since I was here and he was there."

"Except he's here. An hour away, just south of Buffalo. He never reached out to you?"

She shook her head. "No. I didn't know he was around until you mentioned it the other day."

"That alone is suspicious, Kelsea," Dunn said.

She shrugged. "Not to me. We haven't spoken to each other. We dated, but we both agreed it wasn't right between us before. Why would now be different?"

"Does it matter that he moved here ten months ago? Right around the time you started talking to Maxwell."

She shrugged, but a chill ran down her spine. "We haven't talked."

"But the timing is pretty coincidental."

She shrugged, trying not to be concerned. "It wouldn't be if someone wasn't stalking me."

"But someone is stalking you, Kelsea. That's the whole point."

She sighed and tried to imagine Dane lusting after her all this time. It was a stretch, but she didn't know him any more. He was a different person than the last time they were together. So was she.

"Talk to us about Mason."

Kelsea groaned. "From one to another. These guys have nothing to do with it. Mason is a friend. He's a good guy. He paid for what happened with his wife, and he hates himself for it. He still loves her. He couldn't care less about me."

"Do you know that you bear a striking resemblance to his late wife?" Dex asked.

"What? No. He said she was a blonde."

Dex nodded and slid a picture across the table to her. "She was, but that doesn't mean you don't look alike."

Kelsea stared down into the face of a woman she'd never met but felt like she knew. All the stories Mason told her about his wife ran through her head. She caught him looking at her sometimes and wondered what was going through his mind. He always brushed it off, but she had a hard time, staring at his wife, thinking it was all completely innocent.

"I've never seen a picture of her."

"She looks a lot like you," Archer agreed.

Kelsea nodded. Had she been working side-by-side with the man who she feared all this time? Was she really so blind that she didn't even notice that Mason was dangerous? Everyone knew about him. Why hadn't she ever paid attention?

JAYMES TOOK in the conversation around him and did his best to focus on what he was doing. He could feel Kelsea's fear from across the table and wanted to take her away from all of this. She didn't deserve to have her life ripped to shreds and everyone in it investigated. But it was necessary if they were ever going to find out who was watching her.

Stalking was one thing. It was disturbing and frightening. But when the guy went from stalking to murder, Dunn and the others couldn't help but get involved. Jaymes was both happy to hear that and terrified for Kelsea.

His stomach rumbled loudly, prompting him to look at the clock. It was after ten, which meant it was far later than he realized. He was starving, and he had no doubt everyone else was, too.

"Why don't we pick this all back up tomorrow?" he suggested.

"We still have more questions," Dunn argued.

"Yeah, and we need something to eat and a few hours of sleep. Kelsea and I aren't SEALs. We can't survive on adrenaline and caffeine like the rest of you."

Dunn glanced around the room and finally nodded. "I'll get Slade."

Slade followed Dunn into the room a minute later with a smile. "Let's get some food."

The three of them headed out, leaving the rest of the team behind to keep working into the night. Dunn promised he'd call if they learned anything but said to have a good night.

Slade ordered Chinese food on their way home and swung by to pick it up. The smell filled the SUV and made Jaymes even more hungry.

By the time they got home and ate, exhaustion settled in for Jaymes. He was ready to get some sleep and knew Kelsea was right there with him.

But he had to know one thing.

"Do you think he can get in here?" Jaymes asked Slade.

Slade glanced around and shrugged. "Honestly? Yeah. Absolutely. We're all gone all day. All of us can pick that lock downstairs, and the one to your place. There's no reason to think he couldn't."

"Should we sweep here?"

Slade looked around. "Not a bad idea, but let's stay vigilant. Anything moved? Check it. A weird spot on the wall, get close. Something feels off, don't ignore that feeling. Trust your gut. Both of you."

Jaymes nodded and thanked Slade. He and Kelsea headed to his room. She was quiet. When he closed the door, she sank down on the edge of the bed and stared straight ahead.

"Are you okay?"

She laughed mirthlessly. "I really wish everyone would stop asking me that."

"Why?"

She looked up and rolled her eyes. "Because I'm not okay. I'll probably never be okay again. This all might be no big deal to them, and maybe even to you a little bit, but it's a big fucking deal to me. Someone's been watching me, Jaymes. Someone has video of me naked. Taking a shower, getting dressed, maybe even having sex. Someone violated my privacy in the worst possible way, and for months now. I can't even think straight, let alone be okay. And they could have done the same thing here. I just..."

He sat down next to her and wrapped his arms around her. She turned to him and buried her face in his shoulder and cried. He held her while she cried and cried until she finally fell asleep in his arms.

He got them both under the covers and held her again. She was finally quiet, but tension still filled her body. He laid there, praying for help and promising he'd do anything to save her from the hell she'd been through. He would find the bastard who did this to her. And he'd get revenge for her.

Because he finally had to admit he'd fallen for her. Hard and fast. And he'd do anything for the woman he loved.

19

———

Kelsea didn't sleep well, even with Jaymes right there with her. She woke up once and felt like she was on fire but realized he was just laying almost on top of her. The second time she woke up, her pants had twisted around her and were digging into her belly. She tugged those off. Then she heard something.

She was about to give up even trying to sleep when Jaymes snuggled up against her and slid his big hand around her waist. He held her tight, his jeans a stiff barrier between them, and kissed her shoulder sweetly.

"You okay?" he whispered in the darkness.

She nodded. "Better now."

He kissed her shoulder again and nuzzled her neck, then fell back to sleep. Knowing he was right there with her finally gave her peace and she managed a couple of hours of good sleep.

When she stirred again, the sun was streaming through the window and Jaymes was sitting on the edge of the bed.

"Okay. Thanks. See you soon."

"Everything okay?" she asked.

He gave her a sheepish grin over his shoulder. "Isn't that my line?"

She smiled. "You look like you needed someone to ask."

He set the phone down and crawled back under the covers with her. "You can always ask me anything."

"Yeah?"

He nodded and kissed her softly. "Absolutely."

"I can ask about Lily?"

He stiffened for a moment, then nodded. "Yes. I'll tell you anything you want to know."

She was surprised to hear that since he didn't want to talk about it before, but she no longer cared that much. Lily was getting married to Archer, and Jaymes wasn't the kind of guy who would steal his brother's girlfriend. Not to mention, Kelsea wasn't all that happy about the thought of hearing him talk about another woman.

She shook her head. "I think you should tell me about the phone call you just took instead."

His eyes went from resigned to bothered in a flash. She tried to brace herself, but she knew whatever he had to share was not good news.

"They found something. We need to go in."

Kelsea nodded and sucked in a breath. She wanted the whole thing to be over, but she wasn't ready to face whoever was behind the whole thing. She didn't really have a choice in the matter.

"Let's go. I need my life back."

They got up and showered quickly, then got dressed. Slade stopped by a coffee shop for caffeine and breakfast for everyone, then headed to the office. The rest of the team was already there when they walked in.

Everyone grabbed food and coffee and made small talk, avoiding Kelsea the entire time. She took her coffee and sandwich and sat at the table, waiting the rest of them out.

When they couldn't delay any longer, they all finally sat. Dunn took the chair next to her with Jaymes on her other side.

"Just tell me," she said.

"English was able to trace some of the cameras."

"Some?"

He nodded. "Apparently, there were two cameras in most places because there were two people watching you. One set we're still looking for the end site, but the other English was able to find because he knew where to look."

"Where?" she asked, dreading his answer.

"Dane Lewis's office."

"What?"

"English looked at feeds going to all of our prime suspects' homes, plus their places of work, and found one of the feeds going to Dane Lewis's office. We're going to pay him a visit this morning. We want you to go to school. Act like nothing is going on. You need an alibi in case this goes bad."

"Bad? Like what? Someone else is going to die because of me?"

Dunn shook his head. "No one is going to die today, Kelsea."

"Then why do I need an alibi?"

Dunn glanced around the room. "Because we never know how things are going to go. We could go in there and he could have a gun trained on the door waiting for us. He could have any number of things going on. We need to be prepared for anything."

"Wouldn't it be better if I stayed here?"

Jack shook his head. "No. I get that it feels right since

you'll be safe here, but we need someone outside this room to be able to say you were where you said you were. We operate on the edge of the law. That means not everything we do is on the right side of it. The reason Dunn got called when Maxwell's house blew was because they thought we might have had something to do with it."

"What? Why?"

Jack shrugged. "Because we have the skills and were asking questions about the guy just days before he died. We're still new around here. The local PD doesn't know us yet. The border patrol is a little more interested in working with us, but we're getting pushback. We don't want to drag you into the middle of it."

Dunn flashed a glare at Jack, but he just stared right back. "She needed to understand."

Dunn was not happy Jack told her all that, but it was too late. "I'll go to work, but I want someone in touch with me throughout the day. I can't get another video of someone I used to date getting killed."

Dunn shook his head. "You won't, Kelsea. We're just going to talk to him. He'll still be alive when we leave. I promise."

HE LET himself into the office without bothering to knock. He had to hurry.

"What are you doing here?" Dane asked, looking up from his computer.

"I could ask you the same thing," he said, nodding to the computer screen where pictures of Kelsea's house were on display.

He leaned back in his chair and smirked. The bastard

acted like he owned the whole fucking world. Getting involved with him was a mistake, but he didn't know it at the time. How in the fuck could he have predicted that the one PI he picked to work with was actually Kelsea's sniveling ex-boyfriend who left her high and dry before med school?

It all worked out in the end.

"I have just as much right to watch her as you do. She hasn't been around much lately. What's going on?"

He shook his head. "None of your damn business. Did you get what I asked you for?"

Dane nodded and handed over a folder. "Not much on either of them. The brother's a fucking war hero. He almost got his ass handed to him, but there's a sealed report that he shouldn't have been discharged when he was."

"How the fuck did you get that?"

Dane smirked again. "I'm just that good."

He had to give him that one. The fucker was good. So good he never realized Dane added cameras for himself to be able to watch Kelsea until those SEAL bastards were talking about it an hour ago. He was just glad he was smart enough to slip a bug into her purse. She carried it with her everywhere so he stayed one step ahead of them.

Barely.

"What about the mother?"

Dane shrugged. "Nothing special with her. She goes to church, lives off her dead husband's retirement. She doesn't do much."

He knew all that already. He was hoping for something a little more from him, but he would take what he could get. Besides, he'd already laid the groundwork with her, and his plan was in motion to get Kelsea away from Baby Boy.

"Did you get anything on the other chick?"

Dane shook his head. "Nah. She's even less interesting.

She went to school with Golden Boy and has known him for years. It looks like after his kidnapping she shacked up with the brother. Engaged. I've heard that Jaymes has a thing for her, but who knows if that's true."

"You should know. That's what I pay you for."

He shrugged. "Not enough. I'm doing half of this shit as a favor."

"Yeah, and you're watching her in the shower as a thank you."

He scoffed. "You didn't know I was doing that. Hey, how did you find out?"

He shook his head. "The same way I found out that they're on to you and coming here to question you."

"What?" he asked, jumping to his feet. All humor vanished just that quickly.

"Sit down. They're not going to do anything about it."

Dane turned a glare his way, suspicion reining in his eyes. "Why not?"

He pulled out a gun and shrugged. "Because you'll already be dead."

He squeezed the trigger before Dane could react. He took a step back, then slumped into his chair. He groaned, clearly still alive. He wouldn't be for long.

He went through Dane's computer and deleted any evidence of them working together. He grabbed the files in the cabinet that he'd asked Dane to pull together, knowing he always kept paper copies for himself, and tucked all of it into the briefcase he carried in.

Dane was still gasping for breath when he walked out of the room and closed the door behind him. He was planning to kill him quickly, but the fucker was watching Kelsea. *His* Kelsea. He deserved to die slowly.

THE LATER IN the day it got, the more anxious Jaymes was. Slade told him he expected to hear from Dunn and the rest of the team within a couple hours. They were going on six hours since they'd spoken. Something was definitely wrong.

"Have you heard from them?" Kelsea asked, walking into her office.

She had a couple of classes to teach but turned them into study sessions for her students to ask questions if they needed to. She also gave them the option to leave the classroom if they didn't want to study there. Most took that option.

Slade shook his head. "I haven't."

"At what point do you call them?"

Slade opened his mouth as his phone rang. "Yeah." Slade listened for a few minutes, then hung up without a word. "We have to go."

"What happened?" Kelsea asked.

"We have to go, Kelsea."

"No. I want to know what's wrong. I could feel it all day and I can see it on your face. Something happened. Tell me. Now."

Slade glanced around. Students were passing down the hallways, talking. A pair of professors were outside the door having a conversation. Even the classroom Kelsea just vacated next door was starting to fill in. There was no privacy, which meant something bad happened if Slade wanted it.

"Let's just get out of here. I'll tell you everything I know when we get to the car. Dunn will fill us in on the rest."

Kelsea dug in her heels and crossed her arms, plumping up her breasts. Jaymes thought back to the last time he had his mouth on those beautiful breasts and began to harden. He'd never needed someone the way he needed her. It was like a drug to be around her. A part of him understood someone wanting to watch her and believe she was close to him. It was fucked up as shit, but if he ever lost her, there would be a part of him that always felt as though he was missing something and would want to find it.

"Kelsea," Jaymes said, stepping toward her. He grasped her elbow and drew her attention. "Kels, come on."

"He's dead, isn't he?" she asked, her voice shaking. Her lower lip wobbled, and tears filled her beautiful brown eyes.

He wanted to wrap her up and tell her it wasn't true, but he couldn't. With one glance at Slade, Jaymes knew Dane was dead. What he didn't know was how or why.

"Yes, sweetheart. But we don't know why. Let's go find out."

She spun on Slade and got up in his face. It would have been funny if she wasn't so broken about it. She wagged her finger in his face, all five-six of her berating the massive former SEAL. "What the fuck happened? Dunn promised me he wouldn't die, and he's fucking dead? Tell me right now, Slade. Did they kill him?"

He stood his ground and shook his head. "I don't know anything other than he's dead and we need to get to the office. Now, Kelsea."

"Did they kill him?" she whimpered.

Slade shook his head. "I don't know."

Kelsea mechanically gathered her stuff. When she was done packing her bag, Jaymes grabbed it from her and reached for her hand. She let him take it as they walked down the hallway and outside into the bright sunshine.

A fresh blanket of snow fell overnight, leaving every-thing with an even coat of winter. The wind was light, letting the snow lie still as they walked by the other buildings to the parking lot where Slade's SUV was parked.

Jaymes watched the crowd around them, ignoring most of the students in favor of anyone who looked remotely suspicious. Everything about the day was off, but he couldn't figure out how or why.

They almost made it to the SUV when someone behind them called out, "Dr. Arnold!"

Jaymes turned Kelsea behind him and faced whoever was coming at them the same time Slade did. Slade reached for his back, where he had a gun hidden, but Jaymes just wanted to block Kelsea.

"Whoa," Edward said, pulling up short when he took in the two men standing guard in front of her. "I just wanted to give something to Dr. Arnold."

Kelsea put her hand on Jaymes's shoulder and eased him to the side. "It's okay, guys. You both know Edward. What is it?"

Edward handed over a magazine of some sort. "It just came out today. Did you see it?"

He had it opened to a two-page spread with more words than pictures. Jaymes recognized brain scans on one page and when he looked closer, he saw Kelsea's smiling face under the by-line.

She took the magazine from Edward and smiled. She looked up at him with green eyes that sparkled just enough to say she was happy. "Thank you, Edward. I had a long day."

He nodded. "Yeah, I was looking for you. I just got out of class, but your office and the lab were both empty. Is everything okay?"

Kelsea nodded. "Yeah. I just got some bad news about an old friend."

Edward's brow furrowed and concerned slipped into his eyes. Jaymes catalogued his every move as Edward reached for Kelsea's hand. "I'm so sorry, Dr. Arnold."

She nodded and squeezed his hand. "Thank you. I appreciate that."

He smiled at her again and nodded. "I'll let you go, but I wanted to make sure you saw that."

She thanked him and went to give it back to him.

Edward shook his head. "I've got another copy. You keep that one."

Kelsea nodded and thanked him again. Edward waved and walked away, rubbing his hands together to ward off the cold.

Kelsea watched him for a second, then faced Slade. "How could you possibly think he would be behind this?"

Slade shrugged and guided Kelsea to the car. Jaymes sat in the back with her, holding her hand on the drive back to Niagara Falls.

When they finally pulled into the office parking lot, Kelsea was asleep. Jaymes took a second to stare at her. Her long lashes brushed against her cheeks, casting a faint shadow on them. Her mouth hung slightly open as she snored softly. Dark strands of hair snaked around her shoulders and rested on her cheeks. He reached up and brushed them behind her ear, lingering just a bit on her soft skin.

She stirred, blinking her eyes open. She smiled when she saw him, then her face fell as reality slapped her. She sat straight up and looked around, then nodded once. "Let's go."

20

Kelsea followed Slade into the office building with Jaymes at her back. It didn't escape her notice that they were flanking her, keeping her between them. It should have made her feel safe. Instead, it was a stark reminder that she was in danger.

Deadly danger. Whoever this was wasn't playing around. Two people Kelsea was attached to at some point were dead. She hated the thought of Dunn and the others killing Dane, but a part of her hoped it was the case. Then it would mean he wasn't murdered by the psycho who killed Maxwell.

The elevator ride was quick and quiet. Before she knew it, they were walking into the F-BOMB offices again, a place she never dreamed existed until she needed protection from the men inside.

Slade swiped a card at the door and let them inside. They bypassed the conference room they used the last time and headed down a hallway through another secured door. Slade tapped on a door frame when they went by. Kelsea glanced inside to English shuffling papers and getting up to follow them.

There was another conference room at the end of the hall. This one was more basic, but bigger. Large cabinets lined one wall, cabinets Kelsea was sure were loaded with more weapons than she'd ever heard of let alone seen. A glass wall looked into the hallway. The other two walls were solid, one with a large whiteboard and the other with a large projection screen.

The whiteboard was lined with pictures and a timeline. She walked over to it, reading everything they'd laid out so neatly from the last six months of her life. On top were personal events, on the bottom were interactions with suspects. It was pretty sad that there wasn't more going on in her life. In six months, she'd started dating Maxwell, got dumped by him, and worked. That was it. When the psycho stalker caught up to her, her tombstone was going to read, "Here lies Kelsea Arnold. She worked a lot and had no life. Now she's gone, and no one cares."

She swallowed the pain in her throat and read the rest of what they had. Notes to the side mentioned events that didn't fit within the last six months. Her relationship with Dane as kids, meeting Edward, and when she started working with Mason at Best Friends Forever.

Kelsea turned and found the team watching her. Jaymes stood near the door. Her eyes landed on him, watching his reaction to everything. She was most ashamed of everything he learned about her. She wanted him to think she was desirable and sexy, but she wasn't either of those things. She was living with him because she was afraid to be in her own home. And he was letting her because he was a good guy who knew how terrifying it was to not be safe in your own home.

As if to prove her fears, Jaymes ducked his head, snapping the eye contact they had. She'd never felt more alone in her life than she did in that moment. She was surrounded by amazing men, all of whom were working to keep her safe, but none of them really cared about her. She was a job, an obligation.

She was the stupid one who went and fell for Jaymes. He made her feel safe. He protected her and believed her when no one else did. She tried to convince herself her feelings were misplaced hero syndrome, but it was more than that. She didn't love him because he was her hero. She loved him because he was Jaymes. A nice guy who was there for her, but who also was funny and smart and sexy and everything she'd ever hoped to find in a man.

But he was done. Two dead exes were enough for him to step back. She didn't blame him. It hurt, but she understood. If she could put a stop to all this and protect him, she would in a heartbeat.

"Are you ready to get started?" Dunn asked her softly.

Kelsea nodded and took a seat with her back to the whiteboard. She couldn't stare at the lackluster life she'd led any longer.

Dunn took the seat next to her. Slade moved to her other side when Jaymes chose a seat across the table. She avoided his gaze, focusing on Dunn and the others as they told her everything.

"He was unconscious when we got there. He'd been shot. We're not sure how long he was down before we arrived, but I'm guessing it wasn't long. His pulse was faint, and he bled out before we could save him."

"Did he suffer?" Kelsea whispered. She hadn't spoken to Dane in years, but she didn't like the thought of him dying slowly.

Silence around her told her he not only died slowly, but he died in pain.

"So whoever this is killed Maxwell after he beat the shit out of him and killed Dane with one shot designed to make it slow." She glanced around the room, waiting for someone to argue with her. No one did. "Great. And we have no idea who it is."

"Mason is still on the list. So is Edward."

Kelsea scoffed. "So no one. Because I've already told you it isn't either of them."

"Kelsea," Dunn said carefully. "We know it's hard to admit that someone you know and care about could be doing something like this, but every single person in this room had the man we trusted the most turn on us. Our commanding officer not only kidnapped Jaymes, but he killed one of our brothers in combat. He lied to all of us and tricked us. He sent us in the wrong direction and made us believe we were doing the right thing when, in fact, he sent us on wild goose chases and killed the only people who could tell us he was the one behind it all."

"And that's what makes you think this is one of the two men I trust. What motivation would either of them have to hurt me or kill my exes?"

"We can't rule them out just because you don't think they would do this," Dunn said harshly. "They're our best suspects."

"Which means you're not looking hard enough."

"Trust me, Kelsea, we're looking. We've looked into everything we can possibly imagine, and none of the other people we considered had any interaction with you. Stalking is not usually random. As many as eighty percent of stalking victims know their stalker. That tells us it's not likely someone random. We don't believe it's an ex of yours—"

"Since they're dead," Kelsea muttered.

"Dammit," Dunn shouted, slamming his hand on the

table. "Do you really think we don't want to solve this? We might not know you that well, Kelsea, but we give a shit. We're trying. We've looked into the people in your past. We're digging for more and more information. We want to find out who's doing this."

"Why are you dealing with this and not the local police department?" Kelsea asked, not at all deterred by Dunn's outburst. "Why is any of this your business? Aren't you supposed to be watching the borders or something?"

Dunn glanced around the room. "We are watching the borders. We're also watching you, Kelsea. If you'd rather the local PD takes over, we can step back. We're not trying to make you uncomfortable."

Kelsea closed her eyes and rested her head in her hands. She didn't know what she wanted or needed. Best-case scenario would be to put all this behind her, but she knew that wasn't going to happen any time soon.

She shook her head without meeting the eyes of any of the men in the room. "No. It's fine. I just... I want this to be over."

"So do we, Kelsea," Dunn said. "So do we."

JAYMES UNDERSTOOD why Kelsea was upset. It was bad enough that one of her exes was killed. With two, someone was sending a clear message. But there was more to the story, and Jaymes needed to know what it was.

"Did you find the feed? The cameras that were watching Kelsea?" he asked.

The tension in the room both settled and ramped up. That was the whole reason they went to Dane's office. Him dying overshadowed that, but there was nothing they could do for him. They needed to figure out why he was watching, and what else he knew about it.

"We did," Dunn finally said, focusing on Jaymes instead of Kelsea. "But he wasn't watching all the cameras. It looked like he only had some of them, which was what we thought."

"Did you find anything to tell you who he was working for?"

Dunn shook his head.

English spoke up. "His office had clearly been wiped. Files were deleted off his computer and one of the file cabinets was sorted. Whoever killed him is likely the person who hired him."

"And again, we have no idea who that is," Kelsea muttered.

Everyone in the room fell silent. The men surrounding the table were used to solving problems. They figured out the answers and fixed things. This had been hanging over their heads for days, and two men were dead with no one knew how many more to come. Kelsea was safe because they were with her at all times, but that didn't mean she could live her life. If they didn't figure out who was behind all this, she'd live in fear forever.

Jaymes knew all too well how painful that was.

"So what are we going to do?"

The other men avoided looking at Jaymes or Kelsea. Most of them kept their focus on Dunn, but his eyes said he was just as lost.

"We talk to Mason and Edward again. For tonight, everyone needs to get some sleep. We'll start fresh tomorrow," Dex said, the voice of reason.

The room waited for Kelsea's response. All she did was nod, giving the room permission to breathe a sigh of relief.

The men stood, filing out one by one. Slade led Kelsea out with Jack right behind her. Jaymes hung back to talk to Dunn.

"What's really going on?" Jaymes asked when Kelsea was in the hallway.

Archer stayed with Dunn, and the two of them faced Jaymes.

"We don't know. Both Mason and Edward are suspicious, but we can't draw a line from either of them to all this. English is working to figure out where the second feed goes. It doesn't make sense that the PI got caught but not whoever hired him."

"How did he get caught?" Jaymes asked.

"What do you mean?" Archer asked.

Jaymes stared at the table, his mind spinning. "We found him because there was a feed from the cameras going to his place, right?"

The other two nodded.

"Okay, so how is it a PI can run lines that go to a separate location and are secure, but the lines running to his own office are wide open?"

Dunn and Archer exchanged a glance. "It doesn't make sense."

"Neither does the fact that whoever killed him obviously knew exactly when to go looking for him. If he was still breathing when you got there, you didn't miss the guy by much. How did he know you were going then so he could tie up loose ends?"

Dunn rubbed his jaw, but Archer's eyes went wide. "Kelsea."

"No," Jaymes said immediately. "She isn't behind this."

Archer shook his head. "I don't think she is, but she could be bugged."

"We haven't been at her house."

Archer shook his head again. "I'm not talking about her house. I'm talking about her. Her purse or a bag or even her coat. Someone could have bugged any of those things and heard everything we've said. We told Kelsea we were going after Dane. If her stuff is bugged, this guy knew it, too."

"Shit," Jaymes breathed. "How do we handle this?"

"Get rid of it," Dunn said quickly.

"What if we use it?" Archer asked.

Jaymes shook his head. "I'm with Dunn. Kelsea has had her privacy invaded too much. We need this done. Gone."

Arched met and held Jaymes's gaze. "When you were gone, I'd have given anything to have a connection open that we could have used to find where you were."

Jaymes's throat closed up. He loved his brother, but they never talked about his kidnapping. Not since the first few days after he was back. It wasn't something Jaymes liked to relive. Archer never admitted how much the whole thing bothered him. Jaymes always thought he was another job for his brother, but the emotion in Archer's eyes said otherwise.

"Let's ask Kelsea," Jaymes finally said.

Dunn went into the hallway and whispered something to English, then to Kelsea. Kelsea handed her purse to English, then shrugged out of her coat and gave that to Slade. Then she followed Dunn back into the conference room.

Kelsea shook, arms wrapped around her middle. Tears flooded her eyes, clinging desperately to her lashes.

Jaymes couldn't let her stand there and fall apart. He went to her and slid an arm around her waist. She flinched, then settled against him. He kissed the side of her head and gave her all the strength he could spare, and then some.

"If we're right, we can use this to our advantage. We can track the signal from any bugs we find in your stuff, and find the bastard who's behind all this," Dunn said harshly.

Kelsea laughed mirthlessly. "You have all sorts of things to track and haven't found him yet. What makes you think this will be different?"

"Because bugs like this aren't as advanced. If we're right, there's a simple listening device in your bag. They're not high end. They send a signal out like a cell phone. If there is one in your stuff, we can use it to feed bad intel to the person responsible for this."

"Like telling him one thing so you can catch him?"

Archer nodded. "Exactly like that."

"And this will all be over?" Kelsea asked hopefully.

Dunn gave her a half-smile. "That's what we hope, Kelsea."

"Let's do it," she said.

"Are you sure? It means someone will still be able to hear everything you say and do. You can refuse to do this," Dunn said, playing the other side.

"He's been listening anyway. He already knows every-thing. He's killing people. I don't care what it means for me. I can't have him kill anyone else," Kelsea said.

Jaymes turned her in his arms and wrapped her up. Dunn and Archer nodded to him and silently left the room.

Kelsea buried her face in his chest and cried. Silent tears fell as she shook against him. His heart ached for her. When Lily was taken, after him, he was useless to help, but he was also useless to feel much. He'd been through the emotional wringer after believing he was dead for sure. He didn't spend much time on the side of the grieving family and friends. He was the one who was gone. The one who vanished and had to go through all the stages of grief on his own. Watching his life fade away day after day, unsure how long had passed or how many more days he'd live.

"This is all my fault," she whispered.

"No," Jaymes said firmly. "Not even a little bit."

"How can you say that? Two men are dead because of me. And many more are at risk. You're right to pull away from me. I get it. I would, too. I'm not enough to put yourself in harm's way."

"What are you talking about?" Jaymes asked, tilting her chin up so she'd meet his gaze.

"Ever since we walked in here," she said, waving her hand around the room. "You saw my life spelled out in every boring detail. I saw it in your eyes. You know I'm not worth it. Two men I was involved with are dead. You don't want to be number three. I don't blame you. I don't want you to be either." She drew in a ragged breath and took a step back, out of his reach. "I'm sorry I got you in the middle of all this."

Jaymes reached for her. "Kelsea, that's not what's going on here."

"It's okay, Jaymes. I want you to be safe. These guys will find the man behind all this, but until then, I think I should stay with Jack."

Jaymes didn't want her words to hurt, but they did. "If you're more comfortable with Jack, I won't stand in your way."

She laughed mirthlessly. "That has nothing to do with it. I want you safe, Jaymes. I can't be responsible for your death."

He shook his head. "I'm not going to die, Kelsea."

She glanced at the board where the details were written out in black and white. "I never thought Maxwell or Dane would either."

"Kelsea, look at me."

She stared at the board for another few seconds, then lowered her lashes over her eyes and turned her face back to him. He waited until she finally looked up at him to speak.

"When we walked into this room, I hated that you had to see it. Coming in here means they're worried about keeping you safe. That kills me. They have no leads. They don't know what's going on. And you just lost the man you loved once. I wanted to give you space to process all that. This isn't me pulling away. But if you'd feel safer with Jack, I will not stand in your way."

She looked up at him, eyes brimming with tears. "The only place I've felt safe in the last week is in your arms."

He closed his eyes for a second, then reached for her. "Then come here, sweetheart."

She stepped into his arms and sighed.

He knew exactly how she felt.

21

———

KELSEA SLID UNDER THE COVERS AND SNUGGLED INTO THE pillow. Her thoughts turned to Dane and Maxwell. She couldn't shake the guilt. No matter what Jaymes said, it was her fault. She just needed to know he was safe.

She almost told him just how much she cared about him when they were in the F-BOMB office. She had no idea how he thought she wanted to be with anyone other than him, but she had every intention of showing him just how much she cared. She couldn't say the words, but she could prove it with her body.

They left her bugged purse in the kitchen so whoever was listening in didn't overhear anything they weren't prepared for. Slade was on the couch again, with strict orders not to speak to anyone unless it was planned ahead of time.

The bedroom door opened and Jaymes walked in. Her mouth watered at the sight of him. His dark hair was a few weeks overdue for a cut, curling around his ears. His rich, brown eyes met hers and heated instantly. Blue shorts hung low on his hips, teasing her with a vee that pointed to the tented front of his shorts. She couldn't wait to get her hands on his firm chest, blanketed with the same dark brown hair that covered his head.

"Got room in there for me?" he asked softly.

She nodded and scooted toward his side of the bed. She'd never gotten so comfortable with a man so quickly. None of her ex-boyfriends had ever spent the night with her so much that they had their own sides of the bed. With Jaymes, everything felt natural. Like they were supposed to meet, although she could have done with different circumstances drawing them together.

Jaymes pulled the covers back just enough to slide under them. He reached for Kelsea, wrapping his arms around her, then skimming her side down to her ass.

He groaned. "You're naked under here."

She wiggled closer and nodded. "I was too warm for pajamas."

He chuckled and wrapped her tighter in his arms. "You're shivering, beautiful."

She shrugged. "Okay, maybe I hoped it would be too warm for pajamas."

"Oh, yeah? And how were you planning to get warm?"

His voice dropped into that low, sexy baritone, sending a chill up her spine and tingles between her thighs. She ached for him. Her breasts throbbed with need, and her core clenched in anticipation. "First, I was hoping you'd climb into bed naked, too."

He tipped her onto her back and covered her upper half with his body. His erection dug into her hip, but she didn't care when his lips touched hers. He brushed the hair off her face and kissed her with a slow passion that had her ready to kick the covers off in seconds. When he finally parted his lips and licked his way into her mouth, she moaned. She needed to feel safe and loved and happy, even if it was just for a little while.

Kelsea ran her hands up Jaymes's back, loving the feel of his warm, smooth skin under her fingertips. His muscles bunched and flexed, giving her hills and valleys to explore. She could have spent all night learning every inch of him, but she had more pressing things in mind, like the thick length pressing against her side.

She cupped his ass and encouraged him to cover all of her. She parted her thighs and welcomed him between them. He arched into her, the thin barrier of his shorts adding a level of friction that had her throwing her head back and moaning.

"Oh, God. Jaymes, please. I need to feel you inside me."

He arched against her again and kissed his way down her throat to her breasts. He tugged one nipple between his teeth, rocking against her core with each pull. She held on to his shoulders, debating dragging him up, pushing him down, or holding him still. There was no bad option.

He licked across to her other breast, leaving a hand behind to torture the first one. He circled her nipple and flicked it with the tip of his tongue, sending pulses through her entire body.

She'd never come from nipple stimulation alone, but with the beat of his cock against her clit, she was leaping closer and closer to an orgasm.

"Come like this, Kels. Let me feel you let go, baby."

She tried to stifle her moans, but he kept going, dragging them out of her, each one louder than the last. Her body tightened, bracing, tensing, until she snapped, calling out his name and dragging him up to seal their lips together.

She stroked her tongue against his, letting him take over the kiss. He rocked his hips to hers slowly, keeping her on the edge but not letting her fall over again. She panted through their kisses, her head spinning with everything she was feeling.

Jaymes pulled away and rolled over to his side of the bed. He tugged his shorts and briefs off and grabbed a condom from the nightstand. She watched him as he protected them both, then crawled back to her. He positioned himself between her thighs, rubbing against her throbbing flesh.

"Jaymes," she whispered. "You feel so good."

"Kelsea. Look at me, sweetheart. I need to see your face. Know you're right there with me."

She pried her eyes open and met his gaze. The desire in his eyes ramped up her pulse as the tender care calmed her. He reached for her hands and covered her body with his. He stroked into her slowly, filling and stretching her wet channel.

Neither of them spoke as their bodies moved together. With one slow stroke after another, he made love to her. She couldn't think of any other way to describe it. They held hands above her head, their eyes locked on each other's. Every few seconds, he leaned down and kissed her gently, all the while keeping up his slow and steady pace.

Each gentle thrust dragged the base of his cock over her clit. Softly enough that the rise to the top was an easy climb, one that left her surprised when her body tightened and clamped down around him, drawing him in even deeper. Every inch of her trembled with the full body orgasm she didn't see coming.

Just like the man who gave it to her. Kelsea never thought she'd find someone who made her feel the way he did. She told herself a few times over the years that she was in love, but none of the men she'd ever known were anything like Jaymes. He was kind and caring and thoughtful. He called his mother and had dinner with her. He took in a terrified stranger without a second thought. He was a protector and a man she was lucky to know.

He stroked hard into her, hitting her deep. She arched against him, her eyes slamming shut with the sensations flooding her body.

"Look at me, Kels," he said, his voice thick with desire.

She forced her eyes open and stared up at him. He clenched his jaw. He was only inches away, close enough that she felt his breath on her cheeks. The hair on his chest rubbed her nipples as his pubic hair tickled her thighs and belly. She wrapped her legs around his waist, taking him in deeper.

"Oh, damn, Kels. Fuck, sweetheart." He thrust harder, his control faltering.

She met his strokes, tugging the control even further out of his reach. His jaw tightened and his eyes blazed. Through it all, he kept his gaze locked on hers. She was so focused on him that another orgasm snuck up on her and took over her body.

"Oh, God, Jaymes. Yes!"

He squeezed her hands tight and leaned more of his weight onto her, slamming harder into her. She wanted to touch him, to run her hands down his face, but she accepted the torture knowing he was feeling the same way. His eyes betrayed the calm he projected, flashing everything from lust to happiness to fear and back to lust. When he finally let go and thrust hard and deep into her, she lifted up to kiss him so she didn't spill the words that were on the tip of her tongue.

There was no going back from Jaymes Ford. He would forever hold her heart.

Jaymes loved waking up with Kelsea in his arms. There was something addictive about her snuggling her bare ass against his cock and feeling her shock when she realized what she was doing in her sleep. Even better was when she did it again, fully aware of her actions.

He made love to her again, wondering how in the world he got so lucky. He couldn't get enough of her, and she felt the same way. If karma was a real thing, he did something right in his life if he got to share it with her.

Reality slapped him in the face when she curled into his side, their bodies still slick with sweat, and whispered, "Do you think Mason or Edward could be doing this?"

He ran his hand down her spine, cupping her hip, and kissed her head. He gave in to the desire to breathe in the scent of her hair and let her presence calm him. "I don't know, Kels. I hope not because you care about them both, but I don't know."

"If you had to guess, who would you say it was?"

Jaymes forced himself to hesitate, although there was very little doubt in his mind. After a few seconds, he sighed and said, "Mason. He has a history of violence."

"Because of his wife?"

Jaymes nodded. "I know you don't want to hear that."

She shrugged and burrowed tighter into his side. "I don't want to hear any of this, but unfortunately, it's my life now."

"It won't be forever," he said, sliding his hand over her ass. "One day we can wake up like this and know Slade isn't out in my living room listening to our every move."

She giggled. "Yeah, maybe we can go to my house where I won't worry about how loud I'm being every time you make me come."

He flipped her onto her back and covered her again. "I like the sound of that."

She sighed softly and pulled him down for a kiss that left him aching to sink into her again. He would have, too, but Slade pounded on the bedroom door.

"Five minutes."

Jaymes pulled back, considering. He raised one eyebrow.

Kelsea laughed, but the laughter they shared moments ago was gone. Fear and anxiety creased her forehead. She nibbled on her lower lip, and not in the sexy way he liked.

He kissed her again, then rolled out of bed. They dressed quickly, neither of them speaking. Jaymes grabbed his glasses last, making the world sharp again. Gone were the fuzzy edges of reality that he happily lived in for a few days with Kelsea. Reality was back, and they were going to end things with her stalker. He could feel it.

They walked into the living room together, Jaymes leading the way with Kelsea right behind him. He hoped she didn't pick up on the fact that he wouldn't let her walk ahead of him. Even in his own home, he wanted to make sure she was safe.

After all, his kidnapper knew how to pick locks. There was no reason to think her stalker didn't also.

"We're starting with Mason O'Connor," Slade said without preamble. "Are you going to work today? Or are you sticking with us again?"

Jaymes shook his head. "I'm going to talk to him."

"No."

Jaymes blanched. "What do you mean, no?"

Slade shrugged. "It's not a good idea. And Kelsea should have two of us with her."

"I want to be there. I want to look in his eyes and ask why he did all this."

"Dunn and the others can handle it."

Jaymes glanced back at Kelsea and shook his head. "I want to be there. If I had a chance to ask Williams, I'd have done the same thing. I want to understand what these fuckers are thinking when they decide it's okay to destroy someone's life. I need that answer for Kelsea."

Slade and Kelsea didn't say anything for a few minutes. Finally, Slade nodded. "Fine. If Kelsea is okay with it."

Kelsea nodded.

"I'll keep Jack with me." He thumbed out a text. "I told Archer you're going with him."

Jaymes nodded and turned to Kelsea. "You'll be safe with them."

She smiled. "I know. Thank you."

He understood. She wanted the same answers he did. He'd get them for her. Then maybe she could sleep again. Her life could return to normal.

The three of them headed downstairs a minute later. Jack exchanged a look with Jaymes, then smiled at Kelsea. "Just you and me, babe."

"And me," Slade grumbled.

Jack nodded his head. "He doesn't count. We both know you'd pick me over that lump of muscle any day."

Kelsea laughed and winked at Jaymes. He couldn't believe she wanted him when she had six available SEALs at her beck and call, but he was the one she snuggled up to every night. He was the one she turned to. The one who made her feel safe.

Outside, she kissed him and told him to be safe, then walked with Jack and Slade to the SUV. Archer slapped Jaymes on the back and nodded to his SUV.

Archer was quiet for half of the ride to the F-BOMB

office. He shifted in his seat and Jaymes finally asked him what was wrong.

"Are you okay?"

Jaymes laughed mirthlessly. "Ah, no. The woman I love is being threatened by a psychotic killer. And we're going to confront him."

Archer slid him a shit-eating grin. "Love?"

Dammit. Jaymes didn't mean to spill that bit of news. He ran a hand through his hair and sighed. "Yeah."

Archer's smile slipped, and a frown replaced it. "You didn't mean to tell me."

Jaymes considered lying, but decided against it and shook his head.

"I thought we were okay."

"We are. But we were never close. We're... we're still not."

"You talk to Lily all the time."

Jaymes chuckled. "Not as much as I used to. And talking to Lily doesn't mean I'm talking to you. I'm sure she tells you everything we talk about, but I'm not getting to know you."

Archer was quiet again until they pulled into the parking lot beneath the building. He turned off the SUV and sat there. "I'm sorry. For falling in love with her and taking her away from you. If I'd known..."

"She loves you. Even if you'd known, it wouldn't have changed anything."

"And you have Kelsea now," Archer said, giving Jaymes half a smile.

Jaymes nodded. "I do. I wouldn't have fallen for her if I was still hung up on Lily."

Archer thought about that for a minute before he nodded. "I wish things were different. We should get a beer or something. Just the two of us."

Jaymes nodded, although he wasn't entirely sure it was a

good idea. He and Archer were virtual strangers. He wanted to know his brother, but the hero worship was long gone. Archer wasn't the man Jaymes always thought he was. He was still a good man, but he was different. Harder. More closed off, which was hard to believe since Jaymes always knew those things about his brother. Knowing it and seeing it made the harshness of Archer worse. Like it wasn't just in Jaymes's mind. His brother really was a withdrawn ass. Lily brought out another side of him, but Jaymes didn't know that side. He wasn't entirely sure he wanted to.

They walked into the office and Archer swiped them through to the back. The rest of the team was in the conference room, everyone silently studying the details they knew so far.

Dunn flashed Archer a look, but Archer stared him down. Dunn shrugged after a second and nodded at Jaymes. Jaymes nodded back, thankful Dunn wasn't going to keep him out of everything.

He needed this. Even if the rest of them didn't understand, he needed it.

"We discovered a connection between O'Connor and Lewis," Dunn said. "English spent the night looking at Lewis's old case files on his computer and found an old invoice from when O'Connor hired him. It's from a few months ago, but it's enough for us to bring him in and have a conversation."

"So it's him," Jaymes said.

Dex shook his head. "We don't know that yet. There weren't any details in the invoice. It looks like Lewis kept his money trail on the computer but kept the details of all his investigations in a file cabinet. He used some kind of code for the files so we have no way of knowing where to start. The cabinet in his office was only for cases he accepted in the last two months. Everything else is in a long-term storage facility."

"Let me guess," Archer said, "we haven't gotten access to that yet."

Dunn shook his head. "Not yet. That's why we're bringing O'Connor in. We need him to talk."

"Oh, he'll talk. We'll make sure of it," Archer said.

22

DUNN PUT JAYMES IN THE CORNER OF THE FRONT CONFERENCE room when they got word that Mason was there. His eyes said not to say anything, but Dunn didn't spell it out.

Mason walked in with a suspicious look in his eyes, trying to figure out what was going on. He came in on his own, without being forced, but he didn't look like he knew why.

Damn good actor.

Dex offered Mason a cup of coffee, but they didn't say anything about the box of donuts on the table that was clearly not empty. Nor did they offer him cream or sugar for his coffee.

Mason took a sip, then grimaced. Jaymes stared at the man, trying to figure out why. That was all he wanted to know.

"Do you know why you're here?" Dunn asked.

Mason shrugged. "Probably because of Kelsea. Is she okay?"

Jaymes scoffed, drawing Mason's attention. Mason

jerked his head toward Jaymes, but Jaymes didn't return the gesture.

"What is the nature of your relationship with Dane Lewis?"

"The PI? What does he have to do with this?" Mason asked.

"Answer the question," Jaymes growled.

Mason glanced at him again, then focused on Dunn. "I hired Dane to look into someone at Best Friends Forever. Amanda and Jeremy hired this new guy, and he was... suspicious. I couldn't put my finger on it, but there was something off about him."

"What did he find?"

Mason shrugged. "The guy was running an underground dog fighting ring. He used BFF as a feeder. When a dog came in that he thought would do well, he called up one of his many buddies and brought them in to adopt the dog."

"And you figured this out?"

Mason shook his head. "No. Dane did. He shared all the information with me. We went to the police and Amanda and Jeremy at the same time. That way, Amanda and Jeremy didn't get wrapped up and taken down in the investigation. They're doing good things. Dane was a big help in proving that they weren't a part of it. They could have lost the shelter. He's a good guy. And good at his job."

"Then why did you kill him?" Jaymes blurted.

The SEALs turned and glared at him. He really should have heeded Dunn's silent warning to keep his fucking mouth shut.

"What the fuck are you talking about?" Mason demanded, his voice low and menacing.

Dunn answered for Jaymes. "Where were you yesterday morning around ten am?"

"At the shelter," Mason said automatically.

"Can anyone verify that?"

Mason sighed and shook his head. "No. I open up on Tuesdays for Amanda and Jeremy. I'm there between nine and nine-thirty. I feed all the animals, clean all the cages, and get everything ready for the day. They come in by eleven and actually open up front."

"Why don't you open up front?" Dex asked.

Mason held his gaze for a minute. "Do you know who I am?"

Dex paused a second, then nodded.

"Most people don't want to adopt a dog from me. It's better for the animals if I'm in the back, out of sight of the customers."

Jaymes almost felt bad for Mason. He made it sound like he was a victim instead of the other way around. Jaymes knew how manipulative people could be if they wanted to be, though.

"If we call Amanda and Jeremy, they will be able to tell us if you were there yesterday and did everything you mentioned. If you're lying, we'll know."

"Yeah, I get it. I've been through this drill before. Between the Teams and being arrested, I know how all this works. What I don't know is what I'm being accused of."

"As of now, nothing. We're simply trying to find out what's going on."

"Kelsea's stalker killed Dane? And you think that's me. I thought your guys," he jerked his head toward Jaymes, "cleared me. The other two said I was good. I even offered to help. And now I'm a suspect?"

"Of course you're a suspect," Jaymes snapped. "How

could you not be? You killed your wife. Killing two men you barely knew would be nothing for you. Especially if you think it's helping Kelsea. Who you're clearly obsessed with."

"Ford," Dunn barked.

Jaymes and Archer both looked at him, but Jaymes was the only one who got a glare in return.

"Enough," Dunn said.

Jaymes sat back, seething. He wasn't a child Dunn could order around. He was right. Mason was always on the short list because of his past. With the connection between him and Dane, there was no way they could ignore him. The other option was Edward, and Jaymes didn't like the guy, but he didn't think he was psychotic. He already knew Mason was. It made sense.

"So I'm here as a possible suspect," Mason said slowly. "You think I killed... two men you said?" He asked Jaymes.

Jaymes stared past him to Dunn.

Dunn said, "Yes. Dane Lewis and Maxwell Greene."

"Maxwell's dead, too?" Mason slumped back in his chair. "Jesus. That guy was a self-righteous ass, but he... Wow."

"But he what?" Archer demanded.

Mason looked around the room. "He had a wandering eye. He was always checking out customers when he came to the shelter with Kelsea. I don't think she noticed, but I did. Bugged me that he was with Kelsea and staring at other women's asses."

"Did she tell you why they broke up?" Dunn asked.

Mason shook his head. "We don't talk about stuff like that. Kelsea's like a sister to me. And I don't want to know about her personal life. I care about her, but, like you said, I killed my wife. The person I loved more than anyone else in the world. I've never even looked at another woman since Megan died. I can't trust myself."

"Gee, you think?" Jaymes mumbled.

Mason and Dunn shot him a pair of glares.

"He dumped her because she's too fat," Dex said, leaning closer to Mason as he delivered the news. "Said she wasn't pretty enough for him. That he likes curves, but she's not curvy, she's just fat."

Mason held Dex's gaze for a long moment, then swore and leaned back in his seat. "Tell me you're saying that to piss me off and not because it's true."

Dex smirked. "Of course it's true. You've seen her. She's got a hell of a face, but the rest of her..." He shivered in disgust instead of finishing his sentence.

Jaymes gripped the armrests of his chair and tried not to imagine tearing Dex's arms off and using them to beat the shit out of him. What the fuck was wrong with him?

Dex never spoke that way about Kelsea, or Lily. Unless he did it when Jaymes wasn't around. *Fucking asshole.*

Jaymes gave up watching Mason to watch Dex. He plotted all the ways he was going to hurt the other man. Starting with slamming him into the closest vertical surface and choking him until he took every fucking word back.

"I wish I had killed that fucker if he really said that. And if you don't take back what you just said, I'll happily have your blood on my hands."

Dex leaned back in his chair with a grin. "You can try, old man."

Mason jumped to his feet and charged around the table. Dunn was between Mason and Dex, who still laughed. Mason squared off with Dunn, shooting him a murderous look.

Jaymes seriously thought about going after Dex himself. No one stood between them. Dex was supposed to be one of the good guys.

A crash drew his attention back to Mason and Dunn. Archer was shoulder to shoulder with Dunn, both of them fighting off Mason. Every swing Mason took was an opportunity for them to get a blow in on him. The fight couldn't have lasted longer than a few seconds, but it felt endless to Jaymes as the three of them went after each other, all fighting another man's battle.

Dunn and Archer finally pinned Mason, twisting his arm behind his back and slamming him onto the table. Mason spat at them to "let me at that fucker," but Dunn and Archer just held him still.

Dex finally rose from his seat. He leaned down close to Mason's face and grinned. "Tell me again why you shouldn't be on the short list."

Mason growled. "Fuck you. No one should talk about a woman like that. You're a fucking asshole."

Dex rocked back on his heels and nodded. "You're right. Except I only said all that to piss you off. We needed to know what you would do if someone threatened her. Now we know. You just jumped to the top of our list, buddy."

Jaymes tried to process what Dex said. The man was convincing. But Jaymes didn't know which of his statements were true. Did he find Kelsea revolting, or was he lying to get a reaction out of Mason?

English burst into the room with his laptop in his hands. He took in the scene in one glance and shook his head. "Let him up."

"He went after Dex," Archer growled.

"That was the plan. Dex can handle it. He's not our guy. We have an address. We gotta go."

KELSEA STARED at Slade as he talked to Dunn. Or listened, really. The man barely spoke, listening to whatever was going on with Mason. She was going to have a hard time facing him next time she was at Best Friends Forever. She wanted to protect him, and Edward, but Dunn and the others wouldn't listen to her. It gutted her to think of either of them being involved.

Slade finally hung up the phone. He flashed Kelsea a look that she couldn't read then turned to Jack.

"What's going on?" Jack asked.

"English found the other feed."

"That's good, right? Why do you look like it's a bad thing?"

Slade shook his head. "It's good, but it's not someone we've had on our radar." He turned to Kelsea. "Do you know someone named Jennifer Morris?"

Kelsea thought for a second. It sounded vaguely familiar, but she couldn't place it. "It's a common name. I might, but I don't know. Is she my stalker?"

Slade flashed a look at Jack. "The feed is going to her apartment. She lives a few houses down from you, across the street. There's an apartment above a garage."

"And English knows the feed is going to the apartment and not the house?"

Slade nodded. "Something about separate utilities. They're loading up and heading there now."

Kelsea sank into her chair. Not only was her stalker not a male, like she assumed, but the woman lived on her street. She could have been watching her for years. At least months. And she had no clue.

"Who is this woman?" she whispered to herself.

"We don't know yet," Slade answered. "They'll find her, though."

"This will all be over soon, Kels," Jack said, rubbing her back.

She nodded absently and prayed he was right.

JAYMES KNEW Dunn didn't want him involved, but he let Jaymes suit up anyway. Archer gave him weapons to stash in Jack's gear. He was the closest in size to Jaymes so he was outfitted in his friend's vest, helmet, and comms.

They pulled onto Kelsea's street and swarmed the house in question. Jaymes turned and glanced at Kelsea's house, just two houses down across the street. His mom's sat just farther away, but still visible from the driveway.

Dunn called ahead to Jennifer's landlords. The husband met them in the driveway with a set of keys and confirmation that she was inside. Dunn took it silently with a nod, then jerked his head toward the house. The team waited until he was back in his house before taking the stairs on the outside of the garage to the second floor apartment.

Jaymes's heart pounded beneath the bulletproof vest he wore. His palms were sweaty and his breath came in rushed pants. He hadn't been in any kind of combat position, ever. Even during his short time in the Navy, he was assigned to a ship and cruised around the world, parking for months at a time before going back out. The only time he'd ever fired a weapon was during training.

Archer pounded on the door and shouted for her to open up. They waited a few seconds, but there was no response. Dunn reached beyond Archer, all of them squeezed on the tiny staircase and unable to move, and unlocked the door.

As soon as they heard the snick of the lock releasing, they rushed inside, guns up, spreading out.

Archer went right, Dunn left. Rocky followed, then English, Jaymes, and Dex at the end. A second after he walked inside, someone screamed.

Jaymes spun and searched for the woman having a fit. She jumped up, but her headphones were attached to her laptop and yanked her back down. She fumbled to yank them off and threw her hands up.

"Please don't hurt me," she cried.

"Are you Jennifer Morris?" Dunn barked.

She nodded quickly, her whole body trembling. She didn't look like a cold-blooded killer. But Jaymes knew people were terrific actors when they wanted to be.

"Is anyone else here with you?"

She shook her head. "I... I live alone."

English snuck up and snatched her laptop from the floor. Jennifer watched him but didn't say anything as he walked away.

English unplugged the headphones, sending screaming music throughout the apartment. He quickly jammed a button and turned the volume off.

Jaymes looked back at Jennifer. She stood in front of them in a pair of shorts that barely covered her ass and a t-shirt that clung to her curves. She wasn't wearing a bra, or shoes. Her blonde hair was piled on top of her head and her bright blue eyes scanned them all as though trying to figure out what the hell was going on.

After a minute or two of silence, English closed the laptop. "It's clean."

Dunn faced Jennifer. "Do you have another laptop?"

She shook her head.

"Main house?" Dex asked.

English shook his head. "Not possible. Definitely up here. There's another one. She's lying."

English set out searching the small apartment. A door stood open to a bedroom off to the side, but everything else was in the one open room.

Dex joined in the search, then Jaymes and Rocky followed, leaving Dunn and Archer to stand guard on Jennifer.

"Is anyone else here?"

She shook her head again.

Jaymes and Rocky searched the bedroom and attached bathroom. They were about to walk out when Jaymes spotted a strap sticking out from under the bed.

"Rock." He nodded to it.

Rocky moved toward him and drew his weapon. He kicked the side of the bed, but there was no movement. Slowly, he bent down, gun first, and peeked under the bed.

He jerked back up immediately, then lowered himself to the floor. "All clear." He grabbed the bag and carried it into the living room.

"That's my boyfriend's bag," Jennifer said quickly. "He doesn't like me to touch his stuff."

The rest of them ignored her.

Rocky took the bag straight to English. They pulled out another laptop. English powered it up. Jaymes watched as the screen filled with the camera views of Kelsea's house.

"Son of a bitch," Jaymes muttered.

English met Dunn's gaze and nodded. He closed the laptop and put it back in the bag, slinging it over his shoulder.

"Who's your boyfriend?" Dunn asked Jennifer, his voice no longer anywhere close to giving a shit about her.

"Edward. Edward Bailey."

23

———————

KELSEA TURNED THE BOX OVER IN HER HAND AND SMILED. Edward was always leaving her little things. Sometimes it was for work, but once in a while he brought her a gift that toed the line of appropriate. She told him they couldn't be together, but he insisted the things he bought her were because he thought of her as a friend and nothing more.

She knew she would return whatever gift was inside the box, but she was curious.

She untied the bright red bow and opened the box. A small card sat on top with her name scribbled on the envelope. She picked it up and revealed a CD underneath.

She slid her finger under the flap of the envelope. She pulled the card out. The picture on the front was a beautiful woman, fully clothed. Kelsea's eyebrows tugged together. Did he mix up the cards?

Inside he wrote:

```
She's not half as beautiful as you
are. Maxwell was wrong when he said
```

```
you're    fat.    You're    perfect.    I
love you.
    P.S.  This  one  is  my  favorite.  I
watch it every night.
```

Fear shook her hands. Her throat closed up. Every cell in her body vibrated. She lifted the CD from the box and slid it into her computer. Immediately, her bedroom filled the picture.

A few seconds later, she walked in. She disappeared into her closet and returned to the camera view in her bra and panties, the same red ones she was wearing at that moment. She picked them out that day in hopes she could model them for Jaymes that night. After they caught her stalker and she was safe, but she felt dirty watching herself through Edward's eyes.

She vanished again, this time into the bathroom. The picture cut and showed her sitting on the edge of the tub. She added bubble bath to the water and skimmed her hand over the surface.

She knew what was coming. She remembered that night. It was shortly after Maxwell broke up with her. She had a couple glasses of wine and threw herself a pity party. After spending time in front of the mirror, critiquing every inch of her body, she took a bath and touched herself. She needed to feel good, and she figured if she didn't have a man to do it for her, there was no reason for her to feel like shit. So she took matters into her own hands.

And Edward watched her.

Tears flooded her eyes as she watched herself. By the time she was done in the video, she wanted to throw up.

All this time, he was right in front of her. She had no

idea. She thought he was innocent and sweet. He helped her. He was a good student and a nice guy.

Except he wasn't.

Slade and Jack burst into her office together and pulled up short when they saw her face. Neither of them approached her, just watched her.

When she finally looked up and met their gazes, she said, "Edward. It's Edward."

They nodded simultaneously. "Dunn just called. They have his girlfriend in custody. Partly for her own safety, and partly because they aren't sure how much involvement she had. She's Jennifer Morris."

Kelsea sighed and shook her head. "Yep, she is. I knew the name was familiar, but I thought it was just because both Jennifer and Morris are common names." She closed her eyes and pointed to the computer. "He sent me this."

That got them moving. Jack and Slade both rushed to her side. Slade picked up the box and read the note while Jack clicked to start the video all over again.

When she filled the screen in her underwear, she both sucked in a breath and froze.

"Um, we don't need to see this," Slade said, closing the laptop.

Kelsea pressed to eject the CD and put it back in the case. "English will probably want to do something with it. We should take it. My laptop, too. Just in case it had a virus on it."

Slade nodded and took the box with the note and CD in it. He tucked them under his arm and nodded at Jack to grab Kelsea's laptop.

"We need to get you out of here," Jack said. "We don't know where Edward is."

Kelsea glanced at the clock. "He's done with classes for today. He's probably not on campus."

Slade walked to the door. "Still, we need to get you out of here. We need to know you're safe."

Kelsea nodded and followed them. Slade led the way with Jack by her side the entire way. She could feel their presence with every step, solid right beside her, just in case.

Edward. Her head still spun. She couldn't believe it was Edward. He'd been watching her, and he killed Maxwell and Dane. She didn't get it. She wasn't the kind of woman men went crazy over. Why her?

Slade drove them straight to the F-BOMB offices. They checked the garage before they got out of the SUV, then flanked her again as they made their way across the open space. Kelsea only breathed again when she made it into the elevator and up to the F-BOMB suite.

Slade swiped them in, leading the way to the conference room at the end of the hallway. Dunn, Archer, Dex, English, and Rocky all sat around the table, listening to English report on something. Kelsea didn't care. All she needed was Jaymes, but he wasn't there.

"Where's Jaymes?"

Dunn looked up at her, then nodded past her.

Kelsea turned and saw him, decked out like the others in solid black with a thick vest on and straps around his legs full of weapons. She startled for a minute, a slap in the face to remind her of what happened when she was going on with her life and teaching classes like nothing was wrong. Instead, a murderer was wandering the halls of her school, following her, watching her, killing for her.

All the adrenaline of the day finally eased, and she nearly collapsed. Jaymes was there to catch her, lifting her into his arms as she fell apart so fast she wasn't sure she could ever fit back together again.

JAYMES CARRIED Kelsea down the hall to Dunn's office. It was the only one he knew had a couch where she could sit, or lie down, and be comfortable.

He lowered them to the soft leather and pulled her tight against him. She buried her face in his neck and clung tightly to him. He stroked his hand up and down her back, thankful she was safe in his arms.

He still couldn't believe Edward was right in front of them the whole time and none of them realized it was him. Dunn tried to say they knew, but he was full of shit. If they knew, he would have brought that son of a bitch in.

Kelsea's body trembled as a sob tore from her throat. He pulled her closer, rubbing his jaw against her head. She moved her legs, rubbing them together like she was uncomfortable.

Jaymes turned them and stretched out on the couch next to Kelsea, settling her against the back. He faced her, holding her body close as she cried. They held each other, trying to make sense of the whole thing.

A shuffle at the door drew Jaymes's attention. When he turned and saw Rocky standing there, his cheeks red at what he walked in on, Jaymes asked, "What do you want?"

"Just checking on her."

"Why?"

"She almost passed out. Want to make sure she's okay. Can I come in?"

Jaymes turned back to Kelsea, brushing her hair out of

her face. "It's up to you," he whispered. "We can tell him to close the door if you want."

She held his gaze for a minute, then nodded.

"Give us a few. Please."

Rocky nodded and stepped back out of the room. He closed the door, separating them from the noise in the hallway and the entire outside world.

If only it were that easy.

"I'm so sorry, Kels," Jaymes said when her sobs finally slowed to hiccups. "I'm sorry he did this to you."

She laughed mirthlessly. "I don't know how I didn't see it. He's always done little things that I really thought were innocent. But the video..."

"I can't believe he was watching you all this time. I hate that he did that."

She nodded. "Did you guys see the video, too? Did he send it here?"

Jaymes pulled back to look at her. "What do you mean? We have his computer. The live feed is still up, but no one is there."

She shook her head. "He recorded some of the video of me. Taking a bath and... and touching myself. He sent me a CD of it with a note that said he watches it all the time."

Jaymes thought he was going to be sick. "Tell me you're not serious."

She hesitated, then nodded.

"When did he give this to you?"

"It was on my desk this afternoon. He must have dropped it off today some time. They're all in there watching it right now."

"What?" Jaymes barked. "No. They don't get to see that. They have no right to see you."

He was off the couch before she could grab his arm. "Jaymes," she whimpered. "Don't leave me alone. Please."

He turned back to her. For the first time since she walked in, he looked at her. Really looked at her. Her dress was twisted around her hips, the skirt hiked up on one side where it clung to her tights. She wore her fancy boots instead of the snow boots she wore to and from work, telling him they found out and ran. Her hair was knotted on one side and flat on the other.

She was still beautiful to him. But it was her eyes that killed him. Red edged out the beautiful green color, making her eyes look small. Dark purple circles marred her skin from too many sleepless nights and too much fear. Her cheeks were red and blotchy from crying.

And all of it was because Edward thought she should be his.

"Why don't we let Rocky check you out? Make sure you're okay. The last thing I need is for you to get hurt. I can't..." His voice cracked at the thought of anything happening to her. "Please, Kels."

She held his gaze for a minute, then nodded.

He walked back to her, cupping her jaw and tilting her head up for a kiss. He lingered there, needing to confirm she was okay. She was there, and she was safe. They would get Edward.

He pulled back reluctantly and let Rocky in. Dex was standing in the hallway, too. Jaymes shot him a glare and closed the door behind Rocky and Kelsea.

"You owe her an apology," he told Dex.

Dex nodded. "I do, but not because I meant it."

"What the hell does that mean?"

"I said all that to get a reaction out of Mason. I knew it

would piss him off, and I needed to know if he was the kind of man who would attack when someone was nasty to her. That's what started all this. That dickface Maxwell dumped her and we think Edward increased his stalking after that. In his twisted fucking mind, he wanted her to know she was beautiful and loved. He went after Maxwell because he hurt her."

"You said the same things he did."

Dex nodded. "But I didn't mean them. Kelsea is a stunning woman. She's... you're a lucky son of a bitch. And if I didn't like you so much, I might kick your ass for her. She's beautiful. She's not fat, and she doesn't need to lose weight. The only thing she needs to do is be herself. And you've given her that from what I can see."

"You want her?"

Dex smiled and clapped Jaymes on the back. Hard. "I wouldn't steal her from you, but if you two broke up for some reason, I wouldn't let her sit out there for long."

"Dude!"

Dex shrugged. "Just making sure you know I didn't mean it."

Jaymes rolled his eyes.

"So bad transition, but the video..."

"Fuck. She mentioned it. How bad is it?"

Dex grimaced.

"That bad?"

He half-shrugged. "It doesn't leave much to the imagination, but English said it was made by the computer we have in possession. It was definitely him that did all this."

"Where is he?"

Dex shook his head. "That, my friend, is the million dollar question."

Rocky opened the door. He nodded at Jaymes. "She's good. She wants to go into the situation room."

"Is that a good idea?" Dex asked.

Rocky shrugged. "Not sure, but this is all about her. I think she has a right. She might even be able to help."

Dex nodded once, then started down the hall. Kelsea walked out behind Rocky, her eyes scanning. When she spotted Jaymes, she immediately went to him.

He wrapped his arm around her shoulder and kissed the side of her head. "Are you sure about this?"

She shook her head. "No. I'm not sure about any of this. But I have no choice. I'm not going to hide from him. I'm going to fight."

Jaymes smiled and walked with her. She had depths of strength he never had. When he came back, all he wanted to do was hide. He didn't want to be alone, and he sure as hell didn't want to go anywhere near the asshole who kept him hostage.

But Kelsea was ready to kick ass. Jaymes had no doubt she would, too.

They walked into the situation room and took seats against the far wall. The other guys were talking about options, trying to figure out where Edward could have gone. English was doing something on the computer, and Archer and Dunn were arguing about how to find him.

Jaymes's phone vibrated in his pocket. He dug it out and sighed. "My mom," he whispered to Kelsea, who leaned over to see who it was.

"Answer it."

He shook his head. "This is important."

She smiled. "So's your mom. She's the one who brought us together, and if I've learned anything this week, it's that having people you count on makes a difference."

Jaymes smiled at her and swiped to answer the phone. He kissed Kelsea's nose, then stood and left the room, saying hello on his way into the hallway.

"Oh, you are going to answer me! I thought maybe you were ignoring your poor mother."

"No, Ma. Just busy."

"You are? That stinks. I was hoping you were free tonight."

Jaymes stifled a groan. He loved his mother, but ever since his father died, he was the man she turned to for everything. A leaky sink, a frozen computer, a squeaky hinge. He had no problem helping her out, but usually she waited until something was almost beyond repair to tell him about it.

"I'm sorry, Mom. I'm with Kelsea. We're kind of in the middle of something."

"Well, I was going to see if you could both come over."

A man's voice in the background mumbled something Jaymes couldn't hear. He stopped pacing the hallway and strained to make out what he said.

"Mom? Is someone there with you?"

She whispered something to the voice, then chuckled. "Well, we wanted it to be a surprise."

"We? Who is we, Mom?"

She laughed. "I met a very nice young man on Sunday. He came to church, and I invited him to Bible study tonight. He's a student at Erie University. I told him your girlfriend teaches there. We were so surprised to hear he knows Kelsea. He used to be one of her students. We thought it would be nice for all of us to get together."

Jaymes could barely speak when he asked the question he already knew the answer to. "Mom. What's his name?"

"Edward, honey. Edward Bailey. Do you know him?"

Jaymes walked back into the situation room. No one paid him any attention. He had to figure out how to tell them all what was going on.

"Mom, I need you to listen to me very carefully. Edward is not someone you should be alone with. He's not a good man."

"What do you mean?"

Jaymes slapped the table, finally drawing the attention of everyone in the room. He pulled the phone away from his ear and hit the button to put it on speaker.

"Mom, Edward is dangerous. He's been stalking Kelsea for months. He's already killed two men. If you can get out of the house, you need to leave now. Tell him you need to get something from the store, anything. But get out now, Mom."

Silence met his words. Jaymes looked around the room. He met Archer's gaze, fear reflected back at him. Everyone was still as they waited.

"Mom. Are you there? Mom!"

"I'm sorry, but your mother isn't able to talk anymore," Edward said. "She sends her apologies."

"If you hurt her, I'll—"

"You'll what, Jaymes? We both know you aren't the brother I have to worry about. Archer, on the other hand, well, he might carry some firepower, but something tells me he just might agree to my deal."

Archer stepped forward. "We don't make deals with pieces of shit like you."

Edward laughed. "Well, you might. See you have something I want. And I have something you want. It's easy. All we have to do is trade, and everyone gets what they want."

All eyes swung to Kelsea. She stood in the corner, frozen, listening to Edward's words.

Before anyone could say anything, Edward added, "You have one hour, or your mother can say hi to Dane and Maxwell for everyone. Tick-tock, boys."

24

THE ROOM ERUPTED IN CHAOS AROUND HER SECONDS AFTER
Edward hung up.

"An hour? Is he crazy?"

"How did we miss this?"

"What are we going to do?"

"Trading Kelsea isn't an option."

"We need solutions, not more problems."

They all talked. Over each other, around each other.
Sometimes shouting, sometimes calm. Through all of it,
none of them turned to Kelsea.

She dropped back onto her chair and sat there, frozen.
Finding out Edward was behind all this was hard enough,
but hearing the lengths he was willing to go to crushed her.
He wasn't going to give up. Not until he got what he wanted.

Poor Cecelia.

Kelsea's heart pounded at the thought of Edward
hurting her friend. Cecelia had been so kind to Kelsea since
she moved into the neighborhood. She welcomed her when
no one else seemed to care that the eyesore down the street
was finally bought and being fixed up. Cecelia even offered

up her son, Jaymes, to help Kelsea fix up her house if she needed it.

Maybe she should have taken her up on it.

Kelsea's eyes strayed to Jaymes. He stood toe-to-toe with Slade arguing about something. Kelsea couldn't really hear any of them. Her ears were ringing, but she had to see Jaymes one last time.

He was a beautiful man. Someone she would have loved to spend the rest of her life with. She laughed to herself. She kind of did. She only wished he knew how special he was. He would make someone very happy if he would let go of himself. He was kind and helpful. He was the sexiest man she'd ever met, with his glasses giving him a nerdy vibe, but his muscles telling you there was more to him than a computer.

She ached to have him hold her one last time, but she knew he'd never let her go. Not if he knew what she was thinking.

Kelsea slipped out of the room while the men argued about every step. Time ticked by quickly. She couldn't stand by and let one more person she cared about die. She was the only one who could stop Edward. And she would.

KELSEA STOOD on Cecelia's doorstep with her heart in her throat. In her rush to leave F-BOMB, she forgot to grab her jacket. She shivered against the January temperature, made even colder by the sun low on the horizon, barely visible through the trees.

The street around her was eerily quiet. No cars drove by. No one came outside to get their mail or walk their dog. Lights poured from picture windows down the street and flooded porches. She strained to hear a sound, any sound, but the world was silent.

All of it contrasted with the roaring inside Kelsea. Blood pounded in her ears and raced through her body. Sweat poured from her body despite the cold. Her hands were clammy and her pulse thundered.

She never thought of herself as suicidal, but as she stood on the doorstep, she knew that's exactly what she was doing. She was killing herself. Edward wouldn't stop until she was his, so Kelsea had no choice, but there was little doubt in her mind that he would eventually kill her. She wouldn't love him. He was smart, and he would know that. She might be able to talk him down for a little while, but eventually it would wear on him and he would lose interest in her.

And he'd cast her aside.

She didn't know how long that would take. She wasn't sure if she hoped it would be quick or not. Quick meant she wouldn't be with him long. Not quick meant maybe she'd be saved, but she'd be with Edward for longer.

No. She shook her head. She didn't want Jaymes and the others to come after her. She wanted him safe. She couldn't live with herself if something happened to him because of her. If he stayed away, he'd be safe.

Before she lost her nerve, Kelsea rang Cecelia's doorbell. The shrill sound pierced the evening air, startling Kelsea even though she expected it.

Silence returned, wrapping around Kelsea like a blanket. She tried to tell herself it would all be okay, but that was just another lie. Like all the times she told herself Edward's attention was innocent.

"Who is it?" Edward called in a sweet voice from the other side of the door.

Kelsea stood back and looked up at the peephole. "I'm alone, Edward."

"Why should I believe you?"

Kelsea took a deep breath, stifling the urge to throw it in his face that he was the liar in their situation, not her. "I've never lied to you, Edward."

He was silent. After a few seconds, the lock clicked open. The door opened a crack, one eye peering out. He scanned her body, then looked past her to the SUV. "I thought you were alone," he snarled.

"I am, I am!" she yelled at the closing door. "I stole it so I could get here. They don't know I left."

He opened the door another inch. His lips curled up in a sneering grin. "You stole it? I knew you wanted me, too."

Kelsea wanted to lie to him, but she couldn't bring herself to say the words so she stayed silent.

Edward looked around again, slowly opening the door until she could see all of him. He looked like a regular guy. Pressed khakis and a plaid shirt gave him a boy next door look. His hair was combed and styled to make him look like a choir boy. No wonder Cecelia took him in. She always told Kelsea she thought clean-cut men were trustworthy. Of course, Edward was probably listening when she said that.

Fucking asshole.

"Please, come in, angel," Edward cooed.

Kelsea nodded and stepped inside. She had to make sure Cecelia was okay, then she was getting Edward away from her.

"Cecelia!" Edward called. "Kelsea's here!"

Cecelia struggled somewhere deeper in the house, a muffled whimper and the scrape of a chair.

"What did you do to her?"

Edward tsked. "She didn't want to listen."

"Tell me you didn't hurt her," Kelsea cried, rushing toward the sounds. Edward sauntered behind her.

Cecelia was tied to a chair in the kitchen. Her arms were red where she struggled. Duct tape covered her mouth, and tears streamed down her face. Her eyes flashed behind Kelsea and widened.

Kelsea glanced back to Edward. He leaned on the doorframe and crossed his arms, watching them.

"Get her out of this," Kelsea pleaded.

Edward shook his head. "I can't risk her getting away. She's going to stay there for a while."

Kelsea stood and faced him, keeping herself between Edward and Cecelia. "She's not a part of this, Edward. You don't have to hurt her."

"I didn't hurt her," he said, his brows tugging together. "And she wouldn't be tied up if she hadn't threatened to help you get away from me. I've gone through too much for you. I'm not letting you go again."

Kelsea checked the time on the stove. "We need to go."

"Why? We have the rest of our lives together."

Kelsea gulped and nodded. "I know, but the others will be here soon. We need to leave. We should go to my house."

Edward grinned, an evil look filling his eyes. "You're right. We should. I've seen your house so many times, but you've never invited me over. Thank you, Kelsea."

She nodded and led the way outside, leaving Cecelia in the kitchen. Jaymes and the team would be there soon, and they would get Cecelia. She would be safe.

Kelsea shivered in the cold air again, rubbing her arms. Edward walked beside her, warm and cozy in his thick coat. His hand brushed hers, and she jerked away.

"Don't tell me all that was a lie, Kelsea. I thought you wanted to be with me."

She clamped her mouth shut again.

"We're going to be together forever." He reached for her hand again, catching it and weaving his fingers through hers so she couldn't tug away. "Your hand is freezing. You should have worn a jacket."

She scoffed. "I was more worried about a psycho not killing my friend."

Before she could think about what she said, Edward jerked their joined hands up and punched her in the cheek. Pain exploded in her face, radiating outward. She brought her free hand up and touched her face, coming away with bloody fingers.

"I'm not a psycho," Edward growled, dragging her down the sidewalk to her house.

Kelsea stopped on her porch, realizing she didn't have her purse or her keys. Edward pulled out his own set of keys and entered one in her door, unlocking it and pushing them inside.

"How do you have a key to my house?" she stammered.

He shrugged. "I knew I'd move in here with you one day. I had a key made so I could come see you whenever I wanted."

She was going to be sick. There was no way around it. He was a sick motherfucker. Seriously disturbed. And she'd just given herself to him.

She was going to die.

Jaymes ran down the hall to Dunn's office and slammed the door. Empty. Again. Her chair. The bathroom. The offices. All of it. She was gone. He knew where she went, but he didn't want to think about it.

"Anything?" Dunn asked.

Jaymes shook his head.

"Do you think...?"

Jaymes met his gaze and nodded.

"Fuck."

The others met them in the hallway. "My keys are gone," Slade said. "I put them on the board when I came in, but they're gone. We all know what she did."

"She saved our mom," Archer said.

"She killed herself," Dex argued.

"We don't know that," Jack said. "She hated that Maxwell and Dane died because of her, her words. She'd never let anything happen to Cecelia."

"Why are we standing around here talking about this?" Jaymes demanded. "We need to go get her."

"We don't know if she's still at your mom's house."

"Or if she's still alive."

"It's been," he checked his phone, "eight minutes since he called. I'm not leaving her with him. Either of them. We start at Mom's house. And if none of you want to go with me, I'll go by myself," Jaymes said, ready to push past all the SEALs in the hallway and tackle the boogeyman on his own.

He spent too many months afraid of his shadow, fearful that danger was around every corner. For the second time in just a few months, danger was in the room with him when he thought he was safe. No one suspected Williams, and no one thought it was Edward. Both of them were around, walking free and at arm's length the whole time. Yet both of them were evil to the core. Jaymes was done being afraid. And he was not going to let Kelsea pay the way so many others did.

"We're with you," Archer said firmly. "But we need a plan."

"How can we make a plan when we have no idea what we're walking into?" Jaymes asked.

Archer shook his head. "I don't know, but we have to come up with something."

"Fine. We go, knock on Mom's door, and hope we can kill him before he kills them."

"That's not a plan," Dunn said. "That's suicide."

"So is what Kelsea did."

Everyone shut up. Jaymes was right. Kelsea gave up herself to save his mom, to save him. He wasn't going to sit back and talk the whole fucking thing to death. He needed to save her. Or die trying.

"What about Mason?" Dex asked.

"What about him?" Jaymes said.

"We brought him in earlier, but he said, more than once, he would help if we needed it. Edward won't be expecting him. It's one more on the team. One more that could make all the difference."

"Call him," Dunn said.

Five minutes later they all piled into the remaining SUVs, armed to the teeth. Jaymes had never been around so many weapons, but they were second nature to the men with him. They were soldiers, real, true soldiers. They spent their lives defending the country and protecting people. If anyone could save Kelsea, it would be them.

The third F-BOMB SUV was in Cecelia's driveway with keys still in the ignition. The hood was cool, telling them it had been a while since she got there.

Jaymes was full of energy. He needed to move. To see that his mom and Kelsea were okay. Standing outside was killing him. The waiting.

A car pulled up, lights off. They all turned to watch and took a collective sigh of relief when Mason climbed out.

"Did I miss the party?" he asked.

Dunn approached him and shook his hand. "Thanks for being here. He won't expect you. You're our only tactical advantage."

Mason nodded. "I'm ready to take this son of a bitch down."

The others nodded in agreement.

Dunn handed out assignments, and they moved to surround the house. Jaymes stayed with Rocky near the vehicles to catch anyone coming out the front door. The area around the house was quiet, even through the comms.

"I got a visual," Jack said. "Cecelia is in the kitchen, tied to a chair. I don't see anyone else in the room with her."

"Mom," Jaymes whispered.

"No movement on the east side," Archer said.

"No movement on the west side," Dex agreed.

"Quiet out front," Rocky whispered.

"We go on my signal," Dunn said.

Jaymes waited with the others, painfully silent, as everyone held their breath for the command.

"Go!" Dunn called softly, sending them all into action.

Rocky watched the front door, leaving Jaymes to scan the street around them. Everything was silent, not moving, like death had already arrived.

Through the comms, he heard them breach the house and clear it room by room. Archer reached their mom first, telling Jaymes she was okay. Shaken, but not hurt.

It only took a few minutes for them to clear the house and call for Rocky and Jaymes to join them inside.

"Mom, sit. Please," Archer begged as Jaymes walked inside.

"I've been sitting for hours," she argued.

"At least let me have a look at you, Mrs. Ford," Rocky

said, moving past the others to check out Cecelia. "How are you feeling? Any dizziness or nausea?"

Cecelia shook her head in disgust. "Absolutely. That man lied to me, then took Kelsea. I'm just sick about it. I tried to tell her not to go with him, but she couldn't understand me."

"Do you know where they went?"

Cecelia nodded. "She said they should go to her house. She warned him that you were all coming."

"You don't think she's working with him, do you?" Dex asked.

Cecelia shook her head. "Kelsea? No. She's a good girl. She was trying to keep me safe. She was protecting me." Her voice cracked. She sank to a chair and buried her head in her hands. "She's a good girl. You have to save her," Cecelia begged, grabbing Rocky's hand.

He nodded. "We'll do everything we can, ma'am."

Dunn jerked his head toward the living room. Everyone except Rocky followed him. "Now what?"

"We go get Kelsea," Jaymes said.

"It's not that simple."

"Why the fuck not?"

"Because we have no idea what we're up against."

"We're up against a crazy piece of shit who won't hesitate to kill her, and anyone else. We can't leave her with him."

Dunn shook his head. "No, we can't. And we won't, but we have to be smart. We don't know what we're walking into."

"We outnumber him," Jaymes argued.

"He has a hostage," Dex said calmly. As if Jaymes needed to be reminded.

"All the more reason to go now."

Dex shook his head, but Archer was the one who

stepped forward. "I get it. When Williams took Lily... But going in guns blazing isn't going to get it done this time. Not when what he wants most in the world is the one person we're trying to take away from him."

"We did that with Lily," Jaymes argued.

"We did, but Williams didn't care about her. She was a means to an end, just like you were. He wanted to destroy Lauren's new husband, not Lily. Not me. Edward wants Kelsea. And he has her. We need to be smart if we're going to get her out of there alive."

"If they're even still there," Dunn said.

Jaymes dragged in a deep breath. "Fine. Then what do we do? How do we handle this?"

Everyone stared around the room. They all avoided Jaymes's gaze, and his gut sank. He was going to lose her. The men he thought the world of, the men who saved him, had nothing. Kelsea wasn't going to make it out alive, and she was only three doors down.

"I have a thought," Mason said, stepping up to join the circle. "It's a little crazy, but it might work."

"Let's hear it."

25

Edward leaned forward and kissed Kelsea's cheek. She tried to move away from him, but he had a strong grip on her shoulders.

He pulled back and smiled gently at her. "It's okay. I know you don't love me yet, but you will one day. Until then, let me love you, Kelsea."

She shivered with disgust. Did he really think she'd ever willingly let him touch her? Or that she'd ever love him? He was a sick, twisted fuck who killed her exes, kidnapped her friend, and stalked her for months. She'd be crazy to love him.

"Why are you doing all this, Edward?"

His brows pulled together, a crease forming between them. "What do you mean?"

"Stalking me—"

He raised his hand, halting her words. The swift blow struck her cheek, making her dizzy. She was sure she had a concussion, but she wasn't willing to stop goading him.

"I already told you that word isn't okay with me."

"Then what word do you want me to use?" she asked sweetly.

He rubbed his jaw and walked away. A gun stuck out of his waistband in the back, but she couldn't get to it without him knowing. She'd get her chance, but until then, she had to keep him talking. Talking was better than anything else he could do to her.

Just the thought threatened her sanity. What little she had left.

"I was watching over you, Kelsea. You were so hurt after Maxwell said those horrible things to you. I cried with you that night, angel. It hurt me, too. I couldn't let him get away with that."

"And Dane?"

Edward rolled his eyes. "Dane was selfish. When I hired him to install your cameras, I didn't know he knew you. When he admitted it, he forgot to tell me he installed a few cameras for himself. He was watching your house the morning I went to his office."

Kelsea rarely thought about Dane over the years. She didn't know why he would be watching her either, but it didn't matter any longer. He was gone. Thanks to Edward.

"He didn't deserve to die," Kelsea said softly.

Edward's eyes blazed at her. "Yes, he did. He had no right to watch you. You belong to me. Not *him*. He violated your privacy by watching you."

"And what were you doing? Because I never gave you permission to install cameras in my house or watch me. You did the exact same thing!"

"No," Edward said, shaking his head. "No. I was protecting you. I wanted to make sure you were okay. He was just being... he was the stalker, angel. He was the one who was watching you for the wrong reasons."

Edward paced in front of her, rubbing his hands through his hair. He was getting agitated and confused. It was good for throwing him off his game, but it could prove to be a bad thing if she pushed him too far.

She tugged at the cuffs securing her wrists together. "Will you take these off?"

"No! I don't trust you."

"Please, Edward. They're hurting my wrists. And I just want to touch you."

Surprise and delight filled his face, quickly followed by distrust. *Smart man.*

"Why?"

She swallowed the bile rising in her throat and smiled at him. "You've been protecting me all this time. Keeping me safe from the men who hurt me. I want to show you how much I appreciate it."

He narrowed his gaze and studied her for a second. She forced every inch of her body to show him she meant it. She smiled sweetly, hoping he bought what she was selling.

He pulled the gun out of the back of his pants and pointed it at her.

She froze, staring down the barrel. This was it. He was going to kill her.

"If you're lying, I'm not going to be happy," he said. Then he set the gun on her TV stand and joined her on the couch.

She used to love her couch. She used to love every inch of her home. If she survived Edward, she'd never be able to be in her home again without seeing him. He stole everything from her. Her life, her friends, her home.

He unlocked the cuffs and pulled them off her wrists. She rubbed the red marks left behind and thanked him. He took her hands in his, gently guiding his fingers over the raw skin. She suppressed a tremor. She had to stay calm if she was going to get away from him.

She glanced at the clock and prayed Jaymes and the others were still at his mom's house. She knew Cecelia would tell them she told Edward to go to her house. It wouldn't be long before they'd storm her home. If that happened, Edward would kill her. She knew it with every pounding beat of her heart.

He kissed her wrists and smiled at her. "I'm sorry I had to put the cuffs on you. I promise, the only cuffs I'll ever put on you again will be lined with blue fur."

Her favorite color. Of course he knew she loved blue.

She smiled back at him. Her nerve was fading, fear taking control of her body. She couldn't let the fear win. She was not going to sit back and let him have her.

"Thank you," she whispered, reaching up with one hand to cup his jaw.

He nuzzled into her palm, closing his eyes for a long second. His hand landed on her thigh, making her jump. His eyes flashed open.

She smiled again. "Sorry. I was surprised, that's all."

He narrowed his eyes at her. "Are you sure that's all it is?"

She nodded. "Yes. I'm sure. Let me show you."

She held his face between her hands and closed her eyes. She leaned forward slowly until her lips touched his. She forced herself not to pull away from the kiss, knowing it was her only way out.

He growled and slid his hand up her side. He roughly grabbed her breast, squeezing hard enough for her to whimper. He didn't stop, squeezing again. His thumb brushed her nipple.

Everything about kissing him was wrong. She hated the feel of his hand on her. His thin lips were nothing compared to Jaymes's full lips. She didn't want to die with Edward as the last man who touched her.

The thought gave her the courage she needed to continue with her plan. He was focused on kissing and touching her and didn't realize she pulled one hand away. She blindly reached for the vase on the table behind her couch.

Her fingers finally brushed the edge, but it was out of reach. She took a chance and leaned forward, hoping he'd think she was just getting into the kiss.

He groaned happily and wrapped his arms around her back, heading south to her ass.

She reacted on instinct, grabbing the heavy glass vase with one hand. She pulled back from the kiss enough to clamp down on his lower lip with her teeth, hard. He screamed and pushed at her. Before she let go, she smashed him over the head with the vase.

His hands fell away for a second, long enough for her to scramble out of his grasp, but not long enough for her to get out of the house.

He jumped up. "You bitch!"

She drew back to punch him, but he deflected it, swinging back with his own backhand to the cheek.

"You're mine, Kelsea. You're not going anywhere."

She punched his stomach, knocking the air out of him. She inched closer to the door, and farther from his gun, but he was right behind her.

Kelsea refused to give up, swinging and punching and kicking until he grabbed a handful of her hair. He pulled hair, twisting her neck. She couldn't get away from him.

"I told you you're not going anywhere," he snarled in her ear.

"You're hurting me."

He tsked. "I wouldn't have to if you'd just listen to me." He spun her around to face him, releasing her hair and grabbing her shoulders. "You're mine, angel. Always and forever, you're mine."

She shook her head. "I'll never be yours."

She kneed him as hard as she could, then stomped on his instep. He grabbed his crotch and dropped to his knees. She didn't wait to see if he was going to get up and ran. It took her two tries to get her door unlocked, then yanked it open and ran outside.

The cold night air slapped her in the face and froze in her lungs. She just had to get to Jaymes. Three doors down. That was all. She would do it if it killed her. But she wouldn't let him kill her.

"Get down!" someone yelled.

"You're mine!" Edward shouted from behind her.

"Kelsea! Down!" someone yelled again.

Two gunshots rang out, less than a second apart. Kelsea felt a sharp pain, then everything went black.

Jaymes heard a wailing and ran to Kelsea, sliding to his knees on the snow-covered sidewalk she laid on. He lifted her head, setting it on his lap, and shook when he saw the cuts and bruises on her cheeks.

He brushed the hair back from her face and ran his finger behind her ear. "I'm so sorry, Kels. I'm so sorry, sweetheart. I love you, Kelsea. Wake up, honey. You're safe now."

His gaze strayed to Edward, lying in a heap much like Kelsea on her front porch. Mason was the first to Edward, with Dunn and Slade right behind him. Mason felt for a pulse and shook his head. Jaymes breathed a sigh of relief and focused again on Kelsea.

"Fuck. Fuck, fuck, fuck! Get over here. Now!" Jaymes shouted, drawing the attention of every one of them.

They rushed him, surrounding him and Kelsea. Dark blood soaked through her shirt and poured onto the ground underneath her.

"Rocky!" Dunn screamed into the night.

"He's with my mom," Jaymes reminded him. "She's not going to make it."

"Don't you dare say that," Mason growled. He pushed his way through the others. "Back off for a minute."

Jaymes shook his head. "I need to hold her. She's cold."

Mason glared but didn't say another word. He stripped off his shirt and ripped it down the middle, then once more to make two pieces. He pressed one piece into the wound on her front. She groaned but didn't regain consciousness. He did the same to the wound in her back.

"She needs an ambulance," Mason said.

"We already called one for Cecelia. It should be here any minute," Jack said.

Sirens snapped the quiet night as flashing lights led the way onto the sleepy street. Dunn ran out to greet the ambulance and gave them the rundown on Kelsea. The paramedics had her in the back and raced away before Jaymes could jump in with her.

"We'll follow them to the hospital," Slade said, throwing an arm over Jaymes's shoulder and leading him back to his mom's house.

Jaymes was numb as he rode to the hospital. Archer stayed with their mom, who only agreed to go to the hospital when she heard Kelsea had been shot. Slade kept in touch with everyone else, and told Jaymes everything that was going on, but Jaymes barely heard any of it. All he cared about was Kelsea.

"She's going to die," he mumbled.

Slade grabbed his arm. "Don't say that. She's not going to die."

"You don't know that. All that blood. That was a lot of blood. And her face." Jaymes lost the fight to hold on to his control. "Oh, God. I can't believe she did that. I should have protected her."

"She wanted to save you, and your mom. She was worried about everyone else getting hurt. She never gave up. Until the very end, she fought."

"And it might have gotten her killed. He won. He's dead, but he won."

Slade didn't argue again, just drove too fast through the streets until they reached the emergency department of St. Nicholas Hospital.

It took three administrators, four nurses, and a call from Lily before they were allowed to hear anything about Kelsea. She was rushed in for emergency surgery, but that was all they could say.

"Waste of fucking time," Jack swore.

"Watch your mouth, young man," Cecelia snapped at Jack.

"Sorry, ma'am," he said, looking chagrinned.

"We're all worried about her. She saved my life. Rushing the doctors is not going to help Kelsea at all. We'll sit here and wait for some news. And pray. All of us need to pray."

Remarkably, no one argued with her. Jaymes looked around the room as everyone bowed their heads and closed their eyes. He followed suit, asking God to please spare Kelsea. To give her another chance. And that if that chance wasn't with him, he didn't care, as long as she was alive. She deserved to be alive and live after everything that son of a bitch did to her.

Sorry, God.

Jaymes stopped watching the clock two hours after they arrived. Once in a while, someone came out of the OR doors and called out a name, but none of them were Kelsea's. So they just sat. And waited. And prayed she would pull through.

Lily pressed a cup of coffee into Jaymes's hand at one point. He nodded, unable to smile at her in thank you. His entire mind was on Kelsea. He should have told her he loved her when she could hear him. One of the nights they had together. One of the times when she was in his arms and looking up at him like he was her whole world. She was his, but he never told her.

"Kelsea Arnold's family," a doctor said from the doorway.

All eleven of them stood together, moving toward the doctor. His gaze strayed to the dark clothes and empty holsters on each of the men. His eyes locked on Jaymes's jacket, soaked with blood, then lifted to his eyes with sympathy.

All the air left the room.

"Ms. Arnold's injuries were severe. The bullet passed through her abdomen. Her spleen was completely irreparable so we had to remove it. Her stomach was also nicked. We were able to fix the hole in her stomach, but because of the injury, her abdominal cavity was filled with gastric acid. We flushed it, but we'll be keeping a close eye on her for a few days to make sure there aren't any additional complications. When she goes home, she'll need to be careful. Are you all family?"

"Yes, sir," Dunn said for the group.

"Uh, is she married to one of you? Or lives with one of you?"

The group swung their gazes to Jaymes. "Yes, sir," he said, not really answering his question, but making it clear he would be there for her. Whatever it took.

"The first few days will be the hardest. Infection is a very high risk right now. She'll be on antibiotics, probably for the rest of her life. She'll have to eat soft foods for a few weeks, until her stomach heals. I'll make sure you get a list."

Jaymes nodded.

"Thank you, doctor," Rocky said for the group. "Any idea when we can see her?"

"We'll be able to get you back when she's in a room. She's still in recovery right now, so maybe another hour. But only one or two at a time."

Rocky thanked him.

The doctor smiled and turned to go, then stopped. "By the way, whoever covered her wound saved her life. She likely would have bled out before she made it here without that."

They all nodded.

The doctor smiled and left, going back through the doors that stopped Jaymes from getting to Kelsea. All he wanted to do was hold her hand and convince himself she was going to be okay. She had to be okay. She just had to.

26

Kelsea tried to open her eyes, but they were glued shut. Her brain was foggy, stopping her from remembering what she was doing before she went to sleep. Did she stay up late drinking alone?

She shook her head, then winced. *Why does that hurt so much?*

There were voices around her, but it sounded like she was in a pool. Funny. She didn't feel like she was swimming. Swimming and drinking did not sound like a good idea.

She tried to open her eyes again, but was immediately assaulted by the sun. Why did she leave her blinds open? And why were there so many people in her house?

"She's waking up," someone said, still sounding far away.

She pushed her eyelids up, but they revolted and clamped down hard again. She groaned. She had to figure out what was going on.

"Turn off the lights," another voice said. Closer. Familiar. She knew the voice, but she couldn't place it.

Her brain was still fuzzy, like someone replaced parts of

it with cotton instead of leaving her brain matter nice and gooey.

Speaking of cotton.

"Water," she gasped, wondering if whoever was in the room would help her or not.

Fear filled her for a second, a remembered emotion that came out of nowhere.

A hand on her cheek had her jerking away, first in fear, then pain. "Ow!"

"I know, sweetheart. I'm so sorry. Take a sip, Kels."

Something small touched her lips. A straw. She parted her lips. Someone held the straw steady, the scent of soap on the hand near her face. She drank the water slowly, willing her mind to work correctly. Where was she? What was going on? Who was there with her?

She tried to open her eyes again, getting a little farther before exhaustion took over and demanded she sink back to the soft bed and close her eyes. Sleep tugged ruthlessly at her, not giving her a chance to argue before it took over and dragged her under.

The next time she tried to open her eyes, she got a little farther. She was able to catch glimpses of a hospital. Why was she in the hospital? The questions kept piling up.

The third time, she saw a man. He was attractive with dark brown hair and concerned eyes. His mouth moved like he was trying to ask her something, but she couldn't hear him.

"She should be waking up," a new voice said. Female. Official. "The times when she opens her eyes then falls back to sleep concern me."

"I agree. Could she have a brain bleed that they missed?" Male. Authoritative.

Both were there at the edges of her memory.

"Did you see her face? Anything could have happened. And then when she collapsed..."

Who were they talking about?

The woman cried softly, the sound muffled. For the first time, they didn't sound far away. They were close. Like she could find them if she tried hard enough.

"Any change?" another voice said. That one was even more familiar. She knew him. She heard that voice. He talked to her in her dreams. She liked his voice. And he... loved her. He told her that over and over again.

"Nothing yet," the first man said. "It might be time to start talking about taking her home. We can monitor her. She'll get the best treatment in the country if she comes home."

"Dad?" Kelsea groaned.

"She's awake," the woman said.

"Mom?"

They rushed her, both of them suddenly in her space.

"Let me check..." her dad trailed off.

Her eyelid was pried open, and a bright flash of light blinded her. "God, that hurts." Just when she could close her eye, the other one was yanked open.

"Pupils are equal and reactive. She's clearly aware of what's going on. Kelsea, can you open your eyes on your own?" her dad said, raising his voice.

"Stop yelling at me. God, what happened? Am I hung over? Why am I in the hospital? How much did I drink?"

"You don't remember?" her mom asked, fear slipping into her voice.

That captured Kelsea's attention and demanded she start taking control again. Something was obviously going on. Something she couldn't remember. Something big and scary enough to have brought her parents to visit her.

She forced her eyes open and took in her parents. Her mom's hair was perfectly coifed in her signature blunt bob. Strands of gray blended into the blonde, the only indication that she'd aged at all. Her dad stood tall with an arm around her mother. If she could make his lips pinch together in concern instead of disappointment, like a problem he couldn't solve, then whatever happened was really bad.

Kelsea tried to push herself up, but her head still hurt too much.

"Here, let me," another voice said. The familiar one. He was on her other side. She turned and looked at him, and all at once, everything snapped into place.

"Jaymes," she breathed. "Oh, God, Jaymes." She reached for him, the fear and despair and loss she felt all rushing back in. Right behind all that was love. For the man who held her hand the entire time. Who was there for her. Who loved her. "How's Cecelia?"

He took her hand and smiled. "You remember her?"

She nodded, then winced. "I do. Oh, God. I remember everything now. Edward?"

"Dead."

She closed her eyes, grief and relief competing. "I don't know how I feel about that."

Jaymes squeezed her hand. "I know. And that's okay. I'm pretty happy myself."

Kelsea chuckled through the tears that spontaneously fell. "Your mom? You never said."

"She's fine, Kels. We're all fine. Worried about you."

She smiled up at him. "I'm better now."

KELSEA'S PARENTS read her chart and talked to the doctors, offering their opinion on every second of her treatment. Jaymes didn't want to meet them the way he did, but he was thrilled to have them there. He didn't know how to deal with everything. They clearly did, better than most of the population.

They pushed her to go home with them when she was finally discharged, almost two weeks after she was shot, but she refused. Jaymes immediately offered to have her stay with him, something she agreed to just as quickly.

Jaymes went to her house earlier in the day and packed up most of her stuff. He didn't know what she would want, but he didn't think she wanted to be at her house at all, so he took as much as he and Jack could carry.

He pulled up to his apartment building and woke her up. She was still falling asleep all the time, but her parents said it was just exhaustion and that once she got a full night's sleep instead of being woken by nurses at all hours she should be better.

Then they warned him about the dangers associated with head injuries and Jaymes wondered if he'd ever get a full night's sleep again.

"Are we home?"

He smiled and nodded. "Yeah, sweetheart. We're home."

She threaded her hand between his arm and his body and leaned against him as they walked. He didn't have a chance to put his key in the door before it opened in front of them.

"We were waiting for you. How are you feeling?" Jack asked Kelsea.

She smiled and released Jaymes to hug Jack. "I'm so much better being out of the hospital. Still tired, but the headaches are mostly gone."

"You had a hell of a concussion," Archer said, holding the door for them to walk in. "It takes a while to recover from them, especially as hard as you hit your head. And as many times."

Kelsea sucked in a breath. She told Jaymes about Edward hitting her. She'd started flinching whenever anyone made quick movements near her face, but she was getting better. She also told him about fighting back. She was strong.

"Lily made some dinner for you guys. It's in the fridge so you can heat it up. If you're up for it, we thought we'd all come up and watch a movie later or something."

"No stalker movies," Kelsea said.

Archer and Jack looked at her, trying to figure out something to say.

Kelsea broke into a grin. "Sorry. Had to put it out there."

Archer rubbed her shoulder. "Don't worry. Lily has a collection of chick flicks already pulled together. Whatever you want to watch."

Kelsea's eyebrows shot up. "I'm going to have eight former military men watching a chick flick?"

Archer shrugged. "I watch them all the time."

"Yeah, because they get you laid," Jack said with a snicker.

Archer grinned. "Yes, they do."

Jaymes laughed with the other guys. He didn't really want to watch a movie with everyone else, but if he had to suffer through it to get laid, he happily would.

"Seven?" Jack asked.

Kelsea nodded and started up the stairs. Jaymes held on to her the whole way, making sure she was steady on the steps. He paused at his door and pressed a kiss to her temple. She sank into him and sighed.

"Thank you for letting me come here. I just didn't want to go home. I'm not ready."

He slid the key in the lock and nodded. "You can stay here as long as you want to. I have a surprise for you, too."

He opened the door and turned on the light. A loud meow greeted them.

Kelsea tilted her chin up to look at him. "Did you get a cat?"

Jaymes nodded. "I did. One I think you might recognize."

She gasped and rushed to the large cage in the corner where Moby was howling for her. She crouched down and opened the door, cooing for him to come to her.

Jaymes leaned against the wall and watched them. Moby crawled onto her shoulder and wrapped his tail around her neck. She stood and met his gaze with tears in her eyes. "You adopted Moby?"

Jaymes nodded. "I did. I thought it was time he had a good home."

She sniffed and nodded. "He does deserve a good home. I think you'll be good for him."

Jaymes laughed and moved closer to her. "Not just me, Kels. Us. He's our cat."

"Ours?"

Jaymes went to her, stroking a hand down her back, then petting Moby. "Yes, sweetheart. Ours. I don't just want you here for now. I want you here forever. If you want to be. Or we can move into your house. Or buy something else. Whatever you want."

"Jaymes," she breathed.

He tilted her chin up with his finger, making sure she was listening to every word he said. "You're the strongest woman I've ever known, Kelsea. You're smart and brave, and you make me a little crazy."

She chuckled.

"When I thought you... I would have died with you, Kels. The thought of not having you in my life..." He dragged in a slow breath. "I love you, Kelsea. So much, sweetheart. And I want you to be in my life as long as you want to be. Forever, if you'll have me."

Tears ran down her cheeks, over the fading bruises that were a stiff reminder of everything they went through to be together. He ached to brush her tears away, but he didn't know what they meant, and he didn't want to hurt her more than she already did.

"I love you so much, Jaymes."

He wrapped her in his arms, pressing her to his chest so he could feel all of her. His hands ran down her curves, enjoying the feel of her body beneath his fingertips again. He ached to touch and tease her until she was boneless with pleasure. It had been far too long since he'd held her, really held her, and she felt just as amazing as she always did.

"I'm so happy to hear that, sweetheart," he breathed into her hair.

A feline growl had him pulling away. Kelsea laughed and ran her hand down Moby's back. "He'll grow to love you just as much as I do."

Jaymes rolled his eyes. "You'd think I was the one who put him in the shelter instead of the one who saved him from certain death."

Kelsea laughed. "Best Friends Forever is a no kill shelter. He wasn't going to die."

Jaymes flashed her a look. "He doesn't know that."

Kelsea grinned. "Well, I think Moby needs to go back into his cage for a few minutes. Good call on that, by the way," she said, putting him back in. "He'd have destroyed this whole place if you left him alone."

Jaymes nodded. "That was what I figured."

Kelsea smiled and wrapped her arms around Jaymes's waist. "Do you know what I want to do now?"

He shook his head.

She tilted her face up. "I'd really like to make out with the man I love. I wouldn't pass up having a little naked fun, too."

Jaymes hardened at the thought. He nuzzled against her neck, kissing his way from her jaw to her collarbone. "Your doctor said you have to be careful for another month."

She pulled back and smiled at him. "Then I guess you have to do all the work."

He groaned. "I will definitely not argue with those plans."

KELSEA LAUGHED with Lily when the opening credits of Drive Me Crazy came on. It was obvious the men in the group had seen it more than once and weren't big fans. Kelsea, on the other hand, loved the movie. Lily definitely had the same taste in movies, bringing many of Kelsea's favorites to their impromptu movie night.

Kelsea snuggled into Jaymes's arms. Moby was perched on the couch behind them, swishing his tail in Jaymes's face every few minutes. He took it in stride.

For all the protesting the guys did, they all sat quietly and watched the movie. Howler was curled up next to Slade on the floor, snoring. The rest of the group was scattered between the couch, the chairs they pulled in from the dining room, and the floor.

When the final credits rolled, Lily jumped up and went into the kitchen. "I stashed dessert in here earlier. Anyone up for some?"

The men all followed her like moths to a flame, drooling over whatever amazing creation Lily made. Kelsea and Jaymes hung back on the couch, still cuddled close together.

"I have to warn you, this will be pretty normal," he whispered.

"Everyone being here?"

He nodded. "They all stayed here and at Lily's place when I was gone. This is their unofficial office. They're comfortable here."

"What if we decide to move one day?"

He shrugged. "One of them will probably move in. Do you want to move?"

She thought about it for a second, then shook her head. "No. I like it here. It feels like home."

Jaymes grinned and tilted her chin up to kiss her lips. He kept it soft, gentle, but he grew hard against her hip. "I think it might be time for our company to go home," he groaned.

Kelsea laughed softly. "They'll leave soon enough. Besides, we have the rest of our lives, Jaymes."

He smiled and kissed her again. "Hell, yeah we do."

THE RHYTHMIC SOUND of synchronized steps on the pavement soothed Jack. He'd always found running to be relaxing, and having a buddy to run with again was good for him.

"Let's stop for a minute," Jaymes said, pulling up short. "Something's in my shoe."

"I told you to tie those tighter," Jack said with a smile. He didn't like stopping when they were in a groove, but he also knew Jaymes would keep going as soon as he was set. "How's Kelsea doing?"

Jaymes nodded and shoved his foot back into his sneaker. He kneeled to tie it and said, "Good. Headaches are pretty much gone. She's going to start teaching again next week."

"Good. I know you're happy to have her with you."

Jaymes stood with a shit-eating grin. "Hell, yeah, I am. I never thought... I'm happy."

"Good. With Lily... Kelsea's right for you."

Jaymes chuckled. "I know. I still love Lily, but I'm not in love with her. I'm really not sure I ever was."

"She was safe for you," Jack said easily. He understood the feeling. Safe was easier than not safe. Jack was willing to risk his life on a regular basis, but risking his heart wasn't an option for him. It never had been, and it wasn't going to change.

"That might have been it. I don't know. Everything is different with Kelsea, though. Easier. Like it was meant to be all along."

"Good for you, man. I'm happy for you."

"Thanks."

Jaymes nodded toward the road again, and they resumed their run. The sound lulled Jack back into his mindless state, so mindless that he didn't notice the man running toward them until he was right in front of them and Jack had no choice but to stop.

"There's plenty of road here," Jack said, trying to move around the man with dark hair and a dangerous glint in his eyes.

The man moved into Jack's path, not letting him by.

The hairs on the back of Jack's neck stood up, and he

instantly catalogued everything about the other man. A few inches shorter than he was, with chin-length dark hair and red dyed streaks. His eyes were brown, and his skin was a few shades lighter. But the most striking thing about the man was the way he held his hands up to show he wasn't armed.

"I need to speak to you," the man said, his accent telling Jack he was not a local.

"And who are you?" Jack demanded. He wasn't armed. He hadn't carried a weapon when he ran since he came back from the desert. He'd never thought about it. Until a stranger stepped into his path.

"My name is Juan Luna. I am a former falcon for the Castillo cartel."

Jack snorted. "Not possible. You don't get out."

Juan lifted a brow and leveled Jack with a fierce gaze. "I did. And now I want to bring them down, and I need your help to do it."

THANK you so much for reading Forgotten! I've really loved writing romantic suspense and getting to know a whole new set of characters! Jaymes was a character I loved from the beginning, and Kelsea stole my heart as soon as I met her. I just love them together!

The series continues with *First*. Jack is tasked with protecting the sister of a kidnapped informant. Pilar is curvy and beautiful, but love is a foreign concept for Jack. There's no way he'll fall for her, even if keeping her close is his favorite part of the job. Get First now!

. . .

ARE YOU READY FOR MORE? Newsletter subscribers get *exclusive* bonuses like short stories, bonus scenes, and a first look at everything new. Sign up for my newsletter today so you never miss a thing!

AMBER HAS BEEN TRYING to straighten out her life since she lost her scholarship and left college. Just when she thinks she might have it back on track, Caleb walks in and throws her off all over again. Check out Playing By The Rules today.

ABOUT THE AUTHOR

USA TODAY Bestselling Author Mary E Thompson spent most of her childhood wishing she had a few less curves. She hid in the pages of books because her favorite characters never cared what size her clothes were. Now, neither does Mary, and she writes stories that celebrate women like her. Real women who have curves, chase dreams, and find love, because we should all be happy, no matter our dress size.

Mary spends her non-writing time with her husband and two kids, watching too much TV, cheering for her hometown football team (Go Bills!), and hiding chocolate from her family.

Visit https://MaryEThompson.com/ to sign up for Mary's newsletter, **Romancing the Curves.** Subscribers get free ebooks and other fun stuff, like exclusive, members only content and giveaways, plus are the first to know about new releases and sales!